I Am Not Not Jessica Chen

I Am Not Jessica Chen

ANN LIANG

HARPER

An Imprint of HarperCollinsPublishers

Library of Congress Control Number: 2024944599
ISBN 978-1-335-52312-9 (trade ed.)
ISBN 978-1-335-08110-0 (international ed.)

Typography by Catherine Lee

First Edition

For anyone who's ever wished they could be someone else

One

I've always had this theory that if I want something badly enough, the universe will make sure to keep it just out of my reach—either out of boredom or cruelty, like an invisible hand dangling stars on a string.

Sometimes the universe will be creative with its tricks too. Take, for instance, that morning a snowstorm appeared out of nowhere. It never even snows in our part of town, and the sky had been an especially vivid acrylic blue, the sun fat and golden and rising over the tufted treetops. But I'd left all my notes in the classroom at Saturday Chinese school, and I desperately needed them for Havenwood's monthly language test on Monday—I still couldn't remember half the phrases we'd been taught, which ones meant "this floating life" and which ones meant "the flow of years like water" and "to dream of becoming a butterfly." If I didn't have my notes, I would fail.

And if I failed, I would have to tell my parents. Watch them try to hide their disappointment.

So I'd rushed down to the car, my chest tight, my heart thrumming with urgency, when, as if summoned by a curse, the clouds had flocked together overhead like wild dark birds, and the temperature had plummeted. The snow had fallen fast, in a mad flurry, quickly sweeping across the town and blanketing the elm trees and blocking off the roads. Chinese school ended up being closed for the entire weekend—something I hadn't known was possible, considering that it never closed, not even during Christmas and New Year's or when one of the buildings caught fire—and I learned to never expect any help from the universe.

But I still can't stop myself from hoping it'll be different this time around. Maybe a miracle will happen. Maybe the universe will be kind for once, and when I reach up, the stars will fall into my palms.

Maybe . . .

I lean my head back against my locked bedroom door and draw in a deep, rattling breath. Another. Another. It doesn't work; the terrible tingling sensation in my fingers only spreads down to my feet, mutates into a violent trembling. My laptop is open and laid out on the floor below, the screen staring back at me like a beckoning, the time blinking in the corner.

4:59 p.m.

One minute until the email from Harvard arrives. Until I can know for certain if I was accepted or not. If I'm good enough or not. One minute until my life changes for better or worse, every passing second stirring up the wasps in my belly.

I can almost imagine it playing out like a scene from a movie. The beautiful, life-changing *ding* of my notifications, the words I've been dreaming of unfurling before me in concrete black-and-white text—*Congratulations, Jenna Chen, I am delighted to inform you*—the way my parents will beam and beam when I run downstairs and tell them, just before we head over to my auntie and uncle's house, where they'll finally get to brag about me. That's how it always goes in those Harvard acceptance reaction videos, and I've watched every single one of them, half salivating, my wanting overtaking every cell in my body, pressing down hard on my chest like a physical sickness.

But then I imagine thousands of anxious high schoolers spread out across the world in this exact moment, all making the exact same wish, all staring at their laptops, waiting for the same email to come in. People like my cousin Jessica Chen: people smarter and cooler and objectively *better* than I am. People who've been preparing for this moment since before they could walk, who haven't already been rejected by all the other Ivy Leagues they've applied to so far. The very thought makes me claustrophobic, makes doubt chew a ragged hole through my gut.

Ding!

I jump at the alert. It's louder than I imagined, the sound harsher.

One new email.

My heart lurches into my throat. This is it—oh god, it's here, it's really happening. I'm going to throw up.

I brace myself, all my muscles tensed as if for a boxing match. My fingers are shaking so hard that I have to click the email four times before it loads onto the screen. There's something about the moment, all the buildup before it, that feels almost anticlimactic. The air doesn't change. The ground doesn't shift beneath my feet.

Just a quick, simple action, a blink, and there it is: a few pixels on my laptop that'll determine the entire trajectory of my life.

At first I'm too nervous to even absorb anything, can only gape at the wall of text, the Harvard logo splashed across the bottom like a bright bloodstain.

Then the words creep into my vision:

> *I am very sorry to inform you that we cannot offer you*
> *admission. . . . I wish that a different decision had been*
> *possible. . . . Receiving our final decision now will be helpful . . .*
> *as you make your college plans. . . .*

I read it, read it all over again, and my gut sinks down to my feet. Time seems to warp around me, trapping me within it like an insect in amber. Distantly, I can still hear Mom and Dad moving downstairs, the sharp rattle of car keys, the clack of shoes, their muted bickering over how many wontons to bring with them to the gathering at Auntie's place. But they might as well be thousands of miles away.

I pick my way through the rest of the email, as if there might be some other piece of information I'd missed, some final thread of hope. But all I see is further confirmation of what I've always known, deep down in the core of me.

> *In recent years . . . faced with increasingly difficult*
> *decisions. . . . In addition, most candidates present strong*
> *personal and extracurricular credentials . . .*

I'm simply not that good.

Not in academics. Not in extracurriculars. Not as a student, or a daughter, or a human. It doesn't matter if I crammed my brain to the point of breaking with formulas and dates, threw myself into my classes, painted until the skin on my hands blistered and split open. Here is incontrovertible proof. Something in me is missing. *Lacking.*

"Jenna! Are you ready to go?" Mom always sounds like she's yelling from across a crowded marketplace. I startle at her voice, then, stomach churning, slam my laptop shut. Wipe roughly at my eyes. Ignore the dangerous ache building at the back of my throat. "I already told your uncle and auntie we've left the house."

A recent memory resurfaces: my mom resting her chin against my shoulder as she watched me send my applications off, one by one, exhaling alongside the *whoosh* of every email. Later, she had spent hours in the kitchen making eight-treasure rice, adding in so many extra red dates and nuts the top layer was almost completely covered. *To celebrate all your hard work,* she'd said, smiling. *It's going to pay off, I can feel it. We'll have a bigger celebration once you get in.*

"Jenna? Did you hear me?"

The wasps inside me grow louder, their buzzing incessant.

"I—I'm ready," I call back, even as I reach for my coat as slowly as possible, comb my hair back strand by messy strand, take the stairs one step at a time, delaying the inevitable.

How am I supposed to confess to my parents that everything they've done for me—leaving behind their old lives, moving across the world, spending what should've been vacation money on over-priced textbooks, waking up at dawn to drive me to tutoring centers, all so I could have a better education—was for nothing?

★★★

By the time we pull into my uncle's driveway, I still haven't figured out how to tell them.

Maybe, I muse to myself, my head resting against the fogged-up car window, *it would be better if I burst into tears. Told them through hysterical sobs.* Maybe then they would at least feel sorry for me, and spend most of their energy consoling me, instead of scolding me, or wondering where they went wrong. But they've already been understanding enough. That's the thing. Each time a new rejection letter from Yale or UPenn or Brown popped up in my inbox, or in our mail, they'd be the first to squeeze my shoulders and say, *It's fine, we're still waiting to hear back from the others.* Except I'd seen for myself the growing concern in their eyes, how it'd spread over their aging features like a shadow; I bet Jessica's parents had never looked at her like that before in her life.

Besides, what could my parents say this time around? There are no good schools left. The only ones we haven't heard back from yet are my safety schools, the kinds of schools I was embarrassed to even be applying to. Of course *Jessica* hadn't applied for any safety schools at all, because she didn't need them. Her getting into the Ivies was already a foregone conclusion, a fate carved into stone for her probably since she was still in the womb. She's just *that good.* That unreasonably, unfathomably perfect.

And I can never be her.

It's such a suffocating thought—that everything I will ever feel and know and accomplish must begin and end with my own mind.

"It's so beautiful," Mom remarks as she steps out of the car, taking in the full view of Uncle's house. She makes the same comment every time we come here, and every time, it's true. I climb out after her and stare down the wide, windswept driveway, lined with magnolia trees, their petals flushed pink and smooth as wax, their slender branches reaching up toward the vast late-afternoon sky. And beyond that, the three-story house rises like a white-painted castle, with its massive floor-to-ceiling windows and ivy-crawled walls and marble balustrade balconies. It's the kind of house that comes with its *own name*, dated back to the pre-WWI days and stamped in gold over the front door for all guests to see: Magnolia Cottage.

Once, when our mutual friend Leela Patel had come over for a study date with the two of us, she'd raised her brows, both her jaw and her bag dropping to her feet. *"That's* your house, Jessica?" When Jessica nodded, with her signature small, humble smile, Leela had whistled. "Damn. I always thought a bunch of rich white people lived here."

We'd all cracked up laughing, not because it was that funny, but because it was so accurate. My uncle and auntie might have moved over to America from Tianjin just three years before my parents did, but they seem to fit in better than we ever could. Every day, while my dad drives across town at dawn to set up air conditioners and inspect switchboards and my mom balances on her too-tight heels behind a reception desk, Jessica's parents list off tasks to their assistants and close seven-figure deals from inside their spacious private offices. In the summers, when we budget for a two-day road trip to the closest beach, Jessica's family flies business class to a luxurious resort in Italy. Jessica's parents have everything: their lavish house and massive garden and high-end clothes. And they have Jessica.

My parents? All they have is me.

I swallow the bitter thought like poison and hurry to help Mom with the wontons. She's packed five whole Tupperwares of them, all freshly wrapped and uncooked and stuffed with our special pork-and-shrimp filling.

"Is . . . there a festival going on that I don't know about?" I ask, surveying the food.

She flicks my forehead lightly, then fiddles with her fake Chanel scarf. It's the one she always wears when she's meeting Dad's side of the family. "Shush. You can't expect us to show up at your uncle and auntie's house *empty-handed*, can you? They're already too kind to us, hosting these gatherings every time."

Neither of us says the obvious—that the only reason my uncle and auntie always host is because our house is way too small to fit all of us, what with its one-and-a-half bathrooms and living-room-slash-kitchen. Even the dining table Dad dragged home from a garage sale a few years ago is only made for four people at most.

"I told you not to pack so many," Dad mutters as he follows us down the driveway, the gravel crunching beneath his old sneakers. "Nobody's going to finish all of that. And they're already preparing hot pot."

"Better to bring too much than too little," Mom returns.

"Then we should've brought the apples from our backyard. Add more variety—"

"*Apples?* Do you want them to think we're cheap? Besides, some people don't even like them."

Dad looks so affronted you'd think he'd invented the fruit himself. "*Everyone* loves apples—"

We've reached the front door now. When it swings open, revealing my smiling uncle and auntie, I watch my parents pause mid-bickering and switch to bright smiles, the whole thing quick and subtle as a magic trick.

"It's so good to see you!" Mom greets, passing the wontons forward. "We made some extra ones, and thought we'd share them with you."

"Aiya, you're too polite." Auntie makes a big fuss of tutting and shaking her head while Uncle fetches the slippers. It's what she tells Mom every visit; sometimes I swear all the adults are following some kind of secret rulebook on social etiquette. "I keep telling you, you don't have to bring anything. We're all family here."

"It's *because* we're family that we should all share," Mom insists. Another all-too-familiar line, followed by the even more familiar "By the way, you look so skinny. Have you been eating well lately?"

I tighten my grip on the wonton containers, dreading the moment they finish running through the pleasantries and turn their attention to me. I'm not sure how much longer I can keep pretending everything's fine when I'm one wrong question away from breaking down. And I can't imagine anything more mortifying than breaking down over my Harvard rejection at my Harvard-bound cousin's house.

"Jenna!" Uncle greets me first, waving me into the warmth of the living room. As different as he is from Dad, I've always liked him; he smiles more than he laughs, seems to know something about everything, and unlike most grown-ups, he never treats me like a little kid. But today, I just want to get away from him. From all of them. "How have your studies been?"

"Oh, not bad," I say, hoping he can't hear the catch in my voice.

"You're being modest," he says, nodding sagely. "I'm sure your grades are excellent."

They're not. Harvard doesn't seem to think so, anyway.

But before he can pursue the topic, Jessica appears beside him like a living saint. An enviably accomplished saint dressed in arctic-blue cashmere and a perfect plaid skirt. From afar, Jessica and I look so similar that we could easily be confused for each other, and at school, we often are. But one day I overheard a girl in our history class comment, in this flat, blunt way that meant she was being totally honest, that I look like the dollar-store version of Jessica Chen.

Ever since then, I haven't been able to stop seeing it. Obsessing over it. Whereas Jessica's hair is black and glossy, like something out of a shampoo ad, mine is dull and deep brown; whereas her complexion is Chinese-beauty-pageant smooth, mine is sickly looking, even after layers of foundation. She's also taller in a supermodel way, with the long neck of a ballerina and the posture of a princess.

"Oh my god, hey." She beams at me, all her straight white teeth flashing. She's never had to wear braces either, never had to suffer to make them the way they are; her teeth are just *like that*, which pretty much sums my cousin up. Jessica Chen has always been a natural. She was born the best, while I've spent my entire life trying to just be good, and I've failed at even that.

I chew down on my tongue until it's numb and force myself to beam back. "Hi."

"Guess who's here."

Something about the way she says it, how she's bouncing on the balls of her feet, sends a jolt of unease through me.

"Huh? Who?" I crane my neck and scan the room, but all I can make out is the usual casual display of wealth: the chandeliers glittering above the plush couches, the gleaming Yamaha piano set in the corner for every visitor to listen to her play "River Flows in You," the gold-framed abstract paintings adorning the walls, the patterned porcelain vases and decade-old yellow wine stacked on the bookshelf, beside rows upon rows of trophies. All Jessica's, of course, for everything from advanced algebra to badminton to cello.

Then a boy our age steps out from behind the shelf with quiet, unfathomable grace, and my stomach flips.

I almost don't recognize him right away. His hair's grown longer, the thick, dark strands curled beautifully around his head like a crown, his jaw sharper, his shoulders broader than they were a year ago. But that self-assured expression arranged on his face is exactly as I remember it. So is the not-quite smile playing across his lips as he meets my gaze. It doesn't matter that I blocked him on every single social media platform when he left for his fancy medical youth program in Paris on a full scholarship, that I tuned my parents out every time they brought up "Mr. Cai's talented son." He might as well be engraved in my memory, etched into my mind, every part of me. I remember it all.

The shock of seeing him here in Jessica's living room—lovely and real and unexpected—*today*, of all days, feels like a punch in the face. My skin burns, and it takes an impossible degree of self-restraint not to flee in the opposite direction.

"Aaron Cai," Jessica says unnecessarily, gesturing between the two of us as though it's our first time meeting, when I've known him all my life. His father is best friends with my dad, and my family had invited them to move closer to us, after his mother passed and his father stopped cleaning, stopped cooking, stopped almost everything. I can't even imagine a world where I *don't* know him, where I wouldn't pass him ready-made lunches before school, where the three of us didn't spend our childhood summers hanging around on Jessica's porch together, sharing chocolate pies and staring at the stars when darkness fell.

"You haven't changed much," Aaron says, stopping a foot away.

The heat in my skin rises. I know he probably doesn't mean it like an insult, but after our last mortifying exchange, I'd made it a mission to change myself. To metamorphize into someone gorgeous and glamorous and inimitable. Sometimes at night, I'd envision our next meeting. How his eyes would widen at the sight of me. How he'd eat his words, regret everything.

But today is starting to feel like a cruel lesson in the difference between imagination and real life.

"Neither have you," I reply, though when it comes to him,

this is a compliment. When you're so widely known and loved, so soaked in glory you're swimming in it, all you have to worry about is maintenance, not metamorphosis.

"Aaron finished his program early," Jessica explains. "He's going to spend the rest of his senior year back here with us. Isn't that great?"

"Oh" is all I can think to say.

Aaron hesitates, then reaches into his pocket and pulls out a single pen. "As promised," he says, holding it up to me.

I freeze. The pen is intricately designed, plated in rose gold, with a delicate flower charm dangling from the end, the petals carved out of crystals. *He remembered.* My throat burns with the knowledge, every moment from our past coalescing into the present. We were only twelve when he made the promise. He and Jessica had been selected to attend a math tournament in New York, and even though I'd tried to act like I didn't care that I hadn't even been considered for it, he must have seen the disappointment on my face.

I'll bring something back for you, he'd said, smiling, tugging lightly at my hair. *What do you want?*

Nothing, I'd mumbled.

He'd cast me a knowing look. *You always want something.*

I wanted to go with him. I wanted to be on his team. I wanted to be smart like him and Jessica.

How about a new paint set? he'd suggested. *You've been drawing a lot, haven't you? A good artist needs good supplies.*

That was the first time anyone had ever acknowledged that I was good at something, and so casually too, like it was obvious.

Warmth curled inside my chest. *I have enough paints—I just want a pen,* I had told him. It was a small lie. My paints had almost run out, but a pen seemed like a much simpler and cheaper option, something he could find without trouble. *I can use it for my sketches.*

But when he returned, he gave me one of the fanciest fountain pens I'd ever seen, the kind a queen might use to sign her letters. From then on, every time he had to leave for a competition or debating camp or a school excursion, he would come back with a new pen just for me.

As I take the gift from him now, I'm tempted to laugh at myself. An entire fortress, built painstakingly over the year in his absence, threatening to crumble at the light touch of a pen. *Zhen mei chuxi.* The familiar phrase of disdain echoes inside my head. It's what my mom would say whenever I was being slightly pathetic, like when I'd beg her to buy ice cream for me at the mall, or when I'd cry over a tiny scratch on my hand. "I . . . thank you, Cai Anran," I say, his Chinese name falling a little too easily from my lips.

"You really didn't need to bring so many presents for all of us," Jessica adds.

It's only then that I notice the boxes of dark chocolate and bottles of fish oil supplements laid out on the couch. My stomach sinks. He'd remembered his promise, but I had forgotten that Aaron Cai has a dangerous way of making everyone feel special.

I can sense Aaron's gaze on me when he says, "It's no big deal. Both your parents and Jenna's parents have been so nice to me—I mean, you're even letting me impose on your family dinner."

"Are you kidding? The more people the better, especially for hot pot." Jessica shakes her dark, glossy hair out as she laughs.

I breathe through the wire coiling around my ribs, feeling the same way I had the morning they left for the math tournament, my feet rooted to the spot, my eyes following their tall, graceful, receding figures to the bus, the distance between us drawing wider and wider. They've always looked like they belong next to each other.

Then Jessica whirls toward me, her skirt fanning out in a perfect circle. "Oh! We prepared that extra spicy sauce you like. I asked Ma and Ba to put it in a separate pot for you, though, since Aaron wouldn't be able to handle it."

Another thing about my cousin: she's as naturally kind as she is talented. Sometimes—and I know it's awful—I almost wish she were a terrible person. Someone undeserving of her success. Someone I could hate without feeling like the villain.

I tuck the pen away and follow silently after her to the dining room, where all the adults have congregated too, their conversation traveling down the well-trodden routes of real estate prices and our school's extracurricular activities. *Good.* So long as they don't turn their attention to college applications, I might be able to survive this evening.

The hot pot has already been set out on the long glass table, the rich, spice-infused water close to bubbling over, plates of thinly sliced raw lamb and beef and lotus root squeezed around it. Aaron slides into the seat next to Jessica, across from me. I try not to stare at him through the soft, rising steam. Try not to take account of everything both new and familiar about him. New: the way he rests his chin on the back of one hand. Familiar: the way he holds his chopsticks too close to the ends and discreetly picks all the chopped scallions out of his bowl.

Then his gaze catches on mine.

Get a grip, I will myself, quickly turning my head away, my cheeks burning. *He's going to think you still like him, and you don't need to give him a reason to reject you all over again.* Especially not when I'm still reeling from the last time I saw him, an entire year ago.

Once the meat has been thrown into the pot and the ground sesame sauce has been passed around, Auntie sits up straighter in her chair and clears her throat.

"Since everyone's here," she begins, shooting a not-so-subtle look at Uncle, then Jessica, who just smiles down at the table. "I feel like it's a great time to share some *super* exciting news. We found out just minutes before you arrived, and, well . . ."

Even before she says it, I know. My skin tingles, and my breath clogs in my throat, my ribs caving in, bracing for the blow.

"Jessica got into Harvard!" The words come tumbling out in an excited rush, and my sensible, ever-composed aunt actually lets out a little squeal at the end, like a schoolgirl at her first concert. I've never seen her so excited. I've never seen my uncle so excited either—his complexion is as red as his wine, and he's gazing over at Jessica with such fierce, obvious pride it seems to form a warm halo around them, encompassing their side of the family. The good side.

While I remain sitting, my fingers cold and numb, everyone else reacts.

"Wow, that—that's incredible," Mom gushes, reaching out to

ruffle Jessica's hair. "Of course, it's not surprising at all—if anyone's getting into Harvard, it's our Jessica."

Dad gives my uncle a heavy pat on the back. "Congratulations, congratulations. Your job is done, then. Now you can just wait to reap all the rewards of having a successful daughter."

My aunt is grinning so wide I'm scared her face will split into two. "I can't take all the credit—Jessica has always been so independent, so hardworking, so *brilliant*. We've never had to worry about her future."

I swallow, and it's as painful as swallowing glass. All my parents have ever done is worry about me.

"Don't go bragging now," my uncle is saying, but his grin is just as wide, his happiness like the sun, too bright to stare at without your eyes watering.

And there's Jessica, sitting comfortably in all the attention like an empress on her rightful throne. It feels like watching the secret movie in my head playing out in real time, except all the roles have been recast. Instead of Mom and Dad pulling me into a bone-crushing hug, gloating about how smart I am, how successful I'll be, while the others watch on in admiration and joy and envy, it's Auntie and Uncle. And instead of *me* absorbing their compliments, drinking in the euphoria of this moment, it's Jessica.

It's always Jessica.

The moment stretches on long enough to dredge up other memories too, the ones I've worked so hard to bury. Like when I ran home and excitedly told my parents I'd gotten eighty-five percent on our end-of-year exams, only to discover later that Jessica had scored full marks. Or when both Jessica and I entered the school's essay contest, and she'd come in first place, while I came in third, despite preparing for *months*. Or when the principal wanted someone to make a speech on behalf of the school at orientation, and only picked me after Jessica declined, because she'd be busy attending some prestigious awards ceremony with Aaron.

But I should be happy for her. Or I *want* to be happy for her.

"That's amazing news," I tell Jessica, the muscles in my cheeks locked into place. "Seriously. I—I'm so happy for you."

"It's hardly news at all," Aaron says to her. "The three of us have been talking about this since we were kids. If you *didn't* get into Harvard, that would be news."

My whole face stings as if I've just been slapped. I do my best to keep quiet, keep smiling, keep acting like I'm just *overjoyed* about everything, but I can feel Aaron's attention on me.

"What was our elaborate plan again?" Jessica says. "Me and Jenna heading off to Harvard together, and you flying in from Yale to see us every weekend on your private jet—*that* part might have been a tad unrealistic, but everything else might actually work out. . . ."

This is exactly what I've been dreading.

Please don't, I beg inside my head. *Please don't ask me about Harvard.* But of course there's nobody around to answer my prayers.

Just when I'm considering how convincingly and elegantly I could fake-faint on the spot to escape the conversation, my uncle turns toward me. It almost seems to happen in slow motion, like the climactic scene from a horror movie, the air around us as still as death. "That reminds me," he says, snapping his fingers. In my head, the violins from the imaginary horror movie soundtrack screech to a crescendo. "Jenna . . . you must have received the email too today."

I feel, more than see, the effect of his words. The invisible dots connecting in my parents' heads. The sudden pressure in the atmosphere. The weight of their expectations thrust onto my shoulders. I lick my dry lips, stare at my chopsticks, and feel a kind of crushing inferiority that's like being buried under stone. I can't move, can't breathe, can't speak.

"Jenna?" Mom peers at me, and the hope in her eyes makes everything so much worse. She still believes in me. "Did you check your emails today?"

"You should check it now," Auntie says, mistaking my silence for a no. "While we're all here to celebrate. Oh my god, can you imagine? Jenna and Jessica *both* going to Harvard . . ."

My heart squeezes. I can't stand this. Not their faith, not my shame.

"You heard your aunt. Check your emails now," my dad tells me, rising from his seat so enthusiastically he bumps his leg against the edge of the table. He looks like he's one moment away from grabbing my phone and checking my inbox himself. I can see the future he wants for me projected vividly across his face.

I clench my fingers together in my lap, so overwhelmed I can't even think of a way out. I'm trapped.

"Oh, someone should film this!" Auntie says, while Jessica smiles encouragingly. I'm scared to even glance in Aaron's direction, to guess what he's thinking. "Let me get the camera—we'd forgotten to film Jessica's reaction earlier, but we can do it for Jenna. . . . It's such a special memory—"

"Aiya, save the trouble," Uncle interrupts. "I'm sure they're more eager to know the results. Jenna, go ahead. Read what Harvard said."

"Go on," my mom urges.

But I don't reach for my phone. My hands are frozen.

Dad frowns. "Why aren't you—"

"I, um, already checked my emails," I croak out.

"And?" my aunt prompts, the way people do when they're prepared to celebrate good news but want to give you the opportunity to announce it.

The words won't leave my tongue. I can't bring myself to say it, to physically voice my failures, so I just shake my head.

Silence.

Everyone stares at me; nobody speaks. There's only the water boiling in the pot between us, all the white foam and ginger bits and spring onions bubbling up to the surface. I watch as the sliced lamb turns from a raw, tender pink to brown. It'll be overcooked soon, grow too hard to swallow, but no one fetches it out.

"Are you sure?" Dad asks, looking more disoriented than anything, as if convinced I've made a silly mistake. In an alternative universe where I *had* gotten in, he would've been the first person I told. My father, who never got a chance to complete his degree in China, who's always fantasized about sending me off to an Ivy League. Who's already told all his friends and colleagues I was applying to Harvard. Who would glance over at me when my mom was pressing another heated herbal pack to his aching back and sigh and say, *So long as you study hard, you'll be able to find a comfortable job that doesn't take such a toll on your body, do you understand?* He sets his chopsticks down. "You didn't get in? You were rejected?"

I manage to nod.

Another silence, even heavier this time. I catch Aaron's eye across the table—an old habit, muscle memory—and instantly regret it. His gaze is dark, somber, a knife to the throat. It's been a year since he looked at me like that.

"Well." Auntie is the first to recover. She even smiles at me, though maybe I'm giving her too much credit. Maybe it's a genuine smile, just one of relief: *Thank god Jessica is my daughter, and not Jenna.* "That's all right. It's just a school."

"Yes, yes," Uncle adds quickly. "The meat should be ready now. Hurry up and eat."

The second all the platters have been emptied, I slip out quietly through the back door.

Outside, in Jessica's backyard, a cool breeze whips my cheeks, the petal-arched blackness creeping over the edges, blurring the boundary between the trimmed grass and the wilderness of the woods farther up ahead. When we were much younger, we used to imagine monsters living there. *I would kill them,* Aaron had said without hesitation. *I would help them,* Jessica had offered. *I would learn from them,* I had thought to myself. Even then, I felt I lacked something: claws, speed, a hunter's instinct. Now I breathe in, tasting

21

the subdued sweetness of lavender, tipping my head to the dark sky. A few stray clouds drift over the full moon, the light scattering across the city. The stars are visible tonight, sharp as needlepoints and so lovely I'm tempted to paint them, despite knowing I could never get the colors right.

It's cruel, really, how the world tends to present its most beautiful parts to you when you're so profoundly sad. Like a crush who comes up to you in the moonlight and smiles at you each time you insist on moving on—just enough to keep you lingering, to make you wonder how good things could be. If only, if only.

The door creaks open again. I turn around as Aaron and Jessica walk over to join me.

"Hey, are you okay?" Jessica asks, sitting down on the back porch and swinging her legs over the side, her silky hair blowing across her face.

After a pause, I lower myself onto the cold wooden planks too, aware of Aaron stopping on my left. For the thousandth time, I wish he wasn't here. I wish he had never come back. But that's half a lie, because I've missed him too. Sometimes I missed him so much it's embarrassing.

"I'm fine," I say, trying at a laugh, though the sound dies halfway, dissolves into the frigid blue air. "I mean, I only applied as a joke. Harvard's lucky to have you, though," I tell her. "You must be thrilled."

At this, she turns away, the shadows of an overgrown oak cloaking her face. "Yeah. I am. Thrilled."

I glance back at the lit-up house, the vast Victorian-style

structure looming larger than ever against the night sky. Through the thin screen doors, I can make out my parents' silhouettes, both deep in conversation. Auntie's rubbing slow, consoling circles over my mom's back, while my dad has his head in his hands, as if warding off a severe migraine. My chest tightens. Somehow I know they're talking about me. My future. My failures.

"It's really nice out here," Aaron says, leaning back, both his hands propped against the wood. "I've missed this place."

It *is* nice out here, in a way. A cicada chirps from a nearby tree, and the dew-damp grass bends beneath a breeze, and the air feels the way it does after fresh rain: cool and crisp and almost sweet with the scent of earth, ripe with possibility. If I were someone else, I would enjoy this moment, take it, rest my bones in it. But instead, scenes from that better, alternative universe keep unspooling in the back of my mind, one in which I'm laughing with Jessica, both of us giddy over the prospect of Harvard, one where I am whole, convinced at last of my worth.

Then Jessica nudges me, her voice breaking through my thoughts. "Oh my god—look!"

She's pointing at something high above us, and I look up just in time to see it: an astonishing streak of silver, a bright needle of light piercing the sky's black canvas, soaring over the tree skeletons in the woods, over our heads, over everything. I've only ever seen shooting stars in movies before, never like this. It's even more beautiful than I'd imagined.

"Quick, you guys," Jessica says, clasping her hands together. "Make a wish."

Aaron huffs out a soft, skeptical laugh and rolls his eyes, but follows suit after a beat.

I'm skeptical too. The universe has never listened to me before. Then again, I have nothing to lose; everything that could go wrong already has. So I squeeze my eyes shut, the light of stars flickering behind my eyelids. Goose bumps crawl down my arms as the quiet moment expands, takes on a strangely surreal quality, and I can't shake the sensation that something or someone really is listening, shifting closer, their ear pressed against the wall of my thoughts.

My parents' low, concerned voices drift through the cracks in the door behind me, and the cicadas stop singing, and the breeze picks up into a great, billowing wind, shaking the loose wooden boards like a haunting and slashing at my cheeks. The light also grows brighter, glowing a brilliant, pure silver, the kind of color that could belong to another world.

My stomach dips. I feel all of a sudden as if I'm standing on some high precipice, staring down at the sheer drop below. It's like the moment before the fall, before gravity finds me, when everything is sheer potential, the air humming around me.

In the end, I don't even have to decide what my wish is before making it.

I wish I was Jessica Chen.

Two

The drive back home is awfully quiet.

I can tell, from the way Mom and Dad look at each other when we enter the house, pause in our tiny kitchen, all but communicating through charades, that they're working out some sort of script for this. Sure enough, Mom clears her throat and goes first, her voice careful, her words rehearsed.

"We know this might be disappointing news to everyone, Jenna, but it's too late to do anything now. We can't change the past; what's important is for us to look ahead at our options. You still haven't heard back from your safety schools. . . ."

I nod along, just to show I'm listening. Just to stop myself from screaming. The dissonance of coming back to our house straight from Jessica's semi-mansion is jarring. Here, the lights are dimmer, the colors duller, the furniture sparse rather than luxurious, and also completely mismatched, with a traditional Chinese-style chair sitting next to an old Victorian antique table. My dad's work overalls have been draped over the chair to dry, and his toolbox has been crammed into the bottom of the bookshelf, under all the heavy volumes on financial planning and the award-winning

nonfiction titles Dad only pretends to read because my uncle rec-
ommended them. A stack of dirty plates awaits us on the kitchen
counter, neglected from last night, an unopened bag of goji berries
lying beside it.

"I did tell you to sign up for the cross-country team," Dad is
saying, which earns him a pointed glare from Mom. He's going
off-script.

I lean against the kitchen counter. Try to swallow the bitter
lump in my throat. "Cross-country?"

"It's meaningless to talk about this now," Mom says hastily,
stepping between us. "Let's not—"

"It could have helped you look more well-rounded," Dad
presses. "Maybe if you exercised more . . ."

Even though I'd been determined to keep my emotions in
check, accept whatever they threw my way, this is so unreasonable
that I can only stare at him. It seems to be a defining trait of many
parents that they'll pick one *incredibly* specific thing and treat it as
the source or solution of all your problems. For my dad, it's always
been exercise. Have a fever? Too little exercise. In a foul mood?
Go exercise. A bad acne flare-up? Not enough exercise. Existential
crisis? Exercise will help. Find yourself kidnapped and stranded on
a remote island? It could've been avoided if only you'd run a little
more in your free time.

"Whatever," I bite out, knowing there's no way to reason
with him, to explain that the issue isn't my lack of participation
in Havenwood's sports teams. It's that even if I *did* join the cross-
country team and ran six hours a day until my legs failed and my

lungs collapsed, I still wouldn't be half as fast as Jessica, who moves with the athletic grace of a gazelle, who finishes entire marathons *for fun*, breaks records without effort. "I just . . . I don't want to talk about this—"

"You can't avoid the subject," Dad says, his forehead scrunching. "We need to evaluate where you went wrong so you can improve in the future."

"Could we please not?"

His frown deepens. "What kind of attitude is that? Just look at your cousin Jessica," he says, shaking his head hard. "You two came from the same family, attend the same school, are the same age. She's managed to get into Harvard—and what is it, five other Ivy Leagues? Maybe you should learn from her—"

"Laogong," my mom interrupts him with a warning glance. "I don't think that's very fair—"

"Only children talk about fairness," he persists, waving his hands about, his gestures increasingly agitated, the way they are whenever he goes into full lecture mode. "Do you think the world is a fair place? If you're too weak, you'll be eliminated. Look what happened to the Roman Empire—"

If I didn't feel like crying, I'd probably laugh. "First you're comparing me to Jessica, and now you're comparing me to *Rome*?"

He flings a Chinese phrase at me then, one of those four-character idioms I'm not cultured enough to understand, but the sentiment is clear.

I fix my eyes on the window behind him. Outside, the night sky is a somber violet, the silhouette of the Ethermist Mountains curving over the horizon. All the little houses are lined up one by one down our narrow street, made of the same cheap materials, with the same faded redbrick designs. From a distance it looks like the image of the idyllic suburban life, but instead of white picket fences and pretty lawns, we only have wild grass and dark cypress trees, tiny garages taken up by secondhand cars. *Barely bourgeoisie,* I always like to describe it in my head.

Not great. Not terrible. Just suffocatingly average.

We could have lived somewhere better. Somewhere with space to run around in the summer, with modern glass walls and large sunlit bedrooms. But my parents had insisted on staying here, where it costs more for less, so we could be closer to my school, thinking it would boost my chances of success. They've bet every-thing on me—their time and energy and savings—and this is what I have to show for it. Sunk costs. A failed investment.

"Dad. Please." I take a deep breath. "Listen—"

"No, you listen first. I'm telling you that if you'd followed Jessica's example—"

"I tried to." I can barely form the words. I grip the counter, my nails digging into the stone. This feels like a murder scene, all my worst fears, my insecurities, sprawled out and bleeding over the tiles before me. "I tried, I swear. I'm always trying. But I—" My voice catches. "I'm just not that good."

He doesn't agree. But he doesn't deny it either. His eyes are lined with some heavy, weary emotion. Disappointment, most likely.

The back of my throat aches. *Don't cry, don't you dare cry. Not here.* So I leave without another word. Neither of them follows me as I scramble up the stairs, into my bedroom, locking the door behind me. Everything's a blur. I blink, blink harder, catch my heart before it can fall out of my chest. Then, in the dark, deafening quiet, I stare around me.

My latest painting is still sitting in the center of the room, right where I left it. It's the self-portrait I'd been working on earlier this morning, when I was trying to distract myself from college applications, trying not to let my hope consume me. I remember being proud of it, admiring the smooth blend of moss greens and cream whites and smoky pinks in the background, the sharp angles and shadows lining my nose and pursed lips, the bold black brush-strokes layering my hair. In it, my eyes are focused on some distant point beyond the frame, magnolias blooming from the edge of the painting, their petals brushing my cheek. I have one hand lifted, as if I'm waiting for something. Reaching for something.

But now, staring at the portrait, I feel a vicious stab of self-loathing.

I seize the closest acrylic tin and fling it at the canvas, watching the paint drip until my eyes are obscured and the portrait could be of anyone, any sad, nameless girl who yearns for the world. Then, with the violet paint still wet on my fingers, its sharp acid smell burning my nostrils, I bury myself in my blankets and wait for sleep to wash over me.

I wake the next morning with the sun in my eyes.

Strange, I think sleepily, blinking into the bright orange glare of the window. My bedroom is always dark, with its thick curtains and dull view of the brick house next to ours. Then I lift my arms to stretch, and the sense of strangeness digs deeper into my gut. The blankets draped over my stomach are too soft, too light, the pillows stacked higher than I'm used to. Even the air smells different when I inhale: it's oddly sweet, like strawberries, some scent I know but can't place.

I rub my eyes, hoping to wipe away the mist of confusion. But when I squint up at my raised hand, my skin appears . . . smoother. The spilled paint from yesterday is gone, even though acrylic takes ages to wash off. Then I notice something that throws me off-balance, makes everything in my head go fuzzy. There's a birthmark between my fingers, no bigger than a coin and shaped like a flower.

That was never there before.

What the hell?

I sit up slowly, mind spinning, and the strangeness only grows. The sheets are printed with a pastel floral pattern. Definitely not the ones I slept in yesterday. Then the bedroom sharpens into focus, the details registering in pieces. A glass bookshelf close to toppling beneath the weight of medals and certificates and textbooks. A schoolbag set neatly on a desk overlooking the gardens below, a shiny MacBook already placed within it. The Havenwood uniform hanging from the closet doors, the navy plaid skirt longer than mine, the front blazer pocket adorned with so many school badges there's more gold and silver than actual fabric. I've seen those badges before, stared at them during long, monotonous assemblies, marveling at the way they gleamed beneath the spotlight.

Understanding slides into place, offset immediately by more confusion.

I'm in Jessica Chen's room. But . . . how?

I try to recount yesterday's events, searching for clues, an explanation. No, I'm certain I'd fallen asleep in my own bedroom. Did I sleepwalk? Except I've never sleepwalked once in my life. And Jessica's house is at least a fifteen-minute drive from mine, too far to travel on foot in the dead of night. So then . . . then what? Maybe someone moved me here? But that doesn't make sense either. I distinctly remember locking my bedroom door. The only way to unlock it is from the inside.

The creak of a cabinet closing downstairs sends my thoughts bolting like a startled hare in another direction. Would my aunt and uncle know that I'd slept in Jessica's room? How am I supposed to explain this to them? The skin on my face feels stretched full with blood, panic, and mortification taking turns kicking my gut. Had I been so sad that I'd gotten drunk at some point last night? Is that why I don't remember anything?

Out of habit, I reach for my phone on the bedside table. But the wallpaper that glows over the screen is a photo of Jessica from last year's prom, flanked on both sides by Leela and Celine, her other best friend. All three of them look gorgeous—they were the only ones who had worn full-fledged gowns, and the only ones who would be admired instead of ridiculed for it—but Jessica is clearly the center of attention. She's smiling straight at the camera, while the others are smiling at her.

I chew the flesh of my cheek, a third, ugly emotion squeezing its way through my insides. I had skipped prom, because all the dresses that I could afford looked awful, and all the dresses that looked good were too expensive. And because there was no point going, if Aaron wasn't there.

"Focus. Find your phone first," I whisper out loud—

And freeze.

The words are my words; I'm aware of my lips moving in the shape of them. I can feel the vibrations in my throat. But the voice is not my voice. It's higher, gentler, strange, and terribly familiar. I had heard it only yesterday.

A sudden bizarre thought grips me.

Impossible. This can't actually be happening. Not by the laws of physics, or biology, or anything. But I let Jessica's phone fall onto the bed—*her phone*, a voice inside my head notes with new significance, *her bed*—and sprint into the adjoining bathroom, flinging open the doors. I crash to a halt before the mirror, my heart threatening to beat out of my rib cage, my eyes wide.

No, *Jessica's* eyes. The person reflected in the mirror is Jessica Chen. Her glossy jet-black hair. Her long lashes and slender neck and perfectly proportioned body. And yet the expression on her face isn't anything I've seen her show before—it's raw bewilderment. Utter disbelief.

I'm not just in Jessica's room.

I *am* her.

"Jessica!" Auntie's voice cuts through the air, and it takes me another moment to pick my jaw up off the floor, to realize she's technically calling me. Or the body I'm inhabiting.

I'm dreaming.

It's the first possibility that pops into my mind. It must be a hyperrealistic dream of sorts. So instead of screaming, I stare at the single toothbrush propped up on the bathroom counter, hesitate, and search around for a spare, unused one instead, acting as I would after any sleepover. It helps that I've stayed at Jessica's place plenty of times before, when my parents were too busy working late shifts and couldn't pick me up, or when both our parents insisted on getting us together for a study session. Then I put on the uniform already laid out for me, noticing as I do that it's free of wrinkles, and has the same faint strawberry scent as the sheets. *That's* where I know it from. It's Jessica's signature scent.

"This can't be real," I mutter, watching the face in the mirror move as well. I run an agitated hand through her hair, but every strand falls perfectly back into place. Frowning, I repeat the motion with more force, and only end up creating a stunning windswept look, as if a magical beach breeze has fluffed out her hair.

Somehow, it's this ridiculous, unfair detail that pushes aside my initial shock, making room for other possibilities. Maybe I'd inhaled too much of the paint fumes last night. Maybe I'm in a coma, and my damaged brain has decided to conjure up this entire fantasy, weaving the scenes together based on my preexisting knowledge of Jessica and her family. We'd studied something like this in our psychology class. Of course I'd forgotten most of the details as soon as I finished the end-of-semester test, but the general principles still applied.

I'm feeling a little calmer by the time I head downstairs for breakfast, Jessica's phone in my pocket, her bag slung around my shoulders.

Whatever this is—dream or hallucination or simulation—I simply need to ride it out. Wait for it to pass, for me to wake up. Just because the world is vivid enough to seem real doesn't mean it actually is.

Auntie gives me an odd look when I walk in, and my pulse quickens, certain that she'll notice something off, that this will be the first glitch in my new fake reality. I wait for her to ask me what I'm doing in her house. But she only pats the back of my head. "Didn't you sleep well last night? You're never late in the morning."

"Oh . . . uh." I clear my throat, the sound of Jessica's voice still a shock to the system. "I guess I was just tired. . . ."

"Well, hurry," she chides, already moving away to inspect her appearance in the reflection of the wine cabinet. She's all dressed up in a blazer and pencil skirt, her hair gelled back, her lipstick dark. "There are cakes in the fridge—I wasn't sure which ones tasted best and they all looked so good, I just ended up buying one of everything."

I stare at her. Having *cake* for breakfast seems like an impossible concept. Mom would never entertain it. If exercise is my dad's thing, then a healthy balanced diet is my mom's. That meant a steady rotation of boiled eggs, steamed corn, soy milk, and homemade whole-meal mantou. Once every three months or so, we were allowed to buy white bread as a treat (or as a punishment, if you were to ask my mom, because of the damage the extra sugar would do to our bodies).

In disbelief, I make my way to the fridge—*Jessica's* fridge, in her kitchen—unable to shove aside the unsettling sensation that I'm stealing from someone else's house. I feel my eyes widen when I pull the door open. Inside, there are mini cakes of every kind and color imaginable, topped with slices of glistening strawberries, crushed cashews, brown sugar pearls, fresh mango, heavy dollops of cream. They're so intricately decorated, so pleasing just to look at, that I almost feel guilty slicing into the mango cake, with its dotted white flowers and golden flakes.

At Jessica's massive dining table, by the open, sunlit windows, I finish it slowly, savoring the frosting as it melts on my tongue.

"Oh, Jessica, before you go . . . ," Auntie says, her bracelets jingling as she reaches into her Chanel handbag. Real Chanel, I'm sure. I remember Mom pointing it out to me once in an online catalog, this exact design, the kind of bag she covets but can't afford. I had made it my goal to save up enough to buy her one as a surprise. "Here's your lunch money." Auntie extends a thick wad of cash to me.

I choke on my last bite of cake. "This is—" Through coughs, I take the money very gingerly, certain there's been a mistake. "This is, like, seven hundred dollars."

"Oh, sorry." Auntie fishes around in her purse and retrieves another four hundred dollars, pressing it into my palms before I can react. "There. That should be enough. Now, hurry, your friends are waiting for you—and leave the plate," she adds when I start to tidy up. "The cleaner will be here in an hour."

Friends.

I step outside in a daze, the sun a warm balm on my cheeks, the cold morning air stinging my exposed fingers and knees. There's a silver Mercedes parked in the driveway, all the windows rolled down, the paintwork so polished it looks brand-new, and I don't know what surprises me more: the sight of it, or the two girls waiting inside it.

"Get in, babe," Leela Patel yells, sticking her head out, her ponytail spilling over the side like a black stream of water. This, in itself, isn't too different from what I'm familiar with. Leela and I have been friends ever since we were assigned to the same table in art class. We were both painters, both obnoxiously fascinated with the Romantic period, and both eager to be loved by everyone. But the thing about Leela is that she *is* loved by everyone. While I've always considered her my best friend, I doubt that I'm hers. I might not even rank in her top three. Those spots are reserved for special people like Jessica Chen and Celine Tan—who's currently waving at me from the passenger's seat, a half-bitten croissant held between her teeth.

My footsteps falter.

If this really is a dream, it's a bizarre one.

Celine has always scared me. She's been at Havenwood longer than anyone, and she has a reputation as a poet, with a bunch of Pushcart Prize nominations and other prestigious awards to her name already. But while she could go on for pages and pages about how beautiful the moon is in midwinter until you're moved to tears, I've also witnessed her verbally eviscerate people on the spot. Her features are the same: soft and sweet when she's smiling, but hard as stone when she's not, her blue eyeliner drawing out the intimidating angles of her face.

"If we end up running late for English, Old Keller's going to kill me," she grumbles between chews as I climb into the back seat. Then she brandishes another croissant in front of me. "Want one? It's still warm."

"Oh, I'm good, thank you," I manage, trying to hide my shock. There's no way Celine Tan would ever deign to offer *me* breakfast, which means neither of them have detected anything wrong. They all think I'm Jessica. "I've already eaten."

"And we're not going to be late," Leela reassures her cheerily, pulling the car into reverse. "But maybe the teachers would be more lenient with you if you stopped swearing so much in class—"

"Nah, fuck that." Celine dusts the croissant crumbs off her tanned knees, lifts one long leg onto the seat. "My parents aren't paying forty thousand a year for me to watch my tongue everywhere I go. And swearing is *therapeutic*." She glances back at me and wriggles her manicured brows. "You should try it sometime, Jessica."

"Stop trying to drag our sweet, darling Jessica over to the dark side," Leela says, one hand on the wheel, the other reaching out to shove Celine's shoulder. The car lurches slightly, my stomach jolting with the motion, but the two don't seem to notice. "And not to, like, get caught up in the specifics, because you know I'm always on your side, babe—but you only pay twenty thousand a year."

Only a Havenwood student would use the word "only" next to "twenty thousand."

"That's just because of my scholarship."

"Is there a difference?"

"Well, I'm trying to speak on behalf of the student body."

"Please." Leela snorts. The car lurches again as she turns abruptly onto the main road, and I grip the seat belt tighter. "As if most of us aren't on academic scholarships."

"Most of the smart ones," Celine corrects, then considers it for a beat. "But fair. The others don't count."

I bite my tongue. I'm one of the *others* they're talking about; I sat for the scholarship test the same year Jessica did, and failed it by two and a half points. One stupid algebra question, the number six mistaken for a zero, a variable overlooked—and my life marred irrevocably because of it, my parents forced to take up extra shifts, work that much harder for years and years without complaint.

But then Leela catches my eye in the rearview mirror and heaves a theatrical sigh. "Of course Jessica has the least right to complain, what with her full scholarship and all."

"I didn't even realize they gave out full scholarships before Jessica," Celine says, in a tone caught between admiration and envy, her smile sharp as cut glass. Nobody's ever spoken to me like this before. Nobody's ever looked at me as a threat. It feels better than it should. Then she adds, "Guess they make exceptions for the best."

I suck in a silent breath on the word, play it over in my head like an incantation, warmth expanding inside my chest, spreading all the way down to my fingertips. Is this what it's like for Jessica all the time?

"You look so pretty today," Leela remarks, and for five terrifying seconds, she spins around completely in the driver's seat to study me. "Well, you always look pretty, but your hair is *gorgeous* like this. You should wear it down more. If you want," she adds quickly, like she's scared of saying the wrong thing. "You can pull off any hairstyle, really."

I lift a hand to my hair, remembering suddenly how Jessica always ties it up in a high ponytail. "Really?" I ask.

They both nod along, with shocking enthusiasm.

"Oh yeah, for sure," Celine says, tearing off the end of the croissant she'd offered me with her pearly white teeth. "You literally have the shiniest hair I've ever seen. What do you use to wash it again?"

Probably an expensive brand I couldn't pronounce if I tried. "The tears of my admirers," I reply. "It's super organic."

There's a pause.

I tense, waiting for them to realize I'm not who they think I am, to scream "Imposter!" To demand that I bring the real Jessica Chen back. Maybe then this beautiful, unbelievable dream will end.

But they burst out laughing at a volume that feels kind of unwarranted.

"Oh my god," Leela gasps, clutching her stomach. "You're hilarious, Jessica."

As the car speeds down the winding road at least five miles per hour over the limit, with Celine blasting some sad song I don't know from her phone speakers and Leela singing along, my disorientation thickens. There are the familiar, gloomy gray trees spread out on either side of us, with their soft watercolor washes of brown and green, the wild vegetation crawling toward the nebulous horizon; the warmer gray of the concrete pressed beneath the tires; the pale sunlight smudged against the windscreen; the mist-wreathed mountains rising and falling together. There's Frankie's Bakery, famous among the locals for its warm lattes and glazed cinnamon rolls in the fall; the crumbling marble statue of some dead saint standing alone on the corner of Evermore Avenue; the brooding black lake Tracey Davis once tossed her ex-boyfriend's phone into, where one of the boys in our class stayed under for so long on a dare that his friends called an ambulance.

This is the town I've spent my entire life in, its streets and valleys as intimate to me as the lines of my hand, but now everything's different. Because I'm here as Jessica Chen, with her best friends, and for the very first time, I feel like I'm one of them. Someone pretty and smart and talented and full of promise; someone the world bends around, rather than someone who bends to the world.

It's a dream, I remind myself, rolling down the window and letting the wind whip my hair from my face, the crisp air on my skin a counterpoint to what I keep repeating, over and over. *It's a dream.*

It's only a strange, vivid dream.

But I'm no longer sure I believe that.

Three

"Move before we run you over!" Celine calls.

The freshman blinks up at us like a deer in the headlights, wide-eyed and white-faced with alarm, then recognizes the person yelling at her. At once, she scurries away from the last empty parking spot, her open bag hugged tight to her chest, notebooks almost falling out of it in her haste.

"Thanks, Lydia," Celine yells to the freshman as Leela slams her foot down on the gas and swerves sharply into the space, just one dangerous inch away from knocking the sideview mirror off the neighboring BMW. "*Love* your lipstick today, by the way. Is that Dior?"

Lydia flushes, and actually breaks into a shy, earnest smile. "Y-yeah. It is." She hesitates. "Do you . . . want one? I have a spare since my older sister works there. . . ." I cringe slightly at the obvious attempt to boost her social standing, but I can't blame her. There's something about this school, these people, that brings out an almost animal-like desperation in you, a hunger for validation.

"Shit, could you?" Celine bats her long false lashes—a trick that always seems to work on everyone.

"Yeah, of course! I—I'll bring it tomorrow."

I watch the exchange with quiet incredulity. Only Celine Tan could threaten to kill someone one second and compliment them the next, and walk away from it even more adored than before—with a new lipstick, no less.

Leela shakes her head and cuts the engine. "Come on, babe, you need to stop scaring the poor freshmen. I swear little Lydia was about to have a heart attack."

"It's necessary for maintaining social order," Celine reasons without a hint of remorse, sliding smoothly out the car door, her platform heels landing, soundless, on the grass below. "If we don't instill an appropriate amount of fear into the hearts of the young ones, this school will descend into utter anarchy. And we wouldn't want *that*, now would we?"

Leela snorts. "Spoken like a true leader."

"I would be a great leader. I have it all: charisma, good fashion sense, influence. . . ." Celine swings back to me, her long hair almost whacking me in the face. "Back me up here, Jessica."

I resist the urge to look around for someone else, and fall into step behind her. *I'm Jessica now.* She's waiting for *me* to speak. So what would my brilliant, witty cousin say? "Um." *Definitely not that.*

But Leela rescues me. "Stop forcing Jessica to side with you, oh my god."

"I'm only speaking the truth; the evidence is irrefutable—"

"Save your persuasion tactics for your politics essay, 'kay?"

Celine groans. "Don't remind me. I still have two thousand words to write before midnight."

As we continue down the narrow pebbled paths to the main entrance, my attention slips away from their conversation, pulled as always to the view. Havenwood Academy looks exactly how you'd expect a school with such a name to look: like ancient power and old money. The kind of place angels go to rest and artists go to die. The imposing redbrick buildings rise beyond a stretch of balsam firs and a vast sea of deep green grass, with crimson myrtle creeping over the stone gates like spilt blood. Even my dad, who neither knows nor wants to know anything about architecture, couldn't stop himself from pointing out the impressive gardens and carefully clipped lawns and bone-white statues the first time he visited, the school motto etched above all the doors in gold, lest we forget: Ad Altiora Tendo. I strive toward higher things.

A strange prickling sensation snakes down my arms as we take the shortcut around the chapel. This is the latest addition to the campus ("So *that's* where our school fees are going," Leela had commented to me the first time we walked past it), although more students use it to study than to pray, unless it's for good grades.

Soft, flurried whispers from passing students follow in our wake, and soon I realize what the foreign sensation is: I'm being watched.

"God, she's *so* pretty."

"Who?"

"Jessica Chen." A sigh, strained with awe. "I wish I could look like that."

"Is it just me, or has she somehow gotten even prettier?"

"*Right?* Her skin is basically glowing."

"If I had even some of her genes, I swear I'd be invincible."

It's surreal. Everyone in my peripheral vision has me in their central line of view. I feel the ripple in the air, the eyes pinned on my back, bright, envious, eager, the way people adjust their positions to accommodate mine like flowers turned toward the sun, so subtle I wonder if they're even aware they're doing it.

"You know, I heard they recently started a fan club," Celine says when we reach the humanities building.

I'm still trying not to startle at the sound of Celine Tan speaking to me. When I was myself, she had only acknowledged my existence when she wanted to borrow something in class, or when I was blocking her way in the corridors. "A fan club? For who?"

"For *you*, obviously," Leela tells me, smiling. This too is different from what I'm used to. We've been friends for years, but Leela has never looked at me with such sincere admiration, like I'm standing one step above her.

And that's when I decide, firmly, unequivocally, that I can't be dreaming. Because even in my wildest dreams, my imagination wouldn't be able to conjure something so realistic, to create a feeling I've never experienced in all my seventeen years: the kind of joy that springs from other people's awe. The pleasant warmth on my face, the firmness to my steps. Like I've been underwater the whole time, and I'm finally moving up, breaking through the surface, into the sun.

But if this is real life . . . how the hell did it happen? What theory could possibly begin to explain this? And even more importantly, if I'm inhabiting Jessica Chen's body, living her life . . .

Then who's living mine?

Even on days without freakish supernatural events, first period English tends to give me a headache.

All the windows are closed, the single door shut tight, the air in the room stuffy as the inside of a turtleneck sweater and smelling inexplicably of chlorine (the rumor goes that a student was once killed in here, and the school cleaned the body up themselves to avoid bad press). Old Keller is already scribbling out today's learning objectives on the board when we file our way inside, the red marker so faint the words are barely visible. Something about aloneness and selfness and metaphors.

To be fair, Old Keller isn't even that old. Certainly no older than my dad. But he has all the mannerisms and fashion style of someone transported here from the nineteenth century, and he is known to speak fondly of Shakespeare as if they were good drinking buddies.

"Please copy the objectives down," he tells us in a voice like chalk.

He doesn't need to bother; it's what he says at the start of every lesson. Soon the classroom is filled with the soft flap of notebooks flipping open, the scratch of pen on paper, chairs pushing out, people squeezing into their designated seats.

Though nobody ever acknowledges it aloud, there's a pretty clear pattern to the seating arrangement here. An invisible line runs down the classroom. On one side, you have the legacies, the broad-shouldered boys and sun-kissed girls, the wealthy sons and daughters of law firm owners and university professors and construction magnates. On the other side, you have the Asian kids.

Of course, as with any rule, there are exceptions. Like Charlotte Heathers, who's a musical theater nerd, famously has no social media whatsoever, and only spends time with the piano prodigies.

I'm making a beeline for my usual desk in the middle when Leela grabs my arm. Pulls me over with an odd expression on her face, like she's unsure if I'm joking.

"Where are you going?"

"Huh?"

A few heads swivel toward us, all of them looking just as confused as Leela does.

"Aren't you sitting with me?" she whispers, waving at the chair next to her. Jessica's chair.

I falter. Gather myself. "Oh—right. Sorry, I just . . . got distracted—"

"Ladies, ladies, please stop your yapping and take your seats already." Old Keller shoots us a half-hearted glare. As with most teachers, his strictness never seems to apply to Jessica Chen. "Class started one minute ago."

I quickly sit, but I can't stop staring at the empty spot where I should be. My heart beats faster, harder, drowning out the beginnings of Old Keller's lecture. Will some other version of me waltz into class today? Someone with my face and body but not my personality? Or is there some sort of multiverse at work, where two versions of me exist at the same time, my consciousness split between them? The thought drives a chill through the marrow of my bones.

But the seat remains empty, and none of my classmates points out my absence. What's stranger is that Old Keller doesn't remark on the fact that I'm missing either, and he's the kind of teacher who only accepts absences in the event of death. Even if you were *almost* dead, he'd still expect you to drag yourself to class with your last breath to take notes on the symbolism in *Romeo and Juliet*.

". . . before we move on to our next unit, I wanted to hand back your essays. Yes, *finally*, I know, thank you for your patience. I was especially impressed with Jessica's work," Old Keller says, with a rare little smile, the thin wrinkles around his mouth deepening as he turns to me. "Your thesis was, dare I say, groundbreaking. To have interpreted the characters of Edith and Clara as being deliberately unlikable, the personification of the author's own worst fears—indeed, to read their interactions through the lens of self-mockery. . . . It's such a fresh, incisive take, and a true indicator of how well you understood the text and the themes—you were not just thinking *about* the book, but thinking *beyond* it." He pauses dramatically, and clears his throat. "You know I have a policy of never rewarding full marks for essays, as writing can never be perfect, but I was moved to make an exception in this case. Well done. Very well done."

All the questions swirling inside my head take a vacation as a happy flush spreads through my cheeks, my lips kicking up involuntarily. If this bursting, radiant feeling were a liquor, I would be intoxicated. And I can't help myself; I want more of it. I want everything I didn't have. "Thank you so much, Mr. Keller," I say, in Jessica's sweet, angelic voice. I tuck my perfect hair behind my perfect ear and continue with perfect charm, "I honestly don't think I would have gotten into Harvard without your guidance all these years. . . ."

It works even better than I thought.

There's a pause before the whole class reacts. An explosion of noise, color, applause, congratulations, and compliments pouring in from all sides. *"Oh my god,"* Leela shrieks, jumping up from her seat with such enthusiasm it almost scares me. She actually looks like she might cry with joy. "Oh my god—you got into Harvard? That's incredible. Jessica. I can't believe you didn't *tell me right away.* Are you absolutely ecstatic? I'm so ecstatic for you. Do your parents know? What did they say? I'm going to call my mom, she's going to be so excited—she always said you'd make it big—"

"I mean, we all saw this coming," Celine comments on my left, and it's hard to define the emotion in her blue-lined eyes. She hasn't moved an inch, but she's looking right at me, as though still trying to decide what her response should be. At last the corner of her mouth curves. As much in acknowledgment as in challenge. "Congrats, bitch."

"You're literally the only person I know who's been accepted," Leela gushes.

"Wait, didn't Cathy Liu apply as well?" someone asks. "She must have been accepted too, right?"

A few people turn around to search for her. I glance back over my seat at Cathy. She freezes at the sudden attention, her large doe eyes flicking to me. She skipped two grades when she was only in elementary school; that, combined with the fact that her features are naturally younger, with her full cheeks and soft brows, and her tendency to wear heart-shaped jewelry and bright ribbons in her hair, all create the impression of a tween who's wandered into a senior class by mistake. But her scores are proof that no mistakes were made. She's received the academic award for almost as many years as Jessica has, and there was once even a short article about her in the local paper, with a photo of her grinning and holding up all her certificates, her front teeth still missing.

Which is why I'm not surprised when she nods, once.

"Oh, so we have *two* Harvard girls among us," someone calls.

"Quiet down now—the other teachers are going to think I'm running a circus in here," Old Keller tells the class, but there's no real annoyance in the way he shakes his head and leans back against the whiteboard, only pride.

"Congratulations, Cathy," I tell her, surprised by how smoothly the words flow from my lips, how genuine my smile feels. It's so easy to be generous when you lack nothing. To be nice when you're not in pain. It doesn't matter if people are cheering for someone else, because they're already cheering for me.

Cathy smiles back at me. "Congratulations to you too. You're such an icon."

Even after Old Keller starts handing back our essays, someone reaches out and thumps my back, and another person jokes about how they want to be exactly like me when they grow up, even if they're three months older.

It's like a do-over of yesterday night. Like the universe has realigned with all my deepest wants and dreams. Every time I pinched myself awake when I started feeling lightheaded from studying, when I felt close to throwing up before a big exam, when I stayed up until the moon fell and the sky burned red, highlighting and writing and repeating obscure facts under my breath, when I filled in my paintings stroke by stroke by stroke, *this* is the scene I envisioned. Exactly, entirely, this.

The warm glowing bodies around me, the electric pulse of envy, the longing dangling from their faces. For years, I've watched Jessica Chen from the back of the room, how she sat with her chin up, shoulders straight, how her ponytail swayed when she laughed, how the teachers reserved their smiles and praise just for her. I've watched and wondered what it's like to be *that* talented, *that* brilliant—

And now I know.

I feel incredible. Invincible.

I feel like I could claw the sun from the sky and eat it whole.

The first and only time I ever won something, it was for an art competition.

I'd painted a huge family portrait, with Mom and Dad placed at the center of the frame, their eyes sad but smiling, and me standing just off to the side, my features darkened and blurred in their shadow. The setting was meant to be difficult to make out; there was nothing but a vast open field, tendrils of pale purple mist rising around all of us like smoke, a mere suggestion of a place, rather than a place itself. The judges had said there was something unspeakably lonely about the piece that made it stand out. One of the judges had even teared up, studying it.

When I'd gone up to collect the reward for my loneliness, my eyes fastened on the gold medal and the hundred-dollar cash prize, the boy who'd come in second place (he had done an abstract piece, supposedly in the style of Pollock; in all honesty, I just found it very messy) had congratulated me. Then, with all the airs of someone making a bold accusation, he added, "You're just in this competition for the glory, aren't you?"

"Well, yeah," I replied, the medal now clutched to my chest. I loved the weight of it, its polished edges, how it glinted beneath the lights. "Obviously."

He'd stared at me, clearly not expecting me to agree.

I was surprised by his surprise. Why *else* would I have entered the competition, put in all that work, if I didn't care for glory? It seems a common enough motivator for men, and it's never questioned. The realms of history and literature are heavily populated by kings who've gone mad for glory, knights who've killed in search of it, writers who've devoted their lives to capturing it. It's the needle to my compass, what I've mapped my entire life around. It's what my body runs on: food, water, air, and that ceaseless, propulsive desire for greatness.

Now, walking through campus as Jessica Chen, with Leela and Celine falling into step on either side of me, I can taste it. *Glory.* Radiant as the white sunshine slicing through the trimmed lawn. Sweet as the chocolate-dipped strawberries Leela's shared with both of us. The news about the Harvard acceptance has spread all over the school, and the stream of congratulations hasn't stopped yet.

I could live like this forever, I think, smiling, as I lower myself onto the grass, right under the glow of the sun, my skirt fluttering around my thighs, the rich chocolate melting on my tongue. It's only been half a day, and already I can't stomach the idea of returning to my old, small, imperfect self, to my banal disappointments and insecurities.

"Have we heard the news?" Leela asks, lying down flat beside me, one hand raised to shield her eyes.

Celine lies down too, but on her side, in a striking supermodel pose, propped up against her elbow. She somehow manages to stuff two whole strawberries in her mouth and chews. "What news?"

"About *Aaron Cai.*" Leela looks deliberately at me when she says his name. For a moment I forget who I am, and my heart tumbles in my chest. "Apparently he's come back from his Paris program early."

"Seriously?" Celine raises her brows. "Who'd leave a fancy gifted-kid program for this?" She waves a lazy hand toward all the other students milling around the sun-dappled lawn, half of them pretending to study, the wind blowing the clouds into pieces overhead.

"Havenwood isn't bad," Leela says, laughing.

"That's highly debatable."

"Well, he must have his own reasons." Leela turns back to me, a meaningful smile spreading across her glossed lips. "I wonder if he's gotten even prettier. His bone structure was always immaculate."

I can't suppress a scoff, even though I know the answer is *yes*, he has, of course he has. "I honestly don't think he needs to be any prettier. It would become a legitimate public hazard—didn't someone walk into a brick wall two years ago because they were too busy ogling him?"

Leela rolls over, laughing harder. "Can we blame them?"

"Well, I sure hope he's prettier," Celine says, her brows completing their ascent to her hairline. "The ratio of attractive girls to attractive guys around here is actually quite embarrassing."

"I thought you said Blake Chen was getting cute," Leela reminds her.

"Yeah, but then he cut his hair, remember?"

"Blake Chen's still better than Aaron," I mutter without thinking.

Both of them fall strangely quiet, and my stomach jolts. Of course Jessica Chen would never make a comment like that, joking or not. Maybe this is it—they'll realize I'm not her at all. And what will happen after that? Will I somehow snap back into my own body?

Then a familiar voice floats over from right behind me, the last voice I want to hear.

"Conflict of interest aside, I do agree with that."

Heat shoots up my neck as I whirl around and come face-to-face with Aaron. Or more like face-to-waist. He's standing up while I'm sitting, his shadow falling over me, the sun's light circling his head like a halo.

"A-Aaron," I choke out. Apparently the curse about him always

53

appearing at the wrong time is still well in effect, even when I'm no longer myself. "That's not really—I meant . . ."

He folds his arms across his chest. "Yes?"

I can't think of any way to continue without digging myself deeper into this self-made ditch. It doesn't help that I can see, very clearly, Celine mouthing, "He's definitely prettier now." So I just clear my throat and eat another strawberry.

"Do you want to sit?" Leela offers in a bright voice, patting the space next to me. "I can't believe you're back. It's been, like, ages."

Aaron's eyes flicker to her, the patch of grass, back to my face. He hesitates.

"We have so much to catch up on," Leela continues. "Why did you leave Paris early anyway?"

It's like watching a window slam shut; something in his expression tightens, smooths out. Then he straightens, swings his backpack higher up his shoulder. "I'll have to pass today, sorry."

"Oh," Leela says, disappointed. "That's fine."

"Next time," he promises. Just when I think he's gone, a combination of relief and disappointment settling inside me like river sediment, he calls for Jessica.

Jessica.

A delayed beat. I spin around, and his expression shifts again. He looks, briefly, startled. Almost spooked.

"Yeah?" I ask, my pulse picking up.

"Nothing," he says, though he's still staring at me like he's seen a ghost. Shakes his head. "Nothing."

Four

The rest of the school day passes like a perfect movie montage.

In history: the teacher asks a question about the Cold War, and everyone turns instinctively to me, waiting. Before, I could give the correct answer and nobody would even acknowledge it. Now I don't even have to raise my hand to speak. When I make a joke, the whole class laughs. At the end, we play a game of trivia, and people keep trying to catch my eye from across the room, begging silently for me to join their team.

In the corridors: a group of freshmen do a visible double-take and slow down before me, elbowing each other and whispering. I can make out a few words, repeated over and over: "That's her. Jessica Chen. Harvard. So successful. I wish . . ." I lift my chin higher and grin at them, and they flush, as if they've just been greeted by a celebrity. One of them stammers out a compliment about my skirt, even though we're all wearing the same uniform. I walk away to the sound of the others laughing. "I can't believe you just said that to Jessica Chen. That's like, so embarrassing for you."

On the lawn during lunch, after I spend forty dollars of the hundreds I have on a ridiculously overpriced salmon bagel and a pumpkin spice Frappuccino, Cathy Liu skips up to me. Her silver earrings sparkle in the midday brilliance, and a camera dangles from her wrist.

"Congratulations again, Jessica," she says, waving at me first, then at Celine and Leela, who are already lying on the grass, in almost the exact same positions as they were during the morning break.

Leela waves back. Celine just flicks a strand of hair from her face.

This isn't the first time I've seen Cathy approach Jessica's group. She's always hanging around their desks after class, asking Jessica about her grades, trailing after the three of them like an adoring puppy, perking up at the slightest sign of attention. They've never insulted her, of course, or outright excluded her. But you could sense it in the atmosphere, the same inarticulable feeling that made me keep my distance whenever Jessica was with her best friends, when she transformed from my cousin to the girl everyone wanted. *You wish you could be us,* the air around them sang. *But you can't.*

Except the impossible has happened: I *am* her. I take a slow sip of my Frappuccino, the creamy sweetness trickling down my throat, and wait for Cathy to speak.

"I'm actually here on behalf of the yearbook committee," she says, fidgeting with the camera strap. "They're doing a video segment on the school's star students and, well, obviously they wanted to interview you. Do you have, like, two minutes to spare?"

I flash her a dazzling smile. "Yeah, why not?"

"Oh my god, amazing, thank you." She holds up the camera,

and as the lens extends with a faint mechanical sound and focuses on me, I stand a little straighter, shoulders relaxed, chin up. For once, I feel no urge to check my appearance. I *know* I look beautiful. Even the way my shadow falls across the grass is striking, my profile as perfect as a doll's.

"So, Jessica," Cathy begins, "I'm sure you get this question all the time, but we're dying to know—how do you balance everything you have going on in your life? Do you ever even *sleep*?"

I laugh breezily, like an immortal who's just been asked about their secret to longevity. "I never really think of it in terms of balance. There are just so many things I'm interested in, I feel like it'd be much harder if I were to pick only one thing and devote all my time to that. People are always saying that you can't do it all, but, well, why can't you?" The fake answers race each other out of my mouth. *See how relatable I am? How passionate? How humble?* "And in terms of sleep—rest assured that I definitely do sleep. It's why I wake up refreshed every morning. Plus, I love sleeping."

Cathy nods hard. "Everything you said was just—wow. What an absolutely eloquent and inspiring response."

Without any context, nobody could possibly guess that this was a straight-faced reaction to the phrase "I love sleeping."

"I'm glad you think so," I say, taking another sip from my drink as a gentle breeze fluffs out my hair, even nature cooperating with me. It's so irresistibly fun playing this part, like when I would pretend to be a famous singer holding a concert in my shower stall, or when I would deliver an imaginary Oscar acceptance speech from my bedroom.

"Now," Cathy prompts, "what advice would you give to freshmen who might be feeling nervous about their studies?"

I wink at the camera. I don't think I've ever winked before in my life; the one time I tried, someone thought my facial muscles were spasming. But now it comes effortlessly, like everything else. "If I were to give any advice, I would say . . . copy and paste is your friend."

Cathy laughs even louder than I anticipated, a shrill, seesawing sound, the camera shaking with her shoulders.

"I'm just kidding, of course," I say, laughing too. Jessica has the kind of laugh that's instantly contagious, bubbling up through my lips and filling the air. "But really, my advice would be to enjoy the process." In my mind, I see a memory of myself sobbing from sheer exhaustion at three in the morning because I hadn't finished the English project that was due the next day.

"Studying is important, but you can't just coop yourself up in your house with your textbooks. . . ."

Another memory: me lying face down on my bed, my dinner going cold on my desk, a mountain of practice papers stacked up beside it.

"And, you know, don't take things too seriously. . . ."

Me, hunched over and typing into the search bar in the dark: "I don't understand logarithms. Am I doomed?" Throwing my pen across the room when I still couldn't solve the equation.

"That's all there is to it." I beam, the sun spilling over me. "Believe in yourself, and everything will work out."

When the final bell sounds, I take the earliest bus from school in a daze, my head swimming. It already feels like an eternity has passed since I opened my eyes this morning.

How long will all of this last? How long until the spell breaks? A day? A week? I need answers. I need to go home—not Jessica's home, but my own. There has to be some kind of sign, evidence of what's happening to me. And even through the haze of my euphoria, there's another, more crucial question that's been pounding at the back of my skull:

Where is the real Jessica Chen?

I have to find my cousin—but how am I meant to do that if I'm wearing her face?

The sky has already started to darken by the time I stop outside the front door, thick clouds crowding in from the edges, threatening rain. I stamp my feet over the tiles and shakily lift my finger to the doorbell. Then pause. There's a buzzing sensation in my veins, like the moments before I walk into an examination hall. Will some old version of me open the door? Will I bump into myself? Do I run? Attack? Call the police?

No, of course not. Nobody would believe me.

The thought sends another spike of apprehension running through my body. I shiver, wrap my blazer tighter around myself. No matter what happens, I'm completely on my own.

"Don't be such a coward. Just get this over with," I hiss out loud, and the sound of Jessica's voice is enough to jolt me into action.

The bell rings once before the door swings open.

It's not my face that appears in the doorway, but one just as familiar.

"Mo—" I catch myself. Clear my throat. "A-Auntie." The word sounds horribly stiff and unnatural on my tongue. *Wrong.* Like

59

calling our robin's-egg-blue couch green, or pointing at a turtle and calling it a rat.

My mom blinks at me with faint surprise, before her expression quickly arranges itself into a smile. It's a smile I recognize at once, the warm, polite one she always uses in company. I've seen her switch to that smile mid-lecture on countless occasions, when a neighbor popped up with fresh-baked cookies or a relative from China rang her on WeChat. One second she would be scolding me for splashing too much water around the bathroom sink, and the next she would be all gentle mannered and sweet voiced like she was meeting a royal.

But I've never been subject to it. It feels wrong too, even more so than greeting her as "Auntie." It's too nice, everything real forced beneath the surface. It's something I never thought I would experience: being looked at by my own mother like an outsider.

"Jessica," she says. "I didn't expect you here today. Were you looking for something?"

I try to scan the space behind her, but I can't see anyone inside. "Uh . . . I just—wanted to finish a group project Jenna and I were working on. She left the materials in her room. Is that okay?" I watch her reaction closely, looking for signs of—what, I don't even know. Maybe confusion. Suspicion. Maybe for her to clap her hand to her mouth and exclaim: *Speaking of Jenna, I haven't seen her all day.* Or, better yet, *Of course, Jenna is right upstairs.*

But she says neither of those things. Her expression is smooth, her polite smile still perfectly in place. Yet instead of reassuring me, it only drives a deeper sense of unease down my spine. "Oh, certainly. Come on in."

I enter the room without thinking, the way I have a thousand times before: shrugging off my blazer and throwing it over the couch; letting my schoolbag fall to the floor with a thud; sliding into my plastic pink slippers by the closet.

It's only once I've completed my routine that I notice Mom staring at me.

"Uh," I say, panicked, trying to recover in record speed. I manage a short laugh. "Sorry, Auntie, I was . . . I think I'm a little too comfortable around here, you know. It feels even more familiar than my own house."

Her expression clears. "Ah, that's how it should be! We're all family. Let yourself be as comfortable as you want."

"Th-thank you," I tell her distractedly. There's still no sign of anyone else yet. My eyes slide past the empty kitchen and faded furniture and family portraits to my bedroom upstairs. From my angle, all I can see is the closed door. "I'll just . . . go and get started, then."

"Of course," she says, her smile back and brighter than ever, but still strange. Still foreign. It's making my skin itch, the distance and the niceties. She should be nagging me to do my homework or wash my hair in time for dinner, not speaking softly as if I'm someone else's daughter. "Take as long as you'd like."

I run up the stairs, taking two at a time, my heart beating madly in my chest like a wild, spooked creature. Then I burst through the door without knocking, expecting—anything. A duplicate of myself, a phantom, some supernatural force. A banner and camera crew waiting to inform me that I've been pranked.

But I'm greeted with silence.

All I can hear is my own harsh breathing, as if I've just sprinted straight over from school. There's nobody here. In fact, there's no sign that anybody's been in this room since I went to sleep last night. The covers are wrinkled, unmade, the blanket sliding off the bed.

I creep across the space, feeling oddly like an intruder in my own bedroom. My uniform's where I last threw it, crumpled at the bottom of my closet, my skirt spotted with old paint stains that have withstood the strongest laundry detergents our local mall has to offer. Even my homework is in the same place, my math textbook flipped open to the bonus questions, my laptop half open and charging, my Muji highlighters poking out of my pencil case.

Nothing has changed at all, and yet . . .

I can't shake the feeling that something's off. Something important.

Mouth dry, I slowly make my way around the rest of the room, treating it like a crime scene, every pen and yellow Post-it note and half-dry mascara wand evidence of what this is. But what *is* this? What am I now? I keep my hands curled up by my sides, letting my gaze wander.

And that's when I notice it.

The self-portrait I was working on. It's standing up in its usual spot, the paint splattered over the canvas in my rage. Dripping violet, smeared black. I feel that lump of indignation rise to my throat again, but it quickly hardens into fear as I look closer. The difference is small, yes. So subtle I probably could have walked right past and missed it. Confused it for a trick of the light, a lapse in my memory. But it's there.

Somehow, the paint I threw last night has . . . spread. Before, only my eyes had been covered, the rest of my features as clear and vivid as if I were holding up a mirror to myself. Now, the entire top half of my face is hidden, disappearing behind layers of violet. It isn't just that the paint has dripped down—that would make sense, at least. It looks more like someone's come in with a wet brush and run it across the painting in a series of quick, messy strokes, blurring my nose and forehead.

A chill stirs my spine.

"What is this?" I say out loud, into the empty quiet. "What's happening?" My fingers reach out before me, stopping just short of the canvas. Well, not *my* fingers. Not the same fingers that drew this self-portrait, but Jessica's. Longer and more delicate, the birthmark blooming over my skin like a splotch of ink.

I squeeze my temples and try to think like Jessica. If we'd swapped bodies, and she had woken up this morning as me, then what would she have done?

Okay, let's reenact this.

I make my way back to the bed and awkwardly lower myself onto it, the springs creaking under my weight. Then, once I'm in sleeping position, I close my eyes, then open them with a theatrical yawn.

So. I wake up. I'm the real Jessica Chen, or Jessica's soul, in my own body—I mean, in Jenna's body—god, this is confusing. But point is, I'm Jessica. I'm super intelligent, and practical, and responsible, and everyone is in love with me. I never make mistakes. I never have a bad hair day. I don't even know what acne looks like.

I have the perfect life. My life is so amazing that I probably laugh in my sleep, and it would be charming instead of creepy. Now, I've woken up in my cousin's bedroom for some inexplicable reason, so the first thing I do is—

The first thing I had done this morning: look for my phone.

I sit up and pull open the drawer beside the bed. My phone is exactly where I left it, untouched.

Right. My heart patters as I push forward with my line of logic.

Since I'm Jessica, and my brain just magically works ten times faster than the average human being, I quickly arrive at the conclusion that I'm not in my own body. This is *extremely* upsetting, because I love my own body, I love my face, and I love my family and my grades and my expensive collection of summer dresses. I'm desperate to track down where my body is and make things go back to normal, so I give myself a call.

I weigh my phone out in my palm, pausing to think. Of course, as Jessica, I don't know the passcode, but that's fine, because I can just use my fingerprint. . . .

I pretend to perform the motion and then swipe up. *Time to make that call, which should be shown here.* . . . I go back to my call history, and frown. Nothing. No new calls since yesterday.

Okay. Maybe I don't *call* myself. Maybe I send myself a text.

My pulse accelerates in anticipation as I scroll through my messages. But again—there's nothing.

Maybe . . . Uncertainty creeps into the corners of my mind. Maybe I don't message *myself*. Maybe I message someone else for help. Someone I care about, someone who I'm certain cares about me. Someone like . . .

I can't bring myself to say his name, but I pull up my last conversation with Aaron. There aren't any new messages here, either—the last one is dated a year ago. Even without looking, I remember. He had sent it before his flight, only a week after that day in the rain, his tone so uncharacteristically formal I would have mocked him for it under any other circumstances:

> Jenna. I'm sorry this is so sudden, but after some thought, I've decided to accept the invitation to the medical youth program and will be leaving for Paris tomorrow. I've left the math notes you asked for in your locker, if you still need them.
>
> Please don't wait for me.

Don't wait. As if it were that easy. As if I could wipe my memory, forget him the second his plane left the tarmac. As if I could just move past the fact that I wasn't good enough for him, that I lacked some quality that would have made him stay and like me back. Some quality that Jessica would have.

I clench my teeth as I finish scrolling and slide off the bed. "Never mind. I don't contact anyone, because I decide it's easier to go hunt myself down in person. I'm still wearing my pajamas, so I have to change. . . ."

Except I can already see the fissures running through this scenario. Even if Jessica had chosen not to wear my school uniform, she would have had to take *something* from my wardrobe—but a thorough inspection confirms that all my clothes are in order. The more I think about it, the more unlikely it seems that this was a simple body-swapping incident. But if Jessica's soul isn't in my body . . . then where is she?

"Jessica?" I whisper out loud. No answer comes. I clear my throat and try again, with the cautious air of someone attempting to summon a ghost. "Jessica? Hello? If your soul happens to be, um, hanging around, feel free to let me know."

Still no response. Not even a sound.

How else is one meant to locate a soul? Through candles? I still have a few scented ones lying around in my bedroom—all Christmas gifts from people I'm not close to. Or should I draw some kind of diagram? Write out her name? Should I hypnotize myself? Should I do *drugs*?

I don't know what will work. I just know that I need to find my cousin.

So I try everything, except the drugs. I spend the next two hours going through every spiritual trick I've heard of. But the overpowering lavender scent from the candles only makes me cough, and the locket I swing before my eyes only makes me dizzy, and all of it succeeds only in making me feel ridiculous.

Defeated, I plop down on the floor and stare at the altered portrait again, a strange suspicion solidifying inside me. I take out Jessica's phone and unlock it with my fingerprint, then hold the front camera up. The flash goes off, temporarily illuminating the painting in a ghost-white light.

Then I slide Jessica's phone into my blazer pocket and head back down the stairs.

★ ★ ★

"Have you finished everything?" Mom asks, patting the couch. "Here, eat some fruit before you leave. I bought it from the market just this morning. Imported all the way from Sanya, you know—it's very hard to find around here."

The flesh of the dragon fruit has been cut into cubes, the thick purplish shell hollowed out and put to use as a bowl.

"That's okay," I start to say, but Mom's already holding out a small silver fork with a delicate porcelain coating. It's the guest fork. The pretty one she saves for special company. A hollowness forms in the pit of my stomach, the same feeling I would get on the third night of school camp, when the sleeping bags were too stuffy and my classmates were too loud and I started to miss home, or when my mom would drop me off at a gathering I didn't really want to attend, or when I would have a bad dream and tiptoe into my parents' bedroom, waiting for them to wake up and comfort me.

I do my best to ignore it as I take the guest fork and sit down slowly beside my mom. Since I'm here, I might as well test out my theory. If Jenna had appeared or disappeared in the past twenty-four hours in my body, then surely my mom would have seen her. "I haven't had this in a while," I tell her, lifting the fruit to my lips. It's sweeter than I expected, with a faintly tropical, sour edge.

"Ah, yes, we don't buy them often," Mom says, smiling. "But it's one of Jenna's favorites."

I blink at her, trying to recover from the shock of hearing my own mother speak my name like I'm not sitting right here. "Jenna," I repeat, chewing the fruit as fast as I can and swallowing hard, the black seeds scraping my throat like tiny stones. "I was going to ask . . . is she around?"

For the briefest of seconds, Mom's expression goes blank. Like someone's wiped a canvas clean, smoothed out a drawing in sand. Her eyes remain on me, but they shift out of focus, as if staring ahead into a thick fog. Then she shakes her head, and everything about her—her straight posture, her hospitable air—is utterly normal again. So normal I'm not sure if I imagined that odd lapse. "No," she says.

"No?" My heart thuds. "Then where is she?"

"Why, I thought you knew," she tells me, and her voice is still her voice, but it sounds detached. There's a floaty quality to it, sweetness without substance. "She has gone away on that trip."

This isn't right. "What trip?" I press, rifling through my memories. I can't remember ever telling her about a trip, much less planning to go on one last night. "Where has she gone?"

"Away."

Despite all my attempts at composure, I feel myself frown. "Away? How long will she be gone? When did she leave? This morning?"

She pauses, with the kind of confused look I've seen on my classmates when they're working through an impossible math equation, and lets out a light laugh. "I must be getting old," she says. "I'm sorry, Jessica, the details have slipped my mind. . . ."

My heart pounds faster. This is the same woman who memorized my class schedule every semester, who knew the exact minute my lunch breaks started and ended so she could come deliver hot food on time, who kept a mental catalog of all my exams. There's no way she could have simply *forgotten* the details if I were to leave on a trip.

"Are you okay?" she asks suddenly, peering at my face with obvious concern. "You're looking quite pale."

I set my fork down on the table. "I'm fine," I say, but my head is buzzing. "I just . . . remembered something urgent I have to do this evening."

"Oh." She stands up, wiping her hands on her long skirt. "Well, I won't keep you—I know how busy you are, our Harvard star."

I make myself smile, thank her for the fruit, and grab my things, the absolutely surreal exchange already replaying itself in my mind. The cold air hits my face as I shove the front door open. The sky is darker than ever, the clouds layered against each other, the air tinged ash-gray. I'm so absorbed in my own thoughts, the fresh memory of my mom's face, that odd, blank confusion clouding her features, that I don't notice Aaron until I've turned the corner and crashed headfirst into his chest.

"S-sorry," I say, stepping back in a daze, rubbing my forehead.

Then his face comes into clear view: him and his cold beauty, his windswept hair, the clean lines of his nose and jaw. He's staring down at me with a mildly bemused expression, and even through all the noise roaring inside my head, I hear the single beat of my heart.

I wanted this, after he left. To live in the same town, the same city, to be able to bump into him without planning to, to be able to see him just by lifting my gaze. But now he's here, and my wanting has long soured into resentment.

Please don't wait for me.

I drop my hand and straighten with false dignity. "What are you doing here?"

"I should ask you the same thing," he says.

"What do you mean? This is my—" *This is my house,* I'm about to say, until I remember. "This is my aunt's house. I have every right to be here."

"Well, by the same logic, this is my father's best friend's house."

"Can you not hear the obvious distinction?"

His bemusement only seems to grow. "You're a little . . . prickly today. Did something happen?"

"No," I say, too sharply.

"Then have I done something to offend you?"

Your very existence offends me. I swallow those words and shake my head. "Of course not. How could you?"

"Right," he says, but he's studying me too intently, and I feel my skin warming. Just when I'm about to waver under the weight of his gaze, he looks past me to the front of the house. "Is Jenna in there?"

I tense, quiet shock rippling through my body. Not just because he's here in my front yard, looking for me, asking for me, but because he doesn't seem to know that I'm apparently on a trip either. "She's . . . gone."

"*Gone?*" His dark brows furrow. "Where?"

"On some kind of trip, according to her mom. This is my first time hearing of it." I scan his face as I speak, waiting for the same mist of confusion to descend, but his features are perfectly clear, alert. Worried, I would even say, if I didn't know better.

"What trip? We just saw her last night, and she didn't mention anything. Her parents didn't either."

"Are you sure?" I press. "You don't have any impression whatsoever of her leaving?"

"No," he says firmly. "I was trying to find her at school today, but she wasn't there. I feared—" He presses his lips together. "I thought she might be sick."

"Interesting," I murmur, filing this information away in the back of my mind.

"What was that?"

"I just said it's surprising, that she's not around." I pause. I should probably leave it here, before I do or say something that makes him suspicious or breaks the whole illusion, but I need to confirm one last thing with him. "Do you remember the last time you saw her?"

An emotion flashes over his face, faster than I can catch. "Yeah, of course. It was late, she was sliding into the back seat of the car, and she . . ." The corner of his mouth tugs up for a second, an involuntary change, and even his voice sounds softer than it was earlier. "She helped her mother put her bags inside first, and then as she turned around to wave, she bumped her head against the door."

I wince. I had hoped the darkness would conceal the clumsiness of my movements; I hadn't thought he would notice. But how fitting, I guess, that this would be Aaron Cai's latest and possibly last impression of me.

"I haven't seen her since," I tell him, which isn't a complete lie.

"Maybe . . . maybe she really is gone, somewhere far away."

I hope so, I think to myself, all my old self-loathing bubbling back up again in his presence. *I hope that broken, embarrassing version of me never resurfaces again. I hope she remains buried. I hope she's disappeared permanently.*

He nods, though there's still a trace of disbelief in his eyes, like he knows there's more to it than what I'm saying. "Okay," he says after a pause, sliding his hands into his back pockets. "Well, if you do happen to find out where she's gone, could you let me know? Immediately, I mean. I want to talk to her about . . ." He looks down at the wild, uneven grass. Looks up again. "I just want to talk to her."

"Sure. I will," I lie.

I return to Jessica's mansion.

Their cleaner must have already left, because everything is so polished it's almost glowing. There are no dirty clothes strewn over furniture, no leftovers in the kitchen. The massive chandelier glitters in the foyer, throwing flecks of light shrapnel over the obsidian and marble surfaces. I'd always wondered what it was like to come home to what's practically a five-star hotel lobby, complete with the lacquer antique vases on the cabinets and the variety of plush sofas to recline on. I wouldn't be surprised if Jessica had a special sofa just for reading, and another for watching movies, and another one specifically for lying down and contemplating the meaning of human existence.

I cross the living room, the thick wool of my socks padding

quietly over the waxed hardwood floors.

It's only been a day, but it already feels like years ago that Aaron had appeared here without warning, the subject of my sweetest dreams and very worst nightmares. And now he wants to talk to me . . . about what? About how his feelings toward me haven't changed? About how he'd like us to stay friends, and nothing more? Or maybe not even that . . .

I shake away the image of Aaron's face as I enter Jessica's bedroom, calibrating the little information I have.

My body is missing, and so is Jessica's soul. Nobody seems to have detected that anything's wrong, except Aaron. And my own mom believes I'm away on some sort of trip.

Until I can figure out where Jessica is and exactly what has happened to her, my best course of action is to play the part of Jessica as well as I can. Avoid suspicion. Wear her skin convincingly. Familiarize myself with her routine. I don't want to steal her glamorous life—I'm just living it for her until she returns, like how you'd keep a borrowed sports car in good condition by driving it regularly around the block. That way, once she's back in her own body, everything will be able to continue as normal for her.

Still, a bubble of guilt rises up in my chest as I yank open Jessica's drawers, rifling through the contents inside. It feels like a blatant invasion of privacy, even though I don't exactly have any better choices. I flip through old notebooks, stacks of printed-out study sheets, notecards bound with a navy hair tie, past exam papers all marked with a shiny A-plus, the margins filled in with teachers' praise. I take my time reading through them, swinging between awe and annoyance and incredulity. Most of the comments resemble those vague starred reviews you always see in indie movie trailers:

Simply astounding.

A marvel.

Spectacular.

Mesmerizing.

Profound in ways I was not expecting.

This made me weep.

Not only a life-changing experience, but a revelation, and a revolution.

"Okay, this is honestly a little much," I mutter out loud. I would have been lucky to even get a "Good job!" on any of my tests. Yet as my eyes move farther down the paper, I spot a different kind of comment in Jessica's signature curly handwriting. She's circled a date—the only incorrect answer in the entire exam paper, worth merely half a point. And beside it, the red pen pressed so deep it's almost torn through the page: *Did your brain die while you were writing this? How could you get this SO wrong? Fix it. Remember the correct date. Remember, remember, REMEMBER. Don't you dare let it happen again.*

My jaw unhinges.

I don't know what's more alarming: the vicious, unforgiving tone of the comment, or the fact that it's from Jessica . . . to herself. It's how you'd speak to an enemy, someone you hate. I can't imagine the words delivered in her sweet voice, with her easy mannerisms.

There's a sudden prickling over the nape of my neck, the cold sensation of something gone wrong, something misplaced. I snap the test booklet shut and shove it back into the drawer. Then my fingers brush over soft leather. A book I must've missed the first time around.

Frowning, I pull it out.

No, not a book. It's one of those traditional vintage journals I didn't realize people still owned, tawny brown and bound together with a string and rusted key. There's a distinctly used quality to the pages; they're loose and uneven and worn yellow, as if they've been leafed through often in the past.

I never would have considered Jessica the type to keep a journal. It seems too sentimental a habit, too impractical, too time-consuming. I inhale unsteadily, my curiosity warring with my own better judgment. My fingers drift over the clasp, pause at the key. I might be able to justify going through her past exams, but reading her journal is different.

"*No,*" I scold myself, sliding the journal carefully back where I found it, between two folders stuffed full of certificates. "You can't."

But I can't help staring at it a few moments longer before pushing the drawer closed. I can't help wondering if the entries would piece together the Jessica I know: the model daughter, everyone's favorite darling, success incarnate. Or if they're anything like the comment on her test paper: bitter, brutal, brimming with rage.

Five

I go to sleep that night in someone else's body, in someone else's bed. When I open my eyes again, nothing's changed. The sun is streaming in thick through the curtains. I reach out, stretch, and my hands brush over Jessica's silk blankets, her clothes, her bedside lamp.

"Oh my god," I whisper.

It definitely wasn't a dream, then.

I leap to my feet, and instead of horror, I feel nothing but wild, heady relief—then a twist of guilt at just how deep my relief is, how glad I am to still be Jessica. *It's only temporary,* I remind myself sternly. *It's only until you manage to find your cousin again.*

But even that can't ruin my mood.

Everything is more familiar the second time around. I zip up her plaid skirt, smooth out her blazer, tug on her white ankle socks, and this time I even think to brush my hair back in Jessica's signature high ponytail. I find the expensive facial toner she keeps on her bathroom shelf and smear on her pink lip tint. Then I look into the mirror, and recall all those fleeting moments when I was myself and I'd catch my own reflection in the dark window of a store or a passing bus, and think, *I could be beautiful, I could be every-thing I ever wanted. I could be like Jessica Chen.* I'd even imagine my features smoothing out into Jessica's, my lashes lengthening, my skin softening, my lips curving up. But then the moment would pass, and the light would shift, and I would be left with nothing once again.

This time, though, the mirage doesn't break.

When I smile, Jessica's reflection smiles too, showing off her perfect teeth. *It's going to be a good day,* I promise myself, and for once I'm certain of it. It's going to be a good life.

"Wow, someone's happy today," Leela comments from the driv-er's seat twenty minutes later.

I help myself in, shutting the car door behind me, and accept the warm apple cinnamon roll Celine's bought, even though my stom-ach is almost full from breakfast and Auntie had insisted on giving me another five hundred dollars to "buy myself a snack" at school.

The bills rustle in my skirt pockets now as I fasten my seat belt, leaning against the cool leather seats. It must have rained last night. The air has that crisp, earthy scent to it, and there are still droplets of water clinging to the windowpanes, glistening like fragmented glass. All the colors in the roads and trees look deeper: fossil grays and juniper greens. It would be lovely as a painting.

Celine unravels her own cinnamon roll from the middle, so the inside of the car is soon suffused with the fragrance of baked apple and fresh butter. "I'm guessing *you*, unlike us, feel perfectly prepared for the test today. Very typical. Very annoying, but expected."

"Huh?" The smile slips off my face. "What test?"

Leela twists back in her seat to laugh at me. "Who do you think you're kidding? I bet you've been studying for weeks by now. Don't pretend otherwise."

Dimly, I recall something about there being a test on the Cold War unit. But that was meant to be ages away. It had been scheduled for—

Today. The realization pins me to the seat. Of course. Between all the bizarre events and crushing disappointments that have occurred in the past two days, my sense of time has been completely distorted.

"Yeah, I figured," Celine says, misinterpreting my expression for admission. "Well, Leela and I are screwed."

"Oh no, I'm not just screwed—I'm *majorly* screwed," Leela protests, shifting the gear to reverse. The wet gravel crunches noisily beneath the wheels. "I was so desperate that I spent, like, fifty dollars on these crash course notes, but I didn't even understand *those.* At this rate, I'm going to graduate both broke *and* at the bottom of my class."

I try not to look too skeptical. Like many people at our school, Leela has a habit of complaining about tests right before and after she takes them. She'll make it sound like she's about to fail, like the school will expel her for sheer incompetence, only to come back around with a ninety-five percent and a sheepish grin.

The same goes for most claims of being broke. Just last week, I witnessed a group of friends loudly lamenting their meager savings as they sipped their twelve-dollar lattes and swung their designer bags. It's all a performance of relatability, without having to experience any of the actual struggles of the true working class.

"You have to help us, Jessica," Leela's saying, gazing at me through the rearview mirror with her famous puppy-dog eyes. "We all have spares for the first two periods before politics, don't we? Let's hit the library."

"Okay, sure," I say, injecting perhaps a little too much fake enthusiasm into my voice in my attempt to sound like Jessica: generous, upbeat, definitely not intimidated by the idea of a politics test. "I would *love* to. Can't imagine anything better."

Celine snorts. "Did you have too much caffeine this morning?"

"This isn't caffeine talking," I tell her, placing a hand over my heart. "This is my love for learning. We can study together and . . . and ace that test. We've got this."

At least I hope so.

No matter how you feel about Havenwood, nobody can deny that the library is beautiful.

It looks like something that could have been constructed a few centuries ago, during the age of myths and castles. Really, it's every scholar's dream: three levels of rich, dark wood panels and ornate spiral staircases, desks stretching out from the center of the room in the shape of a perfect diamond, the sunlight wobbling gold over the glass displays and white marble pillars. Tall shelves lined with thick bound volumes of books, the most obscure titles, original texts dating back to the eighteenth century, sprayed edges and hard covers with silver foil stampings. The scent of old paper and ink and mahogany. The cool, dark air, stretching up to the domed ceiling, the high windows staring out at the emerald lawns.

Celine pushes the next set of doors open with her elbow, her arms full of textbooks, her steps sharp with purpose. It's never completely silent inside, but it's always hushed, the kind of reverent quiet you might expect to find in a chapel or any other place of worship. Even though it's early, more than half the seats have been taken already, groups of friends hogging the best tables, laptops and notepads laid out between them. We pass a familiar plaque nailed to the wall, the library's dedication written in embossed gold letters.

In loving memory of Katie-Louise Williams, October 3,
1902 to February 13, 1971.

Every time I see it, I'm struck by this sense of unreality. One of the girls in our class is Katie's great-granddaughter. I can't even imagine how it feels, to have history so close to you, to have all that wealth and power passed down from generation to generation, accumulated for you by your ancestors so you need only reap the rewards of what they've sowed. At the start of the twentieth century, my great-grandparents were working as merchants in the Qing dynasty. And with every decade since, we've had to start over, try harder, reinvent ourselves again and again and again.

"Let's go here," Celine whispers, plopping her stuff down on a desk by the window.

A girl is studying alone next to us, half her hair falling out of her messy braid, her glasses sliding down her nose. As I settle into my seat and gaze around, she scribbles a formula down into her notes. Consults something in her textbook. Then promptly bursts into tears.

Leela follows my gaze and makes a soft, sympathetic sound with her teeth. "Oh, poor thing. I bet she's doing calculus."

"It's always the calculus kids," Celine says matter-of-factly. "But don't just pity *her*—pity us. World politics isn't much better."

Leela grimaces down at her study notes. She's brought an entire stack of flash cards, each filled in with her pretty, curly handwriting and highlighted with pastel blues and pinks and sunflower yellows. Next to the title Global Nuclear Tensions, she's drawn a little heart and what may be a doodle of the world exploding. "True," she says with a sigh. "I can't remember these dates for the life of me."

"Should we do something about her?" I ask, staring at the girl just as she slams her head against her textbook with enough force to produce a distinct thudding sound. No one else in the library looks up.

Celine surveys her for a moment, then shrugs. "Nah, she'll be fine. Look, she's already over it."

As she speaks, the girl darts a quick, panicked look at the old grandfather clock in the corner, startles, and like magic, abruptly stops crying. Her tears seem to freeze halfway down her cheeks. She sniffles one last time, dabs her swollen eyes with her blazer sleeve, and resumes studying with remarkable calm. It's as if nothing's happened.

"Smart," Leela comments, spreading her notes out like a fan, her previous question forgotten. "I always schedule in ten minutes a day to cry, so it doesn't interfere with my productivity."

"Damn, only ten?" Celine raises her brows. "When my sister was in her final year, she would cry at least half an hour every day."

"It helps if I scream really loudly in the beginning. Gets most of the energy out that way."

"Ah." Celine nods like this makes perfect sense. "That's a good trick."

"Would definitely recommend."

As Leela leans back in her seat, going over the dates on her cards one by one with a look of pained concentration, my eyes snag on the novel lying underneath her pencil case. The title printed across the spine in block letters is familiar: *Blue Crescent Blade*.

"Hey, why are you reading this?" I ask, pulling the book toward me with two fingers. The cover is a vibrant abstract illustration of blue splotches that form the shape of a doughnut when you squint, though I'm aware this is not a book about doughnuts.

"What do you mean? It's a good book," Leela says, blinking up at me. "I mean, I haven't finished it yet, but it's incredibly thought-provoking. It makes such profound statements on . . . society. It's a masterpiece, I would even say."

I stare in disbelief. Only last week, Leela had called me to rant about the most "mind-numbingly boring book" she'd ever read. This was one of our favorite pastimes: either reading scathing reviews, or coming up with our own. *You would think, for a book called* Blue Crescent Blade*, there would at least be blades involved, right? But no. The closest thing to a blade I've seen so far is a butter knife, which is described at length for seven pages. Seven pages about a butter knife, Jenna,* she'd complained, while I doubled over, cackling into the speaker.

"It's a masterpiece," I repeat, my eyebrows rising. "You're telling me you genuinely enjoyed this."

She nods fast. "Yeah. And I think it's something you'd enjoy as well."

If I weren't pretending to be Jessica, I'd burst out laughing at the blatant lie. Leela has always had a habit of reshaping herself to fit the people she's around; she doesn't find common ground— she creates it. I've watched her slip smoothly between claiming to *hate* cheesecake, to declaring it her favorite dessert, to denouncing anything containing cheese as a show of sympathy for someone lactose intolerant, all within a week. It's why I would feel honored whenever she was honest with me, no matter how unpopular or outlandish her real opinions were.

I would have thought she'd be honest with my cousin too. Then again, anyone would feel self-conscious about their reading tastes around Jessica Chen, whose idea of a beach read is *The Art of War*.

"You'll have to let me read it sometime, then," I say brightly, playing along, before turning my focus to Jessica's notes.

They're the neatest notes I've ever seen, everything organized by theme, then again by chronological order, and divided into three points of significance and main scholarly debates. Keywords have been highlighted and color coded according to a strict system: green for dates, blue for people, red for statistics, orange for quotes. Leela was right, to an extent. *Jessica* was definitely prepared for today's test. She was prepared for everything.

But it's been occurring to me that *I* might not be, even in her body. I might not have her memory, or her intelligence, or her ideas. What if I walk into the exam and fail? Jessica's standards for success are so unbearably high, and her standards for failure so terrifyingly low; all it'd take is one wrong answer, and her winning streak would be ruined. This is my one chance to live my cousin's perfect life, to get everything right. I *have* to do well—as well she would, if she were here.

I spend the rest of the free period trying to sort through the notes and qualm my fears, while Leela mumbles feverishly to herself and Celine sprawls sideways across the desk, her textbook held up in the air with one hand. They get up only to stretch, or to use the bathroom, or to worry out loud about how hard the test is going to be.

More students file into the library and out again, doors swinging, leather shoes squeaking over the hardwood floors. At some point it starts drizzling again, the sound of the rain against the glass strangely soothing, muted and musiclike, the sky outside a sinking, somber gray. And always in the background: the dry rustle of flipping pages, the rapid *click-clack* of the keyboard, the clink of a thermos, someone furiously hushing a group of whispering friends, the brief pause before the conversation picks up again.

"That's it, I give up," Leela says, setting down her books to massage her neck. "I'm just going to accept my fate. I'll simply fail the test. It's whatever."

Celine shrugs. "It doesn't really make a difference. The test doesn't count for much."

"Yeah, *exactly*," Leela says, now rubbing her shoulders. "Why are we even getting worked up over this anyway? It literally does not matter. At all. Grades aren't even an accurate marker of intelligence—there have been, like, numerous studies to prove it."

"And we all know grades alone aren't going to help us get the best jobs," I point out before I can stop myself, glancing up from Jessica's notes.

They both pause, their expressions frozen in matching disbelief. Leela is wearing the look of someone unsure whether they've stepped into an alternate reality. Celine simply stares, as if one of the library's statues of some ancient British lord has sprung to life and started tap dancing right on our table.

"What?" I ask.

Leela shakes her head. "I just . . . never thought I would hear our model student say that grades aren't everything."

"Well, it's true," I tell them. "Even if you get perfect grades, that doesn't guarantee a good future. Not when you've got people like Lachlan Robertson already lined up to be an executive at his father's law firm the second he graduates."

"The system's fucked," Celine concludes, recovering from her shock. "Meritocracy is a myth, academia is corrupt, and grades are irrelevant."

"Agreed." Leela nods hard, her ponytail swishing. "This test means nothing."

"Absolutely nothing," Celine echoes.

A beat passes.

Then we all put our heads down and continue studying.

Ten minutes before the test, Leela rises from her seat and stretches, arching her back like a cat.

"Okay," she says, eyeing the clock. "Okay, oh god. I think it's time to head down."

Celine frowns at her textbook. "Are you serious? I've still got three more pages of content left to memorize—"

"But we can't be late," Leela says, looking visibly queasy at the very idea. "They'll lock us out of the classroom. And you can scan over your notes on the way there."

"Fine, fine," Celine grumbles, and starts to pack up her things. Well, *thing*. Singular. She's only prepared a single ballpoint pen that looks like it might reach the end of its life halfway through the exam. Leela, on the other hand, has brought an impressive array of four different pencils, all sharpened to a lethal point, seven neon highlighters, two erasers, a pencil sharpener and a one-liter bottle of water filled to the very brim.

I glance down at my own equipment: the pens packed neatly in a translucent plastic pocket, Jessica's ID card, and a pastel pink watch. As I stare, the minute hand ticks.

Nine minutes left.

I swallow, try to calm myself. But I'm even more nervous than I used to be before a test. In a sense, I'm facing two tests now: whether I've retained enough information from our world politics classes, and whether I can live up to everyone's expectations for Jessica, fool them all into believing that I'm really her. I can feel the tremors gathering just under my skin, my nerves stretching thinner and tighter than ever. It's as if there's a wild creature scrambling around inside me, desperate to escape, jolting my bones and throwing my heartbeat into disarray. I remember hearing somewhere that the body can't tell the difference between fear and anticipation. All it knows is that something important is about to happen soon, so sit up, stay alert, pay attention.

We file out of the library, move across the vast halls, the Palladian windows throwing great swathes of light over the black-and-white checkered tiles, and join the line of nervous students waiting outside the world politics classroom.

"Wow," Celine remarks dryly. "Everyone sure looks like they're having the time of their lives."

Half of them are fidgeting or muttering to themselves, making desperate last-minute attempts to check their study sheets and quiz themselves and their friends. The other half appear to have given up completely. One guy is busy folding notes into a paper airplane.

"I'm, like, so over it already," a girl is saying to her friend, her voice a bit too loud to be natural. "I didn't start studying until three hours ago. I'm not even exaggerating. It's *so* bad."

Celine snorts and turns her head to whisper to both of us. "Don't buy it for a second. I saw her making flash cards for this test last month."

But even the kids pretending not to care immediately stiffen when the classroom door creaks open and Ms. Lewis steps out. She's probably been at Havenwood the longest of all the teachers—someone found a sepia-toned staff photo of her in the school archives, back when there was still life in her eyes—and she's always reminded me vaguely of a pencil, with her dyed black hair and long, angular limbs and ankle-length skirts.

"Line up in alphabetical order, please," she croaks, consulting the list in her hand. "First up: Hannah Anderson . . ." One by one, she goes through the names. "Audrey Brown. Aaron Cai . . ."

I feel my heartbeat stutter as Aaron brushes past me and strides up to the front of the line. He's shrugged free of his blazer and has on just the plain white collared shirt, his tie loose and askew, his sleeves rolled up casually to his elbows. His expression is bored, his hands empty. He might be the only person here who's actually calm about the test—but that's because he's the kind of genius everyone at Havenwood is either aspiring or pretending to be. The kind of genius who has it easy, who doesn't even have to study to get a perfect score.

Ms. Lewis moves further down the list and pauses at the next name. "Jenna Chen." It's not a question. Without even glancing around, she scribbles something down.

My pulse ticks faster. "Excuse me, Ms. Lewis?" I venture.

She lifts her head. "Yes?"

"Sorry, I just . . . is Jenna Chen not here?" Obviously she isn't. But I have no idea what that means for the school.

"She's absent," she tells me.

"Absent? Do you know where she's gone?"

And just like yesterday, with my mom, her eyes go hazy. Unfocused. Like someone has painted over her thoughts with a white brush. "She's away until further notice," she says in a dreamy, distant voice. Then she focuses on the next name—Jessica's name—and it's like nothing's happened. Everything goes on as usual: the students stamping their feet, the after-rain chill clinging to the air, some girl panicking in the back about forgetting to bring a highlighter.

But all the hairs on my neck stand up.

"I guess she's really not coming to school anymore," Aaron murmurs as I move into place behind him.

"No. Guess she's not."

His brows furrow slightly. Then he stares down at my hands; without meaning to, I've been shaking my pen between two fingers. A nervous habit of mine, not Jessica's. I force my hands to still, but he's already seen it. "Stressed?" he asks.

"Only a little," I lie.

In an even voice, he says, "Jenna was always doing that when she was stressed too."

"W-what?"

"The thing with the pen."

"Oh really?" I cough. "I must've picked it up from her then."

A lie. I remember sitting in the desk behind Aaron all those years ago, watching him spin his pen with the tips of his fingers while the teacher droned on and on at the whiteboard. *You think it makes you look so cool, Cai Anran,* I'd scoffed at him. To which he'd only grinned. *You try it then,* he challenged.

I did try, but to my great humiliation and his amusement, I could only manage a pathetic wobbling motion. He'd laughed so hard the teacher had stopped midlecture and glared at us. I'd gone home that night and spent hours practicing, but in the end I never did master it properly.

"Please take your seats," Ms. Lewis instructs, snapping me back to the present. The test. Jessica's life. "Keep quiet, and don't pick up your pens until I say so."

As we shuffle inside in silence, Ms. Lewis offers me a special little smile, the wrinkles around her eyes deepening. "Good luck, Jessica," she whispers. "I know you'll get one hundred percent, as always."

It should be a compliment, but somehow it feels more like a heavy mallet to the chest, crushing all the air in my lungs. It's Jessica she has faith in—not me. I nod weakly and wipe my clammy palms against my skirt.

The classroom has already been rearranged, the test papers placed face down on each individual desk, a pitcher of water prepared up front next to a box of tissues. The reading and writing times have all been copied out on the board, starting from now and split up into ten-minute intervals.

I sit down. The air feels very cold and compact, and I'm sharply aware of everyone else around me. Celine, crossing one leg over another and squinting at the paper as if to try and see through it, her dark hair falling against her cheeks. Leela, pushing her thick ponytail from one shoulder to the other and back again. Aaron, leaning back in his chair, his eyes straight ahead, the line of his mouth confident, bored, beautiful.

Focus.

I take off my blazer with its stiff fabric and shining badges and shift forward a few inches, like someone about to start a race. All the names and key figures and dates fly around inside my head in a frenzy.

I am Jessica Chen, I remind myself, breathing in, even as doubt scratches the back of my mind. *I am so smart it scares people. I am everything my parents hoped for, everything I used to envy. I am, I am, I am.*

But I don't *feel* like Jessica. I don't feel smart or capable or even remotely confident. I feel more like I'm wearing a beautiful rented ballgown that's a few sizes too small. Beneath the pearls and the silk, it's the same. It's just me.

My teeth won't stop chattering.

A chair squeaks in the back. Somebody sneezes, and Leela immediately whispers, "Bless you," even though we shouldn't be talking. Ms. Lewis glares but says nothing. From outside, you can still hear students laughing, dragging their feet to their next class, the sound rippling like water, distant and indistinct.

"You may begin," Ms. Lewis says.

Six

An hour later, we spill out into the corridors, everyone waving their hands about and talking all at once.

"Oh my *god*," Leela says, yanking out her unraveling ponytail, then retying it with a velvet scrunchie. Her forehead is jeweled with sweat, as though from physical rather than mental exertion. "That was terrible. I mean, I was already prepared for the worst, but that was just inhumanely difficult. At several separate points throughout that test, I contemplated punching a hole through the window and escaping through it."

Celine slumps back against the closest wall, one ankle crossed over another. "No joke. Question six was a bitch."

"What did you write for that one?" Leela asks. "About the lasting consequences of—"

"No, no. We're not doing this again." Celine cuts in firmly, holding up a hand. "No comparing answers after tests, remember?"

Leela sighs and turns to me. "How did you find it, Jessica?"

I try to think back to the questions, to what I wrote, but already the test is a blur in my memory. The most I can recall is the *feeling*—the awful sense of time running out, the cramp in my fingers from gripping the pen too tightly, the pressure at the sides of my skull as I pushed my mind harder than ever before. But before I can say anything, Cathy Liu strides over to join us, her heart-shaped silver earrings bouncing as she walks.

"I'm sure it was easy for Jessica," Cathy says, flashing me a wide smile. "She's going to top the class. As always."

"Of course she will," Leela agrees.

"Not necessarily," I say, my chest constricting. "We don't know that. There's literally no way to know that."

Celine and Leela exchange a pointed exasperated look: it's a familiar one, an old routine, done so many times as to be an inside joke.

"Yeah, but it's *you*," Leela tells me.

Except that it's not. At the end of the day, I took the test alone. Even when I've tricked everyone into thinking that I really am Jessica, the most I can do is maintain the illusion. There is the idea of Jessica Chen people hold in their minds, and then there's me.

"Perfect Jessica," Cathy says with an adoring sigh, her eyes wide and fixed on me. It's probably how I used to look at my cousin when I was younger. "Sometimes I wish I were you."

"Don't we all," Leela says.

I release a silent sigh of relief when the bell rings, sending everyone scattering down the hall.

We have back-to-back classes for the rest of the day, and of course Jessica's picked out the most complex, content-heavy subjects possible. So instead of heading to the art classroom, losing myself in the familiar smell of paints and charcoal and dried flowers, focusing on

93

how to capture the shape of water, the color of light, I'm dropped headfirst into an accelerated physics class I've never taken before. It's like finding yourself in a country where you don't speak the language at all, but you're expected to get around just fine on your own.

I've already filled in three pages of Jessica's notebook when I stare at my notes on torque and angular acceleration, then up at the board, and arrive at the terrible, inevitable conclusion that I have no idea what the teacher's saying. Around me, my classmates are all taking notes too, comparing formulas and whispering. None of them appear to be struggling.

I'm meant to be the smartest person in the room, I think hysterically, *but everyone here is so much smarter than I am.*

". . . your answer, Jessica Chen?" the teacher calls.

I jolt in my seat. "Sorry?"

"Your answer for question nine," the teacher says. Ms. Gonzalez, I think her name was. She's never taught me before, but I know that she's as young as she looks, just a few years out of college, and once went on a research trip to Antarctica, which she brings up at every possible opportunity.

"Oh, I . . . let me look. . . ." I fumble around for my notes, as if the answer might have magically appeared on its own. All the tiny equations and numbers and graphs swim before me, senseless, dense, impossible to comprehend. I can feel people starting to stare, the natural silence stretching out into tension as the moment drags on. My throat closes. *They're all going to find out.* Any second now, they're going to realize that I'm not meant to be here, that I'm not actually Jessica Chen, that I'm not like them.

"It's a fairly straightforward question," Ms. Gonzalez says with a light frown. "Really, this is the kind of question we'd do for fun while we were in Antarctica. . . ." As she goes on a tangent about her trip, the class listening with polite but increasingly strained interest, I sneak a desperate glance at the notebook of the boy sitting in front of me. He'd received some kind of prestigious physics award just last year, and he's on track to study physics at MIT; if anyone were a reliable source, it would be him.

". . . ah, good times, good times," Ms. Gonzalez finishes ten minutes later, wiping her eyes. Then she straightens. "But back to—what was it? Question nine? Jessica?"

"Thirty-four point four," I say, projecting as much confidence into my voice as I can.

"Great. Thanks, Jessica," Ms. Gonzalez tells me, but I've barely breathed a sigh of relief when she pauses. Her brows draw together. "Hang on, I'm sorry," she says slowly, like she's doubting herself. "No, it seems the correct answer is . . . thirty-seven point six. Is that what everyone else got?"

A few nods from around the classroom. More eyes flickering to me.

My face goes hot. The shaky feeling from the test is back, but somehow worse. It's public failure; the mortification of making a known, visible mistake. The sentence of other people's judgment.

I stare over at the boy's notebook again, certain I must have misread it, but the number is the same. Thirty-four point four. He'd answered it wrong.

"That's okay," Ms. Gonzalez says in a hurry, failing to conceal her surprise. "It was a small slip-up. Happens to the best of us."

I hide my burning cheeks with the sleeve of my blazer and nod, even though it feels small in the same way a bone fissure is small, in the beginning, or a crack in a vase: apply the right pressure, and everything breaks.

The only reprieve from class comes in the form of our belated Women's Day and Literature event. It's a somewhat disjointed combination of two topics that the school cares the least about, but must pretend to, for the sake of its image: the arts, and women. Even World Chocolate Day received more than an hour's attention.

We all gather together in the main hall, with its warm brown interior and crimson stage curtains and high cathedral ceiling. Celine slides into the seat on my left, and Leela crosses her legs on my right.

The school made a bad investment last year and installed folding seats, which curve around the raised stage in long rows. Every time somebody sits down and then stands again, or so much as lifts their weight, the seat snaps up with an absurdly loud slamming sound. When we're asked to rise for the school hymn, the heavy silence of the hall is broken by the thud and echo of over three hundred seats bouncing up at once.

The organ drags out its first note, a mournful, eerie tune that reminds me of funerals, the claustrophobic settling of clouds before rain. Our head of music struts up the stage and conducts using a ballpoint pen in sharp, jerky movements. I mouth along to the lyrics: something about courage and light and perseverance through trying times.

Then a girl from our year is invited to do a poetry reading. Her ponytail bobs wildly on her way down the aisle. She takes her time, flattening a crumpled piece of paper that looks like it was ripped straight out of her school notebook, and lowering the microphone down to her height.

"This is a poem about my mother," she says, her mouth so close to the microphone that it makes crackling noises every time she breathes. She clears her throat. "My mother . . ." She pauses deliberately. Gazes out at the crowd like she's just made a significant point. "Once told me . . . that life . . . is a ship . . . and we must . . . take courage . . . and succumb . . . to the waves . . ."

This continues for some time. Every two or three words, she stops, and makes intense eye contact with someone in the audience. It doesn't help that the static from the microphone makes the word "ship" sound like a certain expletive—a fact all the teachers must have noticed as well, but are making admirable efforts to pretend not to.

"Is it just me," I mutter to Leela, "or did that poem just encourage drowning?"

She lets out a startled laugh, quickly muffling it with her blazer sleeve.

Celine glances over at us. "What did you say?" she whispers.

"Oh, um, nothing," I tell her, feeling awkward. I'm still not quite sure how to act around Celine. How *Jessica* would act around Celine. "It's not important."

She frowns slightly, but leans back again.

"Thank you for that incredibly moving piece," Old Keller says as the girl returns to her seat below the stage. "Now, let us turn our attention to our student-nominated Haven Awards. Remember, if there's someone you would like to nominate—and it can be for *anything*, from saving a cat to qualifying for the Olympics to helping a friend with their homework—you only need to email me or Ms. Lewis by Friday afternoon. This week, our first award goes to . . ." He peers down at the card in his hand. "Jessica Chen. For being a model student, a shining example to others, and for her unwavering integrity. Submitted by . . ." His eyebrows rise as he holds the card closer. "An anonymous admirer."

The skin on my neck tingles. *For her unwavering integrity.* Maybe I'm simply being paranoid, but it sounds less like sincere admiration, and more like a taunt. Even when wild applause sounds throughout the hall—even when Leela gives me a friendly shove and hugs her knees to her chest to let me squeeze past—even when I'm walking into the bright glare of the spotlight, I can't help feeling like there's barbed wire coiling tighter and tighter around my insides. That nameless friction, that cold gut instinct that something isn't right, only intensifies when I squint out at the sea of seated students. They're all watching me, their faces obscured by the shadows, too dark for me to make out their individual expressions. To determine if they're staring at me with awe, or with something else.

Her unwavering integrity.

Whoever nominated me for the award is out there, somewhere. And I can't see them, but they can see me perfectly. I've always wanted that: to be looked up at, to be known by people I've never even spoken to before, to be special, distinct, standing up on the tallest, brightest platform. But only now do I realize that when you're out in the open, alone under the lights, and everyone else is in the darkness, you make for such a terribly easy target.

Even after we leave the stuffy air of the hall, my head feels light, and my breathing is a little too quick, too unsteady.

Then it stops entirely when I notice the school photo hanging outside the hall.

The photo was taken two years ago, in celebration of Havenwood's one-hundredth anniversary, and every single student had been forced out onto the lawn to pose. We're all in our best uniforms, white socks and polished leather shoes, hair smoothed back from faces and stiff smiles. Jessica is standing in the front row, next to Aaron Cai, the sun coming in at the perfect angle. Seeing the two of them together is like seeing celebrities on TV; they're larger than life, glowing, untouchable, the subject of everyone's envy. It seems like the most natural thing in the world that they would belong beside each other. Nobody else could reach either of them.

Then there's me at the back. Or at least, that's where I'm supposed to be.

My heart hammers inside my chest.

Somehow, impossibly, my features have all been blurred. As if the photo were drawn using charcoal, and somebody had smudged a finger right over my face. If I hadn't seen it before, I wouldn't even know it was me. But it can't be the photo quality itself. Everything else is clear as ever, of such high resolution I can see the glint of Cathy Liu's silver earrings, the blue cut of Celine's eyeliner, the loose button on Aaron's school shirt.

"Jessica?" Celine glances back at me, brows raised in question, and I realize I've stopped walking completely.

"What's wrong?" Leela pipes up, turning around to study the school photo too. "Did they photoshop an extra arm on someone again? You'd think they'd learn their lesson after that lawsuit three years ago."

I shake my head, my throat tight. "Can you . . . can you see that?" I ask, pointing at my face. Jenna's face.

Leela frowns and looks closer. She's quiet for so long I almost forget how to breathe. "Who's that meant to be?"

"Jenna," I say. There's a great roaring in my ears, my two selves and realities colliding; in the same instant, I feel something shift in the air, like the universe itself is a physical presence, watching from afar.

"Right . . ." Her frown deepens. "It's weird, but I actually can't remember what she looked like."

"What?"

"Jenna Chen." She says the name very slowly, as if she's never said it before, as if unsure it's the right one. "I can't remember," she says again, her voice more distant, her expression clouded over.

A slow chill spreads down my spine.

It's quiet back in Jessica's house. Her parents are out again, and everything is the same as it was this morning.

I stare around their luxurious kitchen, the porcelain dinner sets and marble countertops and modern glass lanterns suspended from the high ceiling, the house I've always dreamed of. Magnolia Cottage: even the name of it is like a place from a fantasy. A place of peace, without any disruptions or distractions.

Back in my house, there was always noise: my mother chopping up garlic in the kitchen, some kind of thriller movie playing in the background; my father listening to the news, repeating snippets to himself to improve his English. More often than not, one of us was complaining about the lack of space, the lack of silence. I remember trying to study for our politics test last semester, and my father practicing outside the door, murmuring over and over the new phrases he'd learned for the day, switching between tenses: *This country . . . is beautiful. This country . . . was once beautiful. This country . . . could be beautiful.*

My heart pinches. It already feels like forever since I heard my father's voice.

But with that comes the memory of our last exchange—the disappointment in his eyes, the bitter accusation in his tone.

Look at your cousin Jessica.

He would be much happier to see me now, like this. The daughter he's always wanted.

I circle the living room a few times before the tug of hunger in my gut pulls me back to the kitchen. There's a thick leatherbound menu sitting next to the microwave. *Phil's Private Dining*, it reads in gold-foil italic letters. I flip through pages and pages of glossy images of appetizers and stop when I reach the number at the bottom. Once, Jessica had flippantly mentioned that nobody in her family cooked, because either her parents brought food home, or they had their private chef deliver Michelin-star dishes straight to their house.

My brief moment's hesitation is broken by the gurgling from my stomach. I enter the number into Jessica's phone, double-checking it against the menu, then wait. It feels wildly overindulgent to order such fancy food for a *snack*, like buying a new fur coat just to wear it once, but it's not like I'm doing anything Jessica wouldn't. Really, when you think about it, I'm just staying in character.

After the second ring, a pleasant, polished male voice floats up from the speaker. "Good afternoon. This is Phil's Private Dining. How can I help you?"

"Hi," I say brightly, leaning against the kitchen cabinet. "It's Jessica Chen here—"

"Ah, looking for an afternoon snack again?" The voice is warm, as if recounting a familiar joke. "I'll get Pete to deliver your usual order—he'll be thrilled to make the trip, I'm sure. Should only take ten minutes."

"That would be great," I tell him, relieved and slightly amazed that he already knows what Jessica would want. I'd been going to the same café down the corner from my house for seven years straight and ordering the same thing each time—a blueberry muffin and lemon tea. But when I'd tried to ask for my usual, the owner had only fixed me with a blank stare. "Thank you so much."

"Always my pleasure. Have a lovely day, Miss Jessica."

The doorbell sounds before I've even finished unpacking my

schoolbag. A breeze kisses my cheek when I open the door, letting in the light and the boy waiting outside. He looks my age, with rumpled gold hair and emerald eyes and perfect teeth, the kind of conventionally attractive guy you would notice from a distance.

"Hey, Jessica," he says. He sets down the giant ribbon-wrapped white box in his arms, then holds up a bouquet of daisies. "These are, um, for you." Color spreads fast through his neck as his eyes flicker to my face, then away, like he's scared of being caught.

"For me?" I repeat, breathing in the flowers' fragrance. The daisies appear to have been hand-picked, bound together with string, a card tied to the end. A phone number is scrawled over it, the first few digits so lopsided I can imagine his hand shaking as he wrote them. My brows rise in disbelief. I'd always assumed that guys only acted this way in romance movies—then again, my cousin's life has always been like a movie. "Wow, that's so sweet," I tell him, offering him a smile.

"I—I'm glad you like them," he stammers. "I wasn't sure what your favorite flower was, and I saw last time I was here that you already had magnolias in your driveway—I mean, not that I was, like, actively taking note of it in a creepy way or anything. . . . Okay," he cuts himself off, his whole face such a bright, vivid red I could match the shade to one of my oil paints. "Okay, yeah, I'm going to go now. Enjoy your meal."

He appears dazed as he steps out into the front yard, spins back around, and promptly walks into a tree.

"Sorry," he calls. I'm unsure if he's talking to me, or the tree.

I feel a little dazed myself as I shut the door and pop the daisies into an empty vase. It's silly, and it's shallow, but it feels good to be wanted. To be so openly adored. I can't stop smiling while I unwrap the ribbons around the box, the cool silk sliding like water between my fingers.

Jessica's usual order is, apparently, an entire afternoon tea set: potato quiche and Parma rolls and hazelnut torte and butter scones with cream and glistening slices of fruit, and a papaya salad containing so many kinds of nuts and seeds it seems almost offensive to call it just a salad.

In the sitting room, I sink back into one of the massage chairs, transporting the tiered tray with all the exquisite bite-sized treats onto the armrest, and open Jessica's laptop.

Time to focus.

After physics class and the Haven Awards announcement, I can't allow for any cracks in my performance. I have to prove to myself that I *can* be Jessica, that perfection isn't so far out of reach from me I can't even emulate it properly. But there's more at stake than my pride—if people find out that I'm a fraud in Jessica's body, who knows what they'll do? They could lock me up, or report me to the police for identity theft, or maybe they'll make a movie about it: the mysterious case of the missing cousin. Even if we were to eventually return to our own bodies, it wouldn't just be my life that's forever altered—it would be Jessica's too. I can't do that to her.

No, I have to make sure nobody finds any reason to doubt me. And that means controlling every detail possible—including Jessica's emails.

I smear the clotted cream thick over the scones and take a large bite, the pastry soft and piping hot in the center and crumbling instantly in my mouth, then click into her inbox.

Right away, a flood of emails come through. Between the reminders about the swimming carnival coming up in two weeks, the automated responses from school reception, and the increasingly desperate reminders to fill out the student feedback survey, it's all just award after award, praise after praise, the world's greatest news distilled into text on the screen.

> *Dear Jessica, I am delighted to inform you that the Admissions Committee has voted to admit you to the Harvard Class . . .*

> *Congratulations, Jessica! In recognition of your commitment to excellence, we are delighted to present you with the Katelyn Edwards Award. You will receive a cash prize of ten thousand dollars . . .*

> *Subject: Some absolutely amazing news! Huge congrats!!!*

> *Dear Jessica, As a highly valued member of the Havenwood student community, your experience matters. That's why we would like to warmly invite you to fill out the following questions—*

Wait. No. That one's still the feedback survey.

> *I'm thrilled to be sending along this early offer from the Dean's Institute. The selection process this year was the most competitive yet, with only two candidates selected out of the thirty thousand who applied . . .*

Jessica!!! I always knew you'd make it big! Just wanted to send a quick note and say I'm SO proud to know you!

It is a great pleasure to inform you that you have been awarded the National Merit Scholarship . . .

Subject: Media Request. My name is Samuel Richards, and I write for Business Insider. *I was incredibly impressed to hear about everything you've accomplished at such a young age—perhaps most notably, the five million dollars you raised for your global education campaign. Because of this, I wanted to reach out and ask to interview you for the next issue . . .*

I stop scrolling and lean back against the couch, catching my breath, overwhelmed by the sheer weight and scope of her achievements. I'd heard somewhere that the imagination is always limited by experience, and that must be true, because no matter how I stretched my mind, I would never even have dared imagine such success.

Then a new email pops up. There's no heading, no sign-off, only one sentence.

I know what you've done.

The world sinks beneath my feet. I drop the rest of the scone back onto the tray and read the email again. My pupils shrink down until all I can see is the black text creeping across the screen. I know what you've done. *I know.*

It feels like my scalp is trying to crawl off my skull.

With shaking fingers, I click into the sender's details, but it's anonymous. Just like the person who nominated me for the award.

The little food I've eaten threatens to lurch back up. I swallow hard, draw in a tight breath, even though it fails to fill my lungs. A clock ticks from the mantel. The wooden boards of the back porch creak. The silence in the house takes shape until it's impossible to distinguish the vibrations of the air from the high-pitched ringing in my ears.

What do they know? Who is the email really addressed to? My cousin? Or have they already found out that I'm an imposter, that I'm only wearing her appearance and her reputation like a stolen crown? And if it is meant for me, and they have found out—*how*? Was it because of my mistake in physics? Or was it something else? Have they been watching me at school?

Could they be watching me now?

Goose bumps break out all over my body. I jerk my head toward the closest window, but all I can see is the burnt orange of flowers, the spreading claws of the trees, the pale yellow light piercing through the gaps in the leaves. Then the clouds shift to cover the sun, and my reflection falls over the darkened glass. Jessica's perfect, angelic face stares back at me, her large eyes filled with my horror.

Seven

In my old life, when everything was terrible and nothing I did felt meaningful, I would always torment myself by imagining Jessica's daily routine. But for the past two weeks, I no longer had to imagine; I could directly compare my routine to hers.

My mornings as myself: wake up to the hostile blare of the alarm. Bury my head in my blankets and press snooze. Repeat until the snooze button gets tired of me. Eventually, find the inner strength to stagger like a resurrected corpse into the bathroom.

My mornings as Jessica: wake up to bright golden air, the open sky beyond the window, somehow already energized. Hum under my breath as I slip into my satin bathrobe and silk slippers. Admire my perfect reflection in the mirror and wonder how it's scientifically possible for a person to not have pores.

Lunch, as myself: wolf down a soggy chicken sandwich and retreat into the shadows of the bike shed, my sketchbook hugged to my chest. Watch Jessica and Leela and Celine from a distance as they laugh together on the lawn, swallow the lump in my throat.

Lunch, as Jessica: lie down in the very center of the school lawn, soaking up the sun, while people like Cathy watch from a distance, desperate to be closer. Catch up with Leela and Celine on the latest gossip. Catch the eye of some beautiful boy passing by.

My evenings as myself: take a hasty shower before collapsing on the couch next to my parents with a bowl of sliced apples, squinting at the light from my phone. Flick through photos and videos of strangers having the best night of their lives, showing off their six-figure brand deals, their shiny new cars, their prestigious art awards, their friends' yachts.

My evenings as Jessica: take a hot bath infused with roses and expensive oils. Wander around the mansion, where every room smells like the magnolias lining the front yard, sweet and clean. Slide into bed and marvel at how different two lives can be.

But Jessica Chen's routine isn't just different from mine—it's also utterly overwhelming. I'd thought that my schedule was already intense, but Jessica's chosen the hardest subjects the school has to offer, and her interests just happen to lean in the opposite direction of mine; instead of history, geography, and art, she's taking chemistry, college-level statistics, and computer science. I find myself rushing from class to unfamiliar class, my anxiety climbing in steady increments with each assignment introduced and each test announced, the work piling up in impossible amounts. It's just one thing after another after another; it feels like I'm being chased. I can't slow down, I can only go faster. By the time I get home, the pressure in my skull is so intense I'm gripped by the very real fear that my brain might explode.

Then there are my self-assigned readings.

In the limited spare moments I can squeeze out of my day, I slip into the library, past the filling tables, to the shadowed corners at the very back, where you can find rare, leather-bound books from decades ago, though few students ever try. I haven't received any new mysterious messages since last week, but the sick, paranoid feeling in my stomach hasn't abated—it's only spread. Every time I catch a classmate's eye, bump into someone in the corridor, I have to suppress a flinch. *Do you know?* The question bubbles up in my mind like bile. *Was it you? Can you tell that I'm not her?*

But in the absence of any real answers, I need to find my cousin now more than ever. There are no reliable answers online, and I don't have either the faith or the intelligence to look into scientific theory, so I turn to lore. Legend. Fairy tales from fallen kingdoms.

Tiny motes of dusts swirl in the air, catching the silver sunlight as I pull out another collection of fantasy stories from the nine-teenth century. It's so heavy that I have to set down the stack of books I'm already holding and balance it against the shelf. My fingers drift over the title. *The Strange and Fantastical Journey of Charles Collins*.

Like most of the other titles I've browsed through, the pages are yellow and thinning, as if the edges had been dipped in water, and flecked with brown, like sunspots. The detailed illustrations curling around the text have started to fade in color too, the dark strokes of ink vanishing with time. But there's a chapter about Charles transforming into the charming, handsome knight he envies. . . .

My heart ricochets inside my rib cage.

I read four pages before my pulse slows its pace again. Nothing happens to Charles's soul, or the knight's. Instead, Charles learns a forbidden spell that only works if he steals the knight's face—which he does in a horrific manner, slicing off the knight's nose and lips, then gouging out his eyeballs, then peeling off the knight's skin. The accompanying drawings are just as vividly gruesome, depicting the two men, one gloating, grinning, his hands crusted crimson, and the other faceless, doubled over in agony, his ruined mouth a gaping abyss. I shove the book back with a violent shudder, the delicate skin on my face crawling with goose bumps.

"I thought it was you."

I jump at the voice, my knees buckling. My first thought of pure black dread is that it's the anonymous student, that they've caught me and everything's over and they'll all know I'm an imposter. But when I spin around, it's Aaron standing in the aisle, a bemused expression on his face.

"Sorry, I didn't mean to scare you," he says.

I can still hear the blood slamming against my eardrums. "I . . . no," I manage, my throat tight. "No, you didn't scare me. I was just . . . surprised. There, um, usually aren't a lot of people here."

"I'm looking for a doctor's memoir," he says, then glances over at the thick volumes lying by my feet. "And you're looking for . . . fairy tales." The faintest lift of his eyebrows. "I didn't think that was your area of interest."

I wince. "It's not. I only . . . I was only looking for inspiration," I say, stringing the lie together as I go, "for my next English project. I thought it might be good to get some, um, unique perspectives from the novelists of the nineteenth century."

"I see." His eyes are too dark for me to tell if he's convinced.

"Well, if you want to read those, you should probably go check them out now. Old Keller might forgive you for being late if you tell him how dedicated you are to your English project, though."

I stare at him blankly.

"Debate." His brows rise higher. "Don't you have the meeting at lunch? I saw them getting ready on my way over."

Right. *Debate*. Because aside from her intensive academics, Jessica has also signed up for every extracurricular under the sun. Student council. The school magazine. Peer mentoring. The English club. Academic decathlon. Yearbook committee. The Chinese Club. And of course the club considered most competitive and elite at Havenwood: speech and debate.

I curse inwardly. "Of course . . . thank you," I babble to Aaron. "I should definitely go—I'll go right now. Nice seeing you . . . as usual." I crouch down, trying and failing to gather all the books in my arms.

Aaron's voice hovers over my shoulder. "Do you need help with—"

"No," I say quickly, using my chin to stabilize the wobbling pile of books. "I'm fine. Really. Thanks again, Cai Anran."

It's not until I've brushed past him that I remember I'm the only one who ever calls him by his Chinese name.

Speech and debate meetings are held in what used to be the world literature classroom. The air tastes bitter, like old coffee and plastic, and the lone window at the back appears to be stuck closed. Two rows of tables have been arranged on opposite ends of the room, facing each other.

"Jessica, you're finally here," Old Keller says when I rush in, and for a confused moment I almost look around to find my cousin. I give my head a quick shake, try to catch my breath, get my bearings. Everything is starting to blur together, my life and Jessica's. "I was just about to announce the topic for today."

I do a quick assessment of the teams, sizing them up instinctively.

On one side is Tracey Davis, Liam Phillip, and Lachlan Robertson. They don't smile at me; they don't seem to notice anyone around them at all. Instead, their heads are bent together and they're joking loudly about something, or someone, a name that sounds familiar but I don't fully recognize. I chew the inside of my cheek, my gaze flickering between them.

Liam is the smartest of the three, without a doubt. Broad shouldered and naturally intimidating, he attended a special debate camp last year and won best speaker at a recent national competition. Tracey is intelligent, sharp-tongued when she wants to be, but not particularly confident. Lachlan is confident, but not very intelligent.

On the other side—my side—is Charlotte Heathers and a girl from Jessica's physics class.

"Hey, Jessica," Charlotte says with a wide, genuine smile. She's one of the only girls in our year who hasn't had her braces taken off yet, and the smattering of freckles across her nose looks more prominent than ever under the harsh fluorescent lights. It's a look that not many can pull off, but she makes it seem cute, even stylish.

"Okay, debaters, please find the topic on the board," Old Keller announces. "Tracey, Liam, and Lachlan—you'll be arguing for the topic. Jessica's team—you'll be arguing against."

I slide into the only seat available, on Charlotte's left, and stare ahead. The topic has been written out with a dying blue marker and circled twice for emphasis.

It reads:

Imperialism is a justifiable means of spreading knowledge
and new technologies to weaker nations.

"What?" I hiss out loud, blinking at the board. "Are we being serious? Is this . . . is this a legitimate topic for debate?"

Charlotte shoots me a look that's half infuriated on my behalf and half apologetic. "Maybe we can ask the teacher to change it," she says. "This is only for a mock debate, anyway."

I feel a low twisting in my gut, but I ignore it. It *is* possible that the teacher would change the topic—but then I'd have to try and explain myself to the room, beg them to understand it from my point of view, and that thought only makes my stomach tighten further. "No, it's fine," I say. "Not a big deal."

Across the room, the other members have already started brainstorming, Liam speaking low and fast with his hand covering his mouth, while Tracey nods enthusiastically and takes notes, her pen flying across the page.

"Wow, they were really prepared for this one, weren't they?" I mutter. "It's great that they can think of so many reasons right away. Not concerning at all."

"We'll win," Charlotte reassures me. "We can come up with better points."

I nod, even though that's not what I'm worried about.

The official debate begins fifteen minutes later. Liam goes first. He stands up slowly, pushing the chair back with an unpleasant, drawn-out screech, and clears his throat twice. His limbs are loose and relaxed, his mouse-brown hair gelled back, his expression smug, as though they've already won.

"I would like to first clarify what the topic is addressing," he says, "in that the real question posed here is: Do the benefits of imperialism outweigh any potential harm? Ultimately, we believe the answer is yes."

It's all I can do to keep my eyebrows from ascending up my forehead.

"What is imperialism?" he continues, now walking around the room as he talks. He isn't holding any cue cards, so his hands move freely about in distracting, elaborate gestures that mean nothing. "Simply put, it is the spread and extension of power, culture, and influence. Let's look throughout history, toward the Opium War, as an example. . . ."

I'm forced to sit there and chew my own tongue as he goes on and on about the economic benefits of opium sales, about the modernizing effects of war, the stimulation of global trade, before arriving at his next point. "We believe that the weaker nations are the ones benefiting the most from imperialism. Look at our education system, our resources, our research—it's universally acknowledged that a Western education is superior. Today, hundreds of thousands of immigrants flock to our country in hopes of attaining exactly that. Those people will spend their whole lives fighting to be recognized by institutions like Harvard." His eyes land deliberately on me, his point clear.

I look away, coldness spreading through my fingertips, unable to think of a response. Because haven't I spent my whole life longing for Harvard's approval?

Charlotte goes next. She delivers a calm but scathing rebuttal, which is then countered by Tracey, and then it's my turn.

I rise to my feet. The notes I've prepared shake so violently in my hands that I almost can't read them. I swallow, open my mouth to speak, even though it feels like there are stones lodged inside my throat. "The second argument in favor of our position is . . ."

The other team looks straight ahead at me. Looks straight through me. Their expressions are totally unbothered, cool, bored. Liam's brows rise higher and higher as I make my points.

"We shouldn't ignore the social ramifications . . . the devastation caused to—" My voice cracks.

Charlotte immediately offers me a bottle of water. I take it, cupping it in my trembling fingers.

"Take your time, Jessica," Old Keller tells me.

I can feel myself growing more and more flustered, an unpleasant heat spreading over my face, my neck, my palms.

"The devastation caused to the local populace," I continue, but it's like I'm not even here. It's like I'm hovering outside Jessica's body, watching everything progress from above. It's all futile. A doomed match. Of course the members of the other team are able to rationalize and intellectualize their way through this argument; they can express their opinions clearly, succinctly, without any personal feelings on the matter, without having to sift through their trauma for evidence, and they'll be rewarded for it.

But here I am, trying to verbalize my own pain, to justify my own existence, breaking it down into digestible points. Every word comes out a double-edged knife. This isn't just a debate for me. This is my history, my life.

Then, finally, it's over. The other team wins.

There's a low sinking sensation in my stomach, but it's more than defeat.

"Good job," Liam says when we're all getting up and shaking hands because we have to. His fingers are ice-cold; mine are warm, clammy. "And just to put it out there, I'm not, like, personally a massive fan of imperialism."

"Right," I say. "Sure."

"It's debating, you know?" he continues. "You can argue things you don't believe in. That's what makes a good debater."

I give him a stiff smile. "I understand."

"Well." He already looks done with the conversation. "Better luck next time."

I watch him as he ambles out of the classroom, his hands in his blazer pockets, Tracey and Lachlan following close behind him. Maybe he'll brag about his win at dinner tonight, recount his finishing statement, and everyone will tell him how smart and eloquent he is. Or maybe he won't, maybe this whole thing will have slipped his mind by the time he reaches his next class. That's how little it matters to him.

★ ★ ★

But I'm still fuming over the debate when I slide into my seat in politics. I feel strangely shaken, like someone's flipped my skin inside out, left a bitter, stale taste in my mouth. The more I think about it, the more my body recoils from the memory.

"Have you heard already?" Leela whispers, misreading the look on my face. She's drumming both fingers on the table in a rapid, erratic rhythm, like a quickening heartbeat. I try to ignore it.

"Heard what?"

"Our tests have been marked," Celine says, with the somber tone of a doctor delivering a medical report. "She's going to hand them back this class."

She's not the only one nervous. All around the sunlit classroom, people's faces are drawn, pinched, turned toward Ms. Lewis at the front of the classroom. Or, more accurately, the test papers stacked beside her.

When the last student has shuffled inside, she closes the door and rests her hands on her hips. She's wearing a darker shade of lipstick today; it bleeds into the fine wrinkles around her lips when she speaks. "I appreciate that this was a difficult test for many of you," she begins.

"Shit," Celine hisses under her breath. "That means we're screwed."

Leela lets out a hysterical sort of laugh.

"We will review it together," Ms. Lewis says. "I'll call your names out one at a time. Whether you're satisfied or not with your score, I suggest you keep your reactions . . . subdued." She shoots a pointed look at Charlotte Heathers, who once famously leapt up onto the desk in joy when she got a ninety-five percent.

I squirm in my seat as the teacher reaches for the first test paper with what can only be deliberate slowness. She lifts it all the way up to her face, then lowers it, adjusts her reading glasses, and squints at the name. Not mine, this time. It's like the moments before we headed into the test, but worse in many ways. Now there's nothing we can do except wait.

And despite the teacher's warning about subduing our reactions, I still can't help assessing everyone's expressions as they head up to retrieve their test. A few people's faces crumple in relief, their tension cracking into a wide beam. They make their way back to their desks happily, patting their chests. Others aren't so lucky.

Only Aaron's face doesn't change at all when he sees his score. As he passes me, I crane my neck and catch the one hundred percent scribbled at the top next to his name.

Typical.

Then a small shock goes through my body, a silent pressure, jolting me from my thoughts. I look up instinctively, and meet his gaze. He's caught me staring. He tilts his head, spelling out a half question I don't know how to answer. Jessica would have simply kept her eyes on her own paper.

"Jessica."

I twist my head, my heart already beating in a frenzy. Ms. Lewis is holding out my test. Every possibility runs through my head, the greatest success and the most crushing failure. I suck in a deep breath and stand up to take it, flipping it over quickly to the first page, the sharp edge of it slicing my thumb.

Ninety-one percent.

My chest inflates, relief flushing through me, the corners of my lips leaping up. *Ninety-one.* I repeat the number inside my head, relishing it. It's so much better than I would have expected. In the past, I had been getting consistent seventies and eighties in my politics tests. Maybe I'm not so bad at this subject. Maybe I could even be *good* at it, and I just didn't have the right notes or study technique—

But then I see the look on the teacher's face, and her eyes are heavy with such obvious concern you'd think I was dying right in front of her.

"Is everything okay at home, Jessica?" she whispers.

I blink, my smile faltering. "Um. Yes?"

At this, her concern only deepens. "Are you certain? Were you sick during the test?" She sounds almost hopeful, like nothing would put her mind at ease more than the idea of me taking this test with a high fever.

"No?" I say. By now I've been standing up here too long, and people are starting to stare.

"Well then, this isn't up to your usual standards, Jessica," Ms. Lewis says, keeping her voice low. "I know some students like to let themselves go toward the end of their final semester. . . ." She peers sternly down at me over her glasses, and out of nowhere, I remember the story my mother used to tell me about Sun Wukong, the monkey king from the myths, crushed under the weight of mountains for centuries. It's hard to breathe. "That's not what's happening here, is it?"

"Of course not," I whisper.

"I certainly hope not," she tells me, patting my arm. "You're the best student I have, Jessica. I would hate to be disappointed."

I can't muster a response, so I just nod and turn back to my desk. As I do, a terrible thought dawns on me: that failure is permanent, but success is always fleeting, it always happens in the past tense.

Jessica's Harvard acceptance only came in last week. In the test before this one, and the one before that, she had received a perfect score. But already I can feel the significance of it fading, the light winking out like a passing comet, there and then gone behind the trees, lost to obscurity. It's not enough to be perfect at one precise moment in time—to stun those around you, to grasp the lightning when it strikes, to move across a stage and gather all the accolades in your arms like fresh roses.

You have to prove yourself over and over, and when the glory for your most recent achievement expires, as it must, as it always will, you have to start again, but with more eyes trained on you, more people waiting for the day when your talent withers, and your discipline weakens, and your charm wears away. Success is only meant to be rented out, borrowed in small doses at a time, never to be owned completely, no matter what price you're willing to pay for it.

Suddenly I feel suffocated, as though I really am trapped beneath mountains, struck down by the gods. I want to escape this classroom, this school. I want to leave this town behind me in the dust and run for miles and miles.

I want to paint, to smear oils over a canvas, but I haven't held a brush since my last night as Jenna Chen.

The second I'm seated, someone taps my shoulder. It's Cathy.

"How did you do?" she asks me.

I manage to smile. "All right."

"Just all right? I'm sure you did great."

She wants the actual score. Of course she does; I don't think Cathy Liu is physically capable of restraining herself from asking about other people's scores, no matter how unwilling they are to share. There was a rumor going around that she keeps a secret spreadsheet on everyone's grades across all her subjects, and that it's more comprehensive than what some teachers have.

I make sure my test paper is fully face down on my desk, so she can't see, and flatten my hands over my lap. Suppress the violent urge to shred my test into pieces. "It was okay," I tell her.

"So, like, ninety-nine percent, then?" she guesses.

I say nothing.

"Ninety-eight?" Her dark brown eyes search my face with anticipation. "Ninety-seven? It must be above ninety-six at the very least—"

"Hey, could you give my friend some space?" Celine interrupts, throwing her a look so disdainful even I feel like withering under it. It's a look that says *Know your place*.

And Cathy does. She shrivels up at once and retreats back to her desk without another word.

"I swear, that girl cannot go a *day* without trying to cozy up to you," Celine mutters to me under her breath. "I bet she was planning to start bragging about her own score next. It's literally embarrassing how eager she is to impress."

Despite myself, I feel a faint jolt of pity. I wonder if that's how Celine saw me, when I was myself: always on the sidelines, trying to cling to Leela and Jessica, to climb higher than I deserved to be. But before I can decide whether to thank Celine or defend Cathy, I'm distracted by the soft creak and click of the door. Leela's slipped out of the classroom.

Nobody else seems to have noticed; they're all busy fussing over their scores, complaining over the questions they misread, the half point they shouldn't have lost. But something's wrong. It's a feeling more than a knowing.

"Where's Leela headed off to?" I ask Celine.

"Probably the bathroom." She shrugs. "She always goes to the bathroom at this time of the day on the dot. Her biological cycle is like a robot's."

That might be true, but I still feel a pang of unease in my stomach. "Well, I'm going too," I say.

"Be quick," Celine calls after me. "We're looking over the answers soon."

The hallway is quiet when I step out. It doesn't take long for me to spot Leela standing alone at the very end of it, her head bowed, her paper crumpled in one hand. Her shoulders are trembling.

Then she seems to hear me approaching, and stiffens. Wipes furiously at her cheeks. Hides the test behind her back like it's something criminal.

"I was just getting some fresh air," she tells me, her voice scratchy even as she shoots me an almost-convincing smile.

"Are you okay?" I ask.

She nods, nods so quickly her ponytail whips around. "Yeah. Of course, silly."

I pause, confused by her reluctance, the wariness in her gaze. As if I'm someone to be guarded against, rather than someone to confide in. No matter what it was, Leela Patel would always find me first when something went wrong. I've listened to her sob uncontrollably over the phone after breaking up with her first boyfriend, after fighting with her mother, after missing the last entry spot for the computer science camp she'd had her eyes on for years. In comparison, this should be nothing.

"You can tell me, you know," I say slowly. "I'm here for you. Whatever it is."

Surprise flashes through her features.

"Really," I continue. Jessica would probably say something much more eloquent and profound, but I can only talk to her the way I know how. "I mean, I bet it can't be *that* bad. You haven't lost a million dollars, have you? Or murdered people? Or crashed a car through the principal's office? Or led a donkey up to the school roof, like those guys did last year?"

She lets out a small snort. "No."

"Then?"

"You . . . wouldn't understand," she murmurs, but her stance is softer, her hands lowering themselves to her sides.

"Try me," I say gently. "I might understand more than you think."

"It's just . . ." She hesitates again. "It's just . . . this test. I bombed it, as expected. Well, even more than expected, if you can believe it."

You couldn't have, is what I want to say, but I stop myself. I've had that line used on me enough times to realize it cuts more than it comforts. It's such a familiar line of conversation I have it memorized. "I did so badly," I would tell someone, to which they'd say, with a flippant air, "I'm sure it wasn't bad—it's not like it was below ninety," which would render me humiliated and speechless, because it very often was.

So instead I just reply, "It's only this one test. Mathematically speaking, it's not enough to affect your average. Plus, we've all bombed at least one test before—it's basically a rite of passage."

There it is again: the surprise on her face, even more pronounced than before.

"Have *you* bombed a test before?" she asks with some skepticism.

"I . . ." I trail off. I want to tell her the truth, but I don't want to lie as Jessica. "I'm familiar enough with disappointment" is what I settle on.

"But you've never felt this way, have you?"

"Felt what?"

"Like you're constantly struggling." She's so quiet I have to read her lips to understand the words. "Like everyone is racing far ahead of you and you're stuck in the same place, or worse—"

"Or slowing down?" I finish for her. "Trust me, I know the feeling."

She stares up at me. "Really?"

I've never known anything else except this. "I told you." I shrug. "Rite of passage. I'll bet half the people in our class are thinking the same thing right now."

"I doubt it. They're all so smart—"

"You're smart as well," I cut in. Sometimes it seems like being called smart is the only compliment that matters at Havenwood. "Everyone knows it. Including the teacher. Remember the presentation you did last month? You literally got a standing ovation at the end like it was a film festival. I don't think that ever happens, but it happened for you."

"Okay, you're just flattering me now," she says, but she's smiling a little, her eyes brighter, clearer. This feels so much closer to what I remember, to the way Leela acted around me, laid-back and honest and never afraid to be too sappy. I've missed it.

"You know what we should do?" I say, eager to make the moment last, to have my best friend back. "Let's head down to the Owl after school." I'm certain this will cheer her up—it's the café where we would spend countless afternoons, racing to reserve the rose-patterned couches in the corner, ordering lemon teas so cold you could see our breath condensed against the glass and platters of fries the size of our head, dipping them in melted cheese and licking the salt and chicken grease from our fingers.

The tables were always decorated with antiques and misshapen mugs and glazed vases, and we'd bring our sketchbooks with us and draw until all the other customers had left. It was one of the few places where I could truly relax, where time didn't seem to shrink, but to stretch out around us.

"The Owl?" Leela looks confused. "I thought you said it was too crowded. And the fries were too oily."

I falter. "Oh. I mean, yeah, but . . ."

To my relief, the classroom door creaks open again, and Cathy skips down the hall toward us.

"What are you two doing out here?" she asks. Then she looks over at me, at Leela's expression, the test she's still holding, and seems to understand at once. "Ah. Didn't get the score you wanted on the test?"

Before either of us can reply, Cathy addresses only Leela. "It's okay if Jessica beat you."

Leela's smile drops completely.

"We should all be used to it by now, right?" Cathy goes on in a matter-of-fact tone. "Jessica is, like, on her own level. She's basically a god, and gods don't have any competition except themselves. It's useless to get upset over it. My best tip? Just accept that she's better than everyone and move on with your life. None of us can be her."

This, I suppose, is a twisted form of praise. Yet all I can focus on is how Leela shuts down, shifts back, her fingers curling over the paper. All I feel is the slosh of ice water in my stomach, the sense that something is slipping away from me.

"None of us can be her," Leela echoes. "You're right. How could I forget?"

"Leela," I try. "That's not—"

"No, no, it's true," she says, and my gut sinks further. She doesn't sound angry. It's hard to detect any emotion in her voice at all. "I'll meet you inside, Jessica. I actually did have to go to the bathroom, so."

"I . . . okay."

I let her go and walk back to the classroom alone, in a daze. Everyone is still obsessing over their test papers, comparing answers, and for a few seconds, standing there in the doorway, the whole thing strikes me as entirely ridiculous. Nonsensical. All this trouble, all this scheming and grieving and competing, for what? A number that will shed its meaning in less than a year?

But when I glance over at my desk, my blood skips in my veins. My test paper has been flipped around, the score exposed. When I go to pick it up, a handwritten note falls out from inside the pages, fluttering onto the desk like the severed wing of a moth.

Not so perfect, are you?

Eight

"How was school?" Auntie asks across the dining table.

Both of Jessica's parents are home today. That's still the only way I can think of them—as *Jessica's* parents, not my own. Because my mom and dad would never be seated so formally for a small family dinner, with their designer blazers and ironed shirts still on, the television turned off in the background, the only sound the light scrape of their chopsticks against the plates. They would never come home with boxes of takeaway from the most famous— and expensive—Chinese restaurant in town. I would always have to beg my mom to let us order food, and more often than not all I ended up with was a stern lecture on how we already had everything we needed at home. And besides, her cooking was better than anything a chef could put together, and didn't I know her friend's uncle's coworker would eat takeout once a week and ended up divorced at twenty-eight, even if the two matters seemed entirely unrelated, and did *I* want to end up divorced at twenty-eight?

I scoop up a piece of sweet-and-sour chicken and pop it into my mouth, the rich flavor bursting on my tongue. "School was . . . okay," I lie through my teeth. My thoughts leave the table and creep into Jessica's bedroom, where her schoolbag sits, the anonymous note folded and hidden inside her pencil case. The mere reminder of it sends dread scuttling down my spine. "I got my test back. For politics."

"Oh?" Uncle glances up. "What did you get?"

"Ninety-one percent."

A very brief silence moves over the room, so subtle I almost don't notice it. I doubt I would have, if I were here as a guest. If the silence weren't directed at me.

"Ninety-one," Auntie repeats. Her tone is light, but there's a quizzical look in her eyes. "Was it a particularly difficult test?"

"No," I say. I feel like *this* is another test, and it's proving very difficult to pass. "I mean, a lot of people did worse."

"But a few people did better than you?" Auntie asks, her tone sharpening.

Uncle shoots her a look. "It's only a score for a humanities subject. It doesn't matter—"

"I don't care about the score," Auntie says, shaking him away. "I care about how Jessica is *reacting* to the score. She doesn't even look upset. How can she improve if she's not reflecting on what she's done?"

I take another bite of the chicken. It's a little too salty, and I'm uncomfortably aware of how dry my tongue feels, but I don't dare stand up for a glass of water—not with Auntie staring me down.

"I'm sorry?" I try.

"No, no, I don't need you to be sorry to me." Auntie stabs her chopsticks into the middle of her rice. *Bad luck,* my mom would say. *It looks like incense; it is associated with death in the family.* "I told you, I don't care about your studies. I'm not like one of those tiger parents. I don't have to care about you at all. Soon you'll be an adult living all on your own and whether you succeed or not will have nothing to do with me. If you fail, then you only have to be sorry to yourself."

I stare. There are a number of things Auntie likes to brag about on a regular basis, and one of them is how she isn't invested in Jessica's studies at all. She would always speak with faint derision of those parents who signed their children up for intensive tutoring in chemistry and math and Chinese, who stayed up to help their children with homework, who closely monitored their children's grades. According to her, Jessica *just happened* to have perfect grades. Jessica *just happened* to be the perfect daughter. Jessica was simply blessed with perfect genes.

But maybe she's never worried about Jessica's grades before because Jessica never gave her a reason to worry.

Because Jessica must have learned at some point that at the first sign of anything less than perfect, her mother would react like this.

"How did your friends do?" Uncle asks. He probably means to help, but my mouth only dries further.

"Yes, good question," Auntie says. "That Leela is a good student, isn't she? Did she do better than you? And what about Celine? You're always telling me she's a genius at those humanities subjects." This time it's clear what the correct answer should be. It won't matter as much if I'm not perfect, so long as I'm superior in some sense.

I remember the tears shining on Leela's cheeks, the way she'd hidden her test behind her, and my gut clenches. To avoid answering right away, I pick at a piece of the fried crab dish and suck on the shell.

Both my uncle and auntie's eyes widen.

"What are you doing?" Auntie asks shrilly.

I'm so startled I flinch. Drop my chopsticks. Blink up at her pale face. My immediate assumption is that this is about the grades, but then my auntie shoots to her feet and—in what I register as a very random, bizarre thing to do—points a shaking finger at the crab.

"How much did you eat?"

"What?"

"How much?"

"I—just that bite—"

"Go rinse your mouth," she demands. "And eat your medicine. Right now."

Medicine? What medicine?

Auntie's features twist with urgency. "Don't just stand there! *Hurry.*"

It's primarily out of confusion that I obey, my feet moving for me while my brain remains at a standstill. Only when I've reached the bathroom and rinsed my mouth twice and glimpsed my reflection in the mirror do I realize what's wrong.

A horrified gasp tears through my teeth.

Red welts have started to swell up all over my neck and cheeks, marring Jessica's otherwise smooth skin. *Crabmeat.* I'd been so caught up in the ominous message and her grades that I'd forgotten one very critical piece of information: Jessica Chen is allergic to seafood.

And as if I'm in need of any further evidence, my whole face starts to itch.

"Crap," I mutter, fumbling around her cupboards for the medicine with one hand while scratching furiously at my skin with the other. In my panic, I send pretty little tubes of face wash and scented soaps and unopened lipsticks tumbling to the ground. The more I scratch, the more it itches, as if I'm driving the sensation deeper into my body.

Finally my fingers close around a white bottle. I check the label, twist the cap open, pour two pills out onto my palm, and swallow them without any water. Then I dig my nails into the flesh of my face, waiting—praying—for the medicine to kick in.

"Jessica?" Two fast knocks on the bathroom door. Auntie's voice. "Jessica? Do you need me to come in?"

"No," I say quickly. "It's fine. I'm fine."

"Are you sure? Do we need to take you to the hospital? I'll ask your father to start the car—"

"No," I repeat. Breathe in. Check my reflection again. It's hard to be certain in the bright yellow wash of the bathroom lights, but the hives seem to have faded a little. It also no longer feels like there are angry poisonous ants crawling over my skin—now they're just plain ants.

Three more deep breaths, and then even the ants disappear.

When I crack open the door, Auntie seizes my shoulders and heaves out a long breath of relief.

"What were you thinking?" she asks. "You've always been so careful."

"I just got distracted, I guess," I say weakly.

She frowns but doesn't pursue the subject. Nor does she bring up the politics test again. "Come on," she tells me. "Let's go down to finish dinner. You barely ate anything."

But I don't feel hungry. Not for the food waiting for me downstairs, anyway. What I want is my mom's cooking. The tender pork ribs and seaweed we'd dip into soy sauce. The vegetable rolls she'd steam herself using white flour and scallions. The rich egg-and-tomato soup she'd serve with rice. The congee she'd make for me when I was sick, the tendrils of dried pork floss she'd sprinkle on top, the scattering of white sesame. When I was younger, I would secretly look forward to catching a cold, because I knew it meant she would let me stay in my bedroom and doodle all day, and she would bring the bowl of steaming congee and a plate of peeled pears and apples. . . .

Stop. I force the thought aside, ignore the ache lodged inside my chest like a blunt arrowhead, the urge to call my parents, to talk to them. I can't simply let nostalgia distort my memories, erase those dinners where the pork ribs and soup went untouched because I was sulking over one of Jessica's accomplishments.

"I've finished dinner," I say, summoning a smile to my lips. "I think I'm just going to go study."

Auntie hesitates, then nods. "All right. Tell us if you have any other symptoms—your dad and I are both flying out tomorrow and we aren't coming back until the seventeenth, but we can cancel our trip."

"Hang on . . . the seventeenth?" I echo. "What's the date today?"

"The thirteenth. Why?"

My heart clenches. I should have remembered what today is. What it means to Aaron.

It's his mother's death anniversary.

His father wouldn't be home. He seldom is, and especially not this evening. Five years ago, on the same date, he'd gone missing for as long as three weeks. Disappeared without a note, without leaving anything in the fridge, no money on the counter, not even an emergency number. Aaron had hidden it from all of us until I noticed that he wasn't bringing lunch to school.

"Just asking," I say. "Don't worry about me. Everything's good here."

Once my aunt is gone, I slip into Jessica's bedroom, letting the door swing shut. My eyes find the ever-growing pile of homework papers and textbooks waiting ominously on the desk. If I want to keep up Jessica's grades, redeem myself after the ninety-one percent, I should really spend the night studying. It's what Jessica would do. It's what a perfect student would do.

But my gaze slides past all the schoolwork and lands on Jessica's phone.

I don't have to search the contacts for his number; I've had it memorized for years. As I lie back on the bed and wait for Aaron to pick up, a series of memories flickers through my mind: Aaron, that first awful year after his mother had passed from her sudden heart condition, still only a child and so quiet it made people nervous. The counselor the school had arranged for, reporting back to my mom because his own father wasn't around. . . . *It would be much less concerning if he threw a tantrum. But he doesn't even cry. He doesn't want to talk about it at all. I'm concerned his emotions are going to consume him from within.* The Mother's Day after that, all the kids showing off their caramel cookies and illustrated cards, while Aaron kept himself distant from them, sitting back, the lines of his face hard. Already, he'd perfected his mask of boredom.

Nobody else connected the dots when he signed himself up for a first-aid course the summer after his mother passed, when he memorized the fastest route to the hospital from every major road and fastidiously refilled their supply of medicine every year, just in case of another emergency. Nobody else seemed to notice how he'd tense whenever someone complained about chest pain or feeling lightheaded, how he'd spend his spare time reading up on every documented illness while other boys his age were partying or playing video games.

"Yes?" Aaron's voice.

Even though I was the one who called, I still feel my pulse jump slightly. I'm used to thinking about him; I'm not used to actually reaching him. "Hi," I say. "Are you busy?"

"Not really." He sounds guarded. Almost suspicious. "Is something up?"

"Oh, no, I just . . ." I pause. I can hardly say the truth, that I was worried about him, that I know how much this day affects him even though he'll never admit it, and the only reason I know is because I've been watching him and wanting him in silence for years. No, I definitely can't say that. But there is something I can ask him about—something I actually need to find out. "I was wondering if you saw anyone move my test today."

"Your test?"

"Yeah. For politics. I'd left it on the desk, and when I came back . . ." The image of the note unfolds inside my head, as clearly as if I were holding it up in front of me. *Not so perfect, are you?* "I don't know. It looked like someone had gone through it while I was outside."

"You're scared someone saw your score?" he asks. "I would have thought you'd love for people to find out your score."

I'm grateful he can't see my expression. "Maybe not everyone is a show-off like you."

"Fair enough," he says dryly. But for the first time since he picked up, there's a hint of amusement to his tone too. "Well, I wasn't paying attention to your desk the entire time, but nobody crossed the room. So if someone *did* sneak a glance at your test, I suppose they would have been sitting near you."

Sitting near me. Celine's face flashes through my thoughts. The look in her eyes when she found out I'd been accepted at Harvard. The edge to her smile.

My heart thuds. The only other person sitting at our table was Leela, and even if I hadn't been outside with her, I knew she'd never do something like that. But Celine—the girl who intimidates everyone, who only speaks to those she deems worthy of her attention, who I was barely acquainted with as Jenna . . .

"Hello?" Aaron prompts. "Are you still there?"

"Yeah," I say, rolling over to cover my stomach with one

corner of the blanket. "Sorry, just thinking."

"Does it really bother you that much? If someone saw?"

"It's a matter of principle." I'm omitting the real truth, but this is true too. "It's such an underhanded move."

"You're right," he says. "Unfortunately, it's the Havenwood spirit. I never did understand why everyone here is so weird about their studies. All the constant competing and comparing—it must require an incredible amount of energy."

Despite myself, I snort.

"What?"

"Of course *you* wouldn't get it," I tell him. "You've never had to worry about your studies."

"I'd never worry about anyone else's studies," he counters. "Which is what most people seem to do." Then he pauses. "Is that the only reason you called? To ask about your test?"

"Yeah," I reply, then realize he's about to hang up. "Wait—no. Um, I still wanted to ask . . . I also needed . . ."

"What do you want, Jessica?"

I only want to distract you. I want to keep you company, so you don't have the chance to feel lonely. Even if it means you're annoyed with me. Even if I haven't forgiven you yet for leaving.

"I wanted to ask . . ." I look around in desperation and spot a framed photo of the three of us on Jessica's bookshelf. It had been Aaron's twelfth birthday, and on my suggestion, my mom had taken us to the Imagine Your Future immersive theme park across town. Aaron is dressed up as a doctor, a faint smile on his lips. Jessica stands beside him in a businesswoman's blazer and pencil skirt, staring calmly ahead. And I'm squashed in the middle in my painting apron, my hair a mess, my face turned away, self-conscious, because Aaron's arm was around my shoulder. An unexpected pang hits my chest. It had been one of those rare days where everything went exactly the way I'd planned, where joy felt simple.

"I just wanted to ask how your whole gifted kid medical program went," I tell Aaron. "I, um, have a friend who's considering applying."

"A friend? Who?"

"You wouldn't know them," I say. "I have so many friends."

He lets out a breath of laughter. "All right. Well, if your friend is really set on this career path, they should give it a try. There aren't that many programs around that'll let you study medicine in such depth before you've even entered college. We had professors and doctors come in to deliver lectures every week. Like, there was this renowned cardiologist, Dr. Zhou, who specializes in basically all aspects of cardiac rhythm management, and he's written these groundbreaking research papers on atrial fibrillation. . . ."

As he talks faster, I can imagine his eyes lighting up with genuine excitement. I tug the blanket higher, stare up at the blank white ceiling, and let his voice fill my head.

". . . and recently, he helped invent this heart monitoring device that's completely noninvasive and more sensitive than anything available. It's smaller than the size of your nail, if you can believe it. Imagine coming up with something like that—an idea, a single device, a new way of thinking, that could help advance disease prevention and treatments all over the world. . . ." He trails off, his next words almost shy. "I realize that was likely far more than what you or your friend are interested in."

"No, no," I say quickly. "No, not at all."

There's a warm, foreign emotion blooming past my ribs: awe, untainted by jealousy. The thing about Havenwood is that it has a way of shrinking everything down inside its ivy-crawled gates. It's so easy to feel like nothing else in the world exists beyond our latest test score, who's valedictorian, who was accepted into an Ivy League and who was rejected, and the reward becomes the glory itself, the validation, the praise. It really is the Havenwood spirit, like Aaron says.

Sometimes I forget that in the bigger scheme of things, it's okay to not be the best at everything. To be surrounded by people who can solve problems you can't, who are talented in different ways, who will go on to change the world. Aaron's intelligence isn't just something that will earn him good grades and compliments at dinner parties; it's what will help him become a brilliant doctor and save lives.

"Tell me more," I say.

He does, even though it's with a kind of incredulous caution, like at any moment I might interrupt and announce that I'm recording him as a prank.

"You know, I believe this is the longest conversation we've ever had," he says later.

I squint up at the dimmed light of my screen. We've been talking for over two hours, long enough that my battery is nearly dead. Still, this information surprises me. I had assumed—*feared*—that

Jessica and Aaron chatted all the time when I wasn't around, that they could talk forever, given how much they had in common.

"I should probably make myself dinner now," he says after a pause. "But if your friend wants to ask me anything about the program, feel free to give them my number."

"Okay. Sure."

"I'll see you at school tomorrow, then."

"Bye, Aaron," I whisper, prepared for him to linger, to repeat himself, the way he always did when we used to call after school, just for the sake of annoying me. But he's already hung up.

The note is still there.

In the pencil case. In the back of my mind. Even when I attempt to fall asleep and squeeze my eyes shut, I can see that sloping handwriting, lit up in the darkness behind my eyelids. And with it, the anonymous email, and the Haven Award. After tossing around on the sheets and fluffing out Jessica's pillow for the seventh time, I flick the table lamp on, wrap Jessica's bathrobe around myself, and crouch down in front of Jessica's drawers.

Then I pull out the very thing I'd vowed to myself I wouldn't pick up again.

Her journal.

My heartbeat accelerates as I touch the cool leather. Guilt drives itself deeper into my gut, but I'm running out of clues. There has to be something in here that I've missed.

I flip open to a random page and scan the first few words—

It happened.

It finally happened. I got into Harvard.

The instant tightening in my chest is all too familiar. But I guess envy is similar to muscle memory, and this has always been what envy feels like for me: like dread. Like physical pain, like raw, pulse-speeding panic, like watching a train run off its tracks. Every time Jessica announced something that had gone well in her life, my stomach would tense and my blood would run cold as if bracing for the threat of violence.

I force myself to keep reading.

> *Even now, it doesn't seem real. When the notification came in, my heart started beating so fast I thought it would explode. I was shaking as I opened up my emails, but then I saw the Harvard logo, and the word "Congratulations." I had to read it three times to be sure. But there was my name, Jessica Chen, and the words I've been waiting to see for years. They accepted me. They want me to be a student at Harvard. The college of my dreams.*
>
> *I ran to the living room to tell my parents and they were so excited—more excited than I've ever seen them. They were hugging me and calling everyone they knew on WeChat, and I delivered the news to my relatives myself, one at a time: my great-grandaunt and second aunt and my uncles and my cousin and her husband and my grandparents on both sides. I didn't even know we had that many relatives, but my mother somehow kept finding more people to call.*

My grandmother cried, and I just remembered the story my mother used to tell me, how she never even had the chance to get her high school diploma before she started working at the hair salon to support her younger brothers. And it was like I could picture our family tree, with my ancestors at the roots, and all those branches spreading out toward the sky, and with every new branch we stretched higher, and more flowers bloomed, and that was how we grew, generation after generation.

They kept telling me how proud they were. I was a genius, I was so incredibly talented, I had worked so hard. I was the one who'd made it, who'd succeeded. It was perfect. For those first ten minutes, everything was perfect.

And now I'm up here alone in my room, the same as always, and the thrill has faded, and I know it sounds awful and so very ungrateful, but all I can think is: that's it? This, right now, is the culmination of all those sleepless nights, every test I cried over, every extra hour I spent studying when I could have been driving down to the coast, eating dinner with my family, going to the mall with my friends, visiting the cherry orchards or swimming in the lake in the high heat of summer. This is as good as life will ever be and . . . I don't have anybody to talk to about it. Sure, there are people I can tell, like I've told my relatives—in the form of an announcement, an opportunity for my parents to brag about me. But who is there I can truly celebrate with? Who else will feel genuinely happy for me?

Then there's Harvard itself—all I could think about was doing the work and getting in, but it's hitting me now that I'll have to keep working once classes begin. I'll have to prove myself all over again to new classmates and new professors. I just feel so exhausted at the idea, like I've been running as fast as I can toward a mountain in the horizon, and it always looks within reach, but I'll never actually get there. Everything exhausts me these days.

A sudden wind howls through the trees.

I jerk my head up. I'm half convinced I'll see Jessica—the real Jessica—right there, hovering behind me, watching in silence. I even whisper her name out loud. "Jessica? Are you there?"

But there's no response. The only person inside her bedroom is me. I swallow back my shock and turn to an older entry.

I shouldn't have done it.

I know I shouldn't have. But I couldn't think of anything else by myself. My brain was blank—my brain often feels blank recently, like I'm too tired to even form a solid thought—and I only had one day left to write it, and I knew the teacher was expecting something phenomenal from me, something that would top everything I've ever written before. I can never just be okay. I have to be perfect. I have to astound them. I *have to prove that I'm intelligent or I'll stop mattering.*

Now it's submitted, and it's too late to turn back.

There shouldn't be any evidence, unless they somehow find out. If they do accuse me . . . I can only pray my reputation will protect me. Everyone thinks I'm good, and they're right, in a way. I'm a good student, a good daughter, a good example.

But I've never been a good person. I don't know how to be.

The journal slips from my fingertips and thuds to the floor.

I'd expected to find clues, but I hadn't expected to find *this*. Suddenly everything looks different. All the ominous notes from the anonymous student. *I know what you've done.* I had been so certain they'd found out that I wasn't really Jessica, but maybe the messages were addressed to the real her.

"What did you do?" I ask the air, wishing more than anything that I had some way to speak to my cousin. Jessica Chen, who's meant to be flawless. Who I've grown up with, who was there to carry my books for me after I twisted my ankle in gym class, who let me stay in her bedroom when my parents were out of town, who'd bake soft lemon cookies for me when I was stressed about exams. Who I've envied for most of my life, who I would follow around everywhere when we were only five, until our parents joked that I was her little shadow. It hadn't stung, then. It had felt like a compliment, because I'd wanted to be just like her. "What could you have done that's so terrible?"

Nine

Jessica's voice echoes in my head all throughout the next day. I hear it as clearly as if she'd read her journal entry aloud to me: *I've never been a good person.*

Maybe it's a blessing, then, that our usual classes are canceled for our annual swimming carnival. The school arranges buses for all of us first thing in the morning and takes us down to the lakes.

It's so early that there's still a light mist rolling in over the slate-gray water and the weeds, the chill of last night clinging to the air.

"We're going to get hypothermia," Celine grumbles as she slips out of her school uniform, kicking her skirt aside into the grass. Like all the other girls, she's already wearing the standard black swimsuit underneath.

Leela removes her blazer and folds it very neatly into the water-proof bag she's brought, then sets her school shoes down in a perfect line facing the lake's edge. "I'm more concerned about getting bitten by a water snake."

Celine laughs at her. "That was only a rumor spread by the boys in the upper year to scare us. There aren't any snakes—"

"You can't be sure of that," Leela protests. "Look at the water. If there were snakes, we wouldn't be able to see them, now would we?"

We both look—Celine, just to humor her, and me, because I secretly share her fear. Venomous snakes might not be *first* on my list of concerns, but they're definitely on it.

The lake waits ahead of us, the surface as dark as the clouded sky, revealing nothing of its depths. The little light that touches the edges is instantly dispersed by the rippling waves. Celine turns away after a brief moment, but my gaze lingers. Water is one of the most difficult things to paint because it's always moving, always shifting shapes; because it cannot exist separately from its surroundings. I couldn't paint the lake without capturing the cluster of bellflowers growing over the banks, or the reflections of students warming up and gathering their towels in their arms, huddling together to escape the cold. And to get the colors right, I would need to mix indigo with Aegean and spruce and find a darker shade for the shadows—

"I still doubt there are snakes," Celine says contemplatively. "Maybe dead bodies, though."

"*Celine.*" Leela glares at her.

"Or friendly mermaids," she compromises. "Happy?"

"Not at all."

"What are you so worked up over?" Celine asks. "Jessica will test out the waters for you. She's getting in first."

"Yeah. Can't wait," I say as I shrug off my school shirt until I'm standing in my swimsuit. The freezing air shocks me, nipping at the skin on my bare arms. In all the years I've been here, I've managed to skip the swimming carnival due to a feigned stomach bug or fever or mysterious skin rash that magically faded by the next day. I wasn't even close enough to the lake to see who was swimming—exactly the way I liked it.

It's not just that I detest swimming. I'm one of the only people in my class who had to take the school's water safety program three times before they let me pass, and that was with the recommendation that I actively avoid large bodies of water.

But Jessica is one of the school's star swimmers, and it's basically tradition by this point for her to swim the first and longest race.

"Speaking of," Celine says, "you should head down now, Jessica." She points to the lake, where the school's swim coach is barking out instructions. "Look, the other swimmers are already lined up."

I take a deep breath and tuck my ponytail under my uncomfortably tight latex cap.

Leela glances over at me and pauses, her eyes widening. "Wow."

"What?"

"No, I'm just impressed by how good you look with the swimming cap on. It makes everyone else look bald. But on you . . . it's basically high fashion," she gushes. "It really brings out the color of your eyes."

I'd think she was being ironic, but as I tread over the grass and join the other swimmers, I catch a glimpse of myself in the dark shine of their goggles. Incredibly, I *do* look good; with my hair pulled back, my cheekbones are more prominent than ever, my neck as elegant as a swan's.

Then I stare ahead. Four parallel diving boards have been suspended over the lake. The wood is rough and freezing under my bare feet as I walk slowly to the end of the board like someone walking the plank, scared I'll slip and fall off before the race has even started.

"Get ready," the swim coach calls, his voice rolling over the water.

In my peripheral vision, I watch the swimmers lower themselves with expert precision, their arms stretched out in a perfect line, the starting position I never learned. Just when I'm imagining myself tumbling headfirst into the lake, Jessica's muscle memory kicks in: my own arms seem to extend on their own, my toes inching toward the edge of the board, my calf muscles steadying me when I lean forward. It's like magic. It *is* magic.

A chorus of excited shouts sound from the banks.

"Let's go, Jessica!"

"You've got this."

"We're all cheering for you!"

"Oh my god, oh my god—Jessica's race is starting."

"Damn, she looks *ready*."

Warmth shoots through my veins the same time adrenaline does. I feel like everything I wasn't: strong, capable, athletic. My fingers flex. My breathing quickens with anticipation. Maybe I could actually win this.

"Set," the swim coach says.

A shift in movement around me. A collective inhale. One final breath.

"Go."

I kick off from the board—there's a heartbeat's moment where it seems I'm weightless, where I've escaped gravity itself. Then my hands pierce through the surface, and the water rushes in around me. It's even colder than the air, but the cold feels separate from my body, from the heat in my limbs.

And then I start swimming.

Though *I* might not be, Jessica's body has been trained for this. Her lungs expand as I dive deeper, and when I come up for air, the oxygen slides sweetly through my teeth in the half second before I go down again. Her arms slice expertly through the white spray. Each powerful kick propels me farther and farther away from the other swimmers; I can hear them splashing behind me, sense the quick, frantic bursts of movement through the ripples. Nothing can stop me. Nobody can beat me. I swim on and on, sleek as an otter, the water parting with every stroke.

There's no exhaustion dragging me back, only elation humming in my veins, pulling me forward, buoying me over the waves.

It turns out that I don't detest swimming at all—I just detest being bad at things.

I'm the first to reach the end. When I break through the surface, drinking in the fresh air, blinking against the water in my eyes, I see them all gathered on the shores: my classmates, clapping, cheering, screaming my name.

"Jessica Chen. Jessica Chen. Jessica Chen."

And I'm suddenly grateful for how similar our names sound, because it's so easy to pretend—at least for a few golden, delirious, glory-soaked moments—that I'm really her, and it's me that they're all cheering for.

The best part about winning the first race—other than the winning itself, of course—is that I can simply stand by myself and watch everyone else for the rest of the carnival.

But I'm not left alone for long.

Aaron approaches in my peripheral vision. Like all the other guys who'll be swimming later, he's taken his shirt off—a fact that's becoming increasingly difficult to ignore the closer he draws.

"Hello," I say to a pebble on the ground, wrapping my towel tighter around my shoulders.

"Hi," he says.

I make the mistake of glancing up and I'm instantly overwhelmed by flashes of dark hair, smooth skin, sculpted shoulders, sharp lines. I'm torn, trapped by the impulse to keep looking and the sense to look away before I betray myself.

"That was quite a race," he comments. "Congratulations on the win."

"Oh yeah, thank you," I say, looking back down to continue my conversation with the pebble. "I mean, I'm definitely not surprised I won. I'm just so naturally athletic."

"Right. That's great." He sounds distracted. "Hey, you haven't seen or heard anything about Jenna, have you? She's still missing, and nobody I've asked can tell me where she is. . . . It's like she's just *vanished*."

"Jenna?" I repeat, lifting my head. I feel like I'm diving

underwater again; everything else grows muted, blurry. "No. Sorry, I—I haven't."

"I'm getting worried." His brows furrow slightly. "It doesn't make sense for her to leave without warning."

"Well, maybe she just doesn't want to be found," I tell him, and turn to go, eager to untangle myself from this conversation. I don't want to think about my old self. I don't want to think at all. I just want to play pretend a little longer, let my classmates come up to me with their pretty words of praise, linger in the lilac haze of my recent victory.

"Wait." Aaron reaches out, his fingertips accidentally skimming over my damp hair, and my breath catches in my throat. It's such a familiar sensation, the kind that drags you back through time, sweeps the ground out from under your feet. With a sudden ache, I remember all those evenings spent walking home after school, in the clear blue summer light, him following behind me. Whenever he was close enough, he would play with a stray strand of my hair, wrapping it around his ring finger, smiling with one corner of his mouth, and I would swat him away. Pretend to be annoyed. But secretly I would always slow my steps on purpose whenever I heard him coming, just so he could catch up. Just so he could tease me and laugh.

But instead of leaning closer, the way he would when he was with me, he drops his hand at once and steps back.

"What did you mean?" he presses, fixing me with a sharp, contemplative look, like he can see something invisible to everyone else, something beyond the overcast sky and pearl-gray lake water.

"That she doesn't want to be found? Do you know why she left? Did she tell you? Is she . . . is she angry at me?"

I swallow, my heart straining against my ribs. I should keep my jaw locked. Bury my secrets under my tongue. But instead I falter. Meet his questioning gaze, so heavy with worry, so sincere. And I miss—something. Maybe what we once were before, maybe the knowledge that when he used to look at me this way, he was seeing my face, not Jessica's.

Tell him, a small voice inside my head whispers. *Tell him the truth. It's Aaron. You can trust him.*

"I . . ." I lick my lips, tasting the lake on them. Overhead, the clouds have scattered, soft beams of yellow light falling over the rippling water, outlining the sides of Aaron's face, so his skin appears almost to be glowing. Beautiful, distant, infuriating Aaron. The boy I would refuse to lend a pencil to, but who I would give up the world for, even after all this time.

Even after all this.

"What's going on, Jessica?" he asks.

Not *Is something going on?* But *What?*

"If I tried to explain," I say slowly, "would you really believe me?"

"Of course."

"Even if it sounds ridiculous?" I press. "Even if it makes no scientific sense whatsoever, and might leave you questioning my sanity?"

The line between his brows deepens, but he nods. "Okay."

"I'm being serious."

"So am I."

"Okay. Then to be completely honest . . . well, I don't really understand it myself yet but . . . the thing is that I'm—" The words push themselves up to the tip of my tongue, but for a few seconds, I hold them there. What if this is it? What if I admit it out loud to him, and the illusion is broken, the spell is shattered? My heart kicks harder against my ribs. It's too late to back out now. He's waiting, watching me. "I'm not . . . who you think I am."

He hesitates. "In a philosophical sense?"

"In a very literal sense," I tell him, shaking my head. "This body . . . this life . . ." I gesture to myself with both hands. "I woke up one day as Jessica. I look like her and talk like her and everyone thinks I am her when I'm not. Not really."

He stares, long enough for my nerves to fly into a frenzy. "That's interesting," he says at last. "You're referring to yourself in third person."

"Because it's *not me*," I say, frustrated. "Don't you get it? I'm not Jessica Chen. I'm—I'm Jenna." My mouth seems to be moving on its own accord, everything tumbling out into the cool air. "I made a wish to be her, and somehow it came true, and now I have no idea where my cousin really is—her soul, I mean, or whatever you want to call it. I've tried searching for her, but I don't even know where to look and I—I just . . . I don't know."

I clamp my jaw shut, and the silence that follows is terrible. All the noise in the background is muted: the faint silver splashing of waves; students laughing and screaming at each other in the far distance; a teacher yelling at them all to be careful, the school isn't responsible if they die, their parents signed that form stating so; the colored banners slamming against the wind. It's just me and him and this uneasy quiet, stretching between us like a shadow.

After an eternity, he runs a hand through his hair, that familiar, agitated gesture he does whenever he's trying to clear his head. "Wow," he says, and it's impossible to decipher the tone of his voice. "I'm not certain what the point of this joke is, but it's definitely creative."

My heart falls. "Aaron, I really mean it. . . ."

But his expression hardens. The sun disappears behind the clouds again, and when he looks at me in the purple darkness, his features are pinched tight, his eyes almost pained. "Look, you can joke about whatever you like, just not—just not her, okay?" He turns his head toward the lake. "Not Jenna."

Before I can figure out what he means, he's already walking away from me. And it's strange, because up until this very moment, my worst fear was that someone would call me out for being an imposter. For faking everything, pretending to be somebody else; a sparrow dressing up as a phoenix. I should be *relieved* he doesn't believe me. It means my act has been convincing enough. But as I watch Aaron leave, his last words echoing in my mind, the heaviness in my chest feels an awful lot like disappointment.

I spend the rest of the day furious at myself.

I should have kept my mouth shut. I should have avoided Aaron altogether. I'd spent the whole year brainwashing myself into hating him, convincing myself I didn't harbor any feelings except resentment anymore, cutting my ties and cleaning my hands for good. And now this.

He still has so much power over me.

He always has.

I don't even know how it happened. When. It came onto me gradually over the years, all the days flowing together, building into something more. There he was, sometimes walking past the window with his hands in his pockets, stopping by for dinner when we made our pork dumplings, standing in our living room with the top button of his collar undone and his black hair falling soft over his forehead.

Aaron Cai, the boy my mother always praised for his manners, the one my father called a prodigy, the student all the teachers fawned over. I was jealous of him—I can be certain of that, at least. His unmatched grace and his faint good-natured smiles and his calm, contemplative air. We were born the same year but he seemed older, somehow, like he understood the world better than I did or he had some kind of trick to navigating it that eluded me. I had this ridiculous idea every birthday that things would be different, and I would grow overnight to become just as mature, just as poised as he was, but my birthdays passed without any luck. Twelve years old. Thirteen. Fourteen.

I was always watching him. Maybe because I hoped to see if he would slip up, even though he never did. I remember studying him in class, his head low, flipping through the faded yellow pages of a textbook, a highlighter held casually between his fingers like a painter's brush. The day in Chinese school, when we were meant to be analyzing the "Song of Divination" by Li Zhiyi, and he was very clearly gazing out the window, his mind on something else.

The teacher had asked me to call on a classmate to read out the poem and I said his name as a challenge, waiting for him to flush, to startle, to stumble over his words. But he had looked me straight in the eye and recited every line perfectly, until the whole class fell into silence, mesmerized. *Impossible,* I thought to myself, fuming. Once the teacher finished praising him, he'd flashed me a smug, crooked smile and turned right back to the window—yet his shoulders shook slightly, like he was trying to keep from laughing.

Then there was the school dance our teachers had insisted on holding in the ballroom, and the many rehearsals that preceded it, with the old woman with the croaky voice who looked like she'd been summoned from the Regency era just to teach us. I remember being paired up with Aaron, how his one hand had closed over mine and his other had rested lightly on my waist, and noticing how warm his skin was, how smooth. When I'd stumbled and stepped hard on his feet, not once but three times, he had merely rolled his eyes.

"If I didn't know better, Jenna, I'd think you were doing it on purpose," he murmured as he spun me, his voice dry.

"How do you know I'm not?"

"Because if you'd wanted to hurt me, I'm pretty sure you'd adopt slightly more effective measures than treading on my toes."

"Don't sound so sure. Maybe it's part of a long-term plan," I cautioned. "Maybe by the end of this session I'll have trampled you enough times that you'll find yourself unable to walk at your normal speed and be late to your next class, and the teacher will mark you down for tardiness."

"How threatening."

"Please." I spun out again and let him pull me back with a tug of my wrist, and for a moment we might've been in a period drama, classical string music rising sweetly in the old halls around us. "Reputational damage matters way more than physical damage around here. You know that."

He laughed then, the sound low in my ear, and I felt a disconcerting rush of pleasure.

And afterward the girls in my class had flocked around me, complaining about their partners, wishing aloud that they had mine. "How did it feel?" they'd asked, giggling. It was no secret that half of them had a crush on him. "To dance with Aaron Cai?"

"Uh. Just . . . normal," I'd replied hastily, but I couldn't meet their eyes.

I remember the weekend after, my parents telling me last-minute that we would be having a picnic by the lake with Aaron, and a strange lump forming in my throat, almost akin to rage. We had been fifteen then.

"Why didn't you warn me Aaron was coming?" I'd demanded, because that was the word that made the most sense to me, even when I couldn't make sense of the emotion inside me yet: *warn*. Like a natural disaster, an impending storm. My mother had cast me a perplexed look while my father frowned and lectured me about my attitude.

"It's just Aaron. I thought you were good friends," he said. "And

Aaron has always been so nice to you."

"He likes to make fun of me when I embarrass myself," I corrected. "I don't think that qualifies as being nice."

But still I went because I had to, painfully, unbearably self-conscious the whole time without understanding why. I squeezed into an impractical strapless dress and refused to wear sunscreen because it made my face look greasy. After three hours on the lake's edge, sitting cross-legged underneath the sun, my shoulders had started to sting and redden from the heat. Even now, the mortification feels fresh, a wound not healed yet: my mother noticing and fussing over my sunburn, rummaging through our bags for some kind of herbal ointment and then smearing it all over me while Aaron politely averted his gaze.

More months passed before I realized it, but something inside me had already shifted. We were studying tectonic plates at the time, and that's what it felt like: something heavy and fundamental rearranging itself beneath my rib cage. He would change a room just by being in it, knock the breath from my lungs just by glancing at me, smiling a certain way. I would invest too much energy into scrutinizing my appearance before school, fussing over my bangs and fiddling with my school skirt, rolling it up and tugging it back down again.

I seemed to fall into a perpetual state of waiting: for my next chance to meet him, my next excuse to linger near his locker, our next class together. I wanted him the only way I knew how to want anything—obsessively, fervently. At times it was excruciating, to be studying next to him in the library, our shoulders almost brushing, to open the front door for him and invite him into the living room, to be *so close* and still have to swallow my heart, seal my lips shut. I couldn't tell him. This too was never a conscious decision I made, just a truth that crept up on me. We knew each other too well, our lives were too inextricably tangled. Anything I felt toward him was my problem. My weakness. My sworn secret.

But then there came that day in the rain, and I forgot, like a fool, and nothing's been the same since. Nothing will ever be the same again.

This was the scene I played over and over in my head on nights I couldn't sleep. Or perhaps this was the scene that kept me from sleeping. We had been riding our bikes home together from school when the rain started. It came without warning—not a drizzle, not even a flicker of lightning, just the serene sky and suddenly the wild, gray rush of water, the streets running dark with it.

And so we'd sought shelter under the almond groves. They'd been in full bloom then, the delicate white-pink petals quivering in the rain, our bikes leaning against the trees, his black hair damp and curling over his forehead, his school shirt soaked through. Even during the storm, he was so casual, so unbothered. Gazing out at the heavy downpour like it was nothing. Sometimes I thought he was the kind of person you wanted on your side during a disaster, someone you could trust to keep a level head no matter what and guide you to safety. Other times, in my less generous moods, I was certain that he was the very last person you wanted next to you if the world collapsed; his calmness could be maddening like that.

We were standing close, maybe closer than we needed to be, and the air was so cold it tasted sweet.

"It looks like we'll be here awhile," he said, and I thought, *Good.*

I thought, *I could stay here forever.*

I said, "God, I hope not. It's freezing."

"You're always cold," he told me, in a flippant sort of way, like it was none of his business, but then he was reaching into his schoolbag and pulling out his sweater. Handing it over to me. Black cashmere. Soft and still dry and wonderfully warm, as though he'd just taken it off.

My heart was beating very fast. I tried not to look too eager. "Oh, you don't have to—"

He snatched the sweater back and draped it over his own shoulders. "Okay, then."

I stared at him for a solid beat, my whole face hot, but then he suddenly grinned at me with quick, unnerving charm.

"Kidding, of course," he said, and this time he didn't just hold the sweater out but stepped forward until I could see the water glistening on his lashes like teardrops. Then he fastened the sweater's sleeves around my neck so that it covered me like a cloak. His eyes turned gentle, his lips wet from the rain. I stared up at him, overwhelmed by his nearness, his scent, by how we had stood together like this a thousand times before but each time it felt different. New. Like we were on the edge of something dangerous.

"Do you always have to tease me?" I grumbled, tearing my gaze away. "You couldn't just be nice?"

The rain fell harder, drowning out the rest of the world.

"It's hard to resist," he said, and he sounded honest. "I don't know why I do it, really. It's only with you."

I swallowed. My throat felt raw, and I didn't understand what he meant, only that I couldn't bear it if it all ended here, if I went home without anything happening, without touching him.

"Maybe it's because you don't like me," I said, seized by a terrible boldness, my heart racing ahead of itself. "Because you hate me."

His brows drew together. "No," he said firmly, despite his confusion. "I could never hate you."

"Really?"

"I swear it."

"Not even if I did this?" And before I could lose my nerve, before I could think about why this was a horrible idea, I grabbed the front of his shirt and pulled him closer, leaving only a hair's breadth of distance between us. I watched him breathe, or struggle to, his chest rising and falling erratically, eyes wide, lips parted, half his face cast in the silver dappled shadow of the petals overhead. I had never kissed a boy before, yet now it seemed so simple. Just one movement, and I'd have him, the way I wanted.

He was staring at my mouth too, like the same thought had occurred to him. But he didn't close the distance. Didn't lean in the way I hoped. Before our lips could meet, he twisted his head away from me.

All the chill in the air seemed to flood into my lungs.

I blinked at him, speechless, choking on my own humiliation.

"We shouldn't," he whispered, his voice strained. "We can't."

"I don't understand." There was no time to polish my words,

make them less embarrassing. I simply said what I thought.

"Jenna . . ."

"You don't . . . want me?" The tears were coming fast now, stinging the back of my eyes and my throat. I stepped back, away from him and out of the shelter, letting the rain pelt my skin. "Is it because I'm—" But I couldn't think of any good reason, other than who I was. *Jenna Chen.* Always the second one, the afterthought, the girl not good enough for anybody. Why had I imagined things would be different? Why did I even still believe in anything? "Why? Why not?"

A low exhale. "It's not like that."

"Like what? You don't even care," I said, and by now my self-defense mechanisms were kicking in, my hurt hardening into pure blistering rage. "You never care about anything, damn it. Do you think it makes you superior, somehow, always keeping yourself apart from everyone? You could have stopped this. You should have—I mean, you knew, didn't you? On some level?"

"What, that you liked me?"

My cheeks felt scalded. Somehow it was a thousand times worse hearing him say it out loud, in that calm, matter-of-fact voice. "Not anymore," I said, unsure who I was trying to convince. "From now on, I hate you, Aaron. I seriously—I hate you so much." The rain was a miracle, in a way; it mingled with my tears, until it was impossible to tell one from the other. My whole face was wet. "I'm going home."

"I can walk you back," he said, taking one cautious step toward me, like I was a bird that might fly away. "Let me—"

I spun around, wiped my cheeks roughly with my sleeves. "Stop it. I'm not talking to you." I could hear how childish I sounded, how foolish, but I didn't care. I closed my eyes in the violent downpour, and there was a sharp pain in my chest, a jagged bone set wrong, and I felt so awfully small, like anything in the world could eat me alive.

One week later, he was gone.

Ten

As the weeks pass, I grow into Jessica's life.

It's like moving from a one-bedroom flat into a mansion. After the first few days of wandering in a daze around your own hallways, tossing and turning on the king-sized mattress, getting up in the middle of the night and hitting your head while fumbling around for the bathroom door, you adjust. You settle in. You don't notice the scent of the magnolias first thing in the morning anymore. You can turn off the night-light with your eyes closed. You know to avoid the creaky step at the top of the stairs and twist the kitchen tap harder to the right.

But I'm still slightly disoriented when Celine calls me on Saturday.

"Why haven't you been answering any of my texts?" she demands the second I pick up.

I swallow, straighten in my seat. So maybe there *is* something I haven't fully adjusted to yet. "Sorry," I tell her, rolling the chair forward to shut my bedroom door with one foot. "I've been really busy." I'm not lying, exactly. When I haven't been watching crash courses on physics, I've been poring over the fables I borrowed from the library, rifling through Jessica's wardrobe and textbooks for any other mysterious messages or hints as to what terrible thing she might've done, and brainstorming increasingly unrealistic solutions for how I might locate my cousin's soul. My last idea had been to buy Jessica's favorite food—roasted duck, dipped in sweet-and-sour sauce—and leave it on the back porch like an offering at a shrine. I had gone so far as to set the plate out on the wooden planks, then rapidly aborted the plan when the ants appeared.

"But I hear you've been replying to Leela," Celine is saying, her voice too casual to be convincing. "So I guess you're not *that* busy."

Yes, well, that's because I'm not concerned that Leela has been writing vaguely threatening notes to my cousin. But if Celine really is the one behind it all, then I shouldn't rattle the grass and startle the snake, as my mom always says. She can't know that I suspect her. Not yet. Not before I figure out my next steps. "I have time now," I say brightly. "I promise I didn't mean to be so, um, absent. I was just overwhelmed."

"Well, in that case," she says, "I take it you're free to go horse-back riding with me and Leela?"

"Like . . . on actual horses?" I ask, just to be clear. "Those animals people used as a primary form of transportation two hundred years ago?"

"Yes, Jessica," she says. "I know it's not your favorite sport in the world, but the horse needs exercise."

"The horse?" I repeat.

"The *horse*," Celine says. "My horse. Hello?"

"Oh. That horse," I say. Three years ago, Charlotte Heathers had bought Celine a horse for her birthday. It was an incredibly nice, incredibly generous, and incredibly impractical gesture. Because Charlotte Heathers comes from a family where horses and twenty-thousand-dollar handbags and sports cars can be casually exchanged as gifts. Because Charlotte Heathers owns three villas and a vineyard and a literal castle that's often rented out to be used as the set for period dramas. Because Charlotte Heathers, sweet as she is, probably doesn't have an accurate grasp of how costly it is to own a horse.

I didn't know either of them well enough to see how the whole thing played out, but I heard through the usual channels of gossip that Charlotte had led the horse straight into Celine's backyard and handed the reins over.

There weren't many updates after that, and so I'd naturally assumed that Celine—being the less nice and more practical person—had found a way to give the horse back or maybe donate it to whatever production team was renting Charlotte's castle. Apparently not.

"So you're coming, right?" Celine asks.

"Well, I don't know—"

"I thought you said you had time," she says, a question in her voice.

I hesitate. If I refuse, she'll definitely realize I've been avoiding her on purpose. Besides, horseback riding is one of those upper-class hobbies I was desperate to try when I was a child, if only I had the money and the opportunity and the athletic ability—and now I have all three. "Okay," I say slowly. "I mean, why not?"

★★★

The doors of the stables open up to a rolling meadow and saturated blue sky and cool afternoon air.

I sink into the saddle, my heels automatically dropping lower in the stirrups, my fingers curling around the reins. Then, mimicking Leela and Celine up ahead of me, I squeeze my horse a few times, my boots thudding dully against the great animal's belly. With a snort, he breaks into a fast, bumpy stride that ought to bounce me right off, but my body—or Jessica's body—adapts at once, rising and falling in a steady rhythm with every momentary loss of gravity.

Soon, without much effort it seems, I've caught up to the others.

". . . did you hear that Cathy completely broke down during our chemistry test yesterday?" Celine is saying.

I turn to her in surprise. "Broke down? How?"

Celine shrugs. "Twenty minutes in, and she just started crying. Like, really bad, serious crying. The teacher had to lead her out of the room."

"Damn," Leela says. "You know, now that I think of it, she has seemed pretty stressed lately."

"Who *isn't* stressed?" Celine says briskly, leaning forward to pat her horse's neck.

"She could be under a lot of pressure," I point out, unable to stop myself from jumping to the girl's defense. Just thinking about her panicking halfway through the test—her wide eyes swimming with tears, her round face splotched red and helpless—makes sympathy simmer low in my stomach. Or maybe not just sympathy; if I think long enough for it to hurt, I can picture my old face superimposed on hers, like soft charcoal lines mapped over tracing paper.

"I guess I do feel bad for Cathy and all that," Celine allows. "It must be hard when you're smart but not the smartest. I actually think it's better to always come in tenth than to always be second-best in everything."

Second to who? I'm about to ask, when I realize the obvious answer. Second to Jessica.

"No, I disagree," Leela says. "At least being second means you get good grades, and you get more opportunities. I feel like it's much more depressing to be average."

"That's like one of Cathy's friends," Celine says. "I kid you not, I completely forgot this girl was even sitting behind me until I was paired with her for a group project. . . ."

We ride for miles like this, with Leela and Celine comparing notes on who's smarter and who's more suitable and who's lacking in this department but not that one, and I feel my skin begin to prickle uncomfortably. Surely, at some point, they must have had a similar conversation about me. And then I realize I no longer have to guess. I can find out for myself.

I breathe in. Speak up before I can back out. "What about my cousin Jenna?"

"Your cousin?" Celine's brows furrow, like she's struggling to place a memory from years ago. "Oh right. Jenna."

So at least they still remember me. They still know I exist. I don't know whether to be relieved or disappointed. Not until Celine sighs and says—

"You're not going to tell her this, are you? I mean, I know you won't. But she's always struck me as, like, the kind of person who's really hardworking. Just really, ridiculously hardworking in order to make up for her lack of natural talent. We can't blame her for that, though. At least she's self-aware—"

"*Celine.* Don't be so mean," Leela chides her, but she doesn't seem to disagree either.

And my stomach is falling, my blood is freezing, my lungs are failing me. Still, I persist, like someone standing on a twisted ankle, testing the extent of the damage. "Is that . . . really a bad thing?"

"Hey, being hardworking isn't anything to be ashamed of," Celine says, adjusting the reins with one hand. "But just hard work isn't going to get you very far, either. Look at all the famous athletes and screenwriters and singer-songwriters and scholars. All the people who've left an actual mark on the world. That writer we were learning about in literature the other day. She wrote her first award-winning bestseller when she was, what, sixteen years old? She showed promise when she was, like, ten. And she said that she barely even practiced, all she did was read a lot. For people like that, do we think they worked hard or were born as prodigies?"

It's not an actual question.

I already know the answer, anyway. I've known it this whole time.

"But your family already has you, Jessica." Celine flashes me a smile that's probably meant to be flattering, meant to make me feel better. I feel like I want to throw up. "One prodigy is enough. You work hard *and* you're talented and everyone knows you'll be successful. If Jenna ever needs anything, she can always ask you for it."

Leela nudges her horse forward just to shove Celine's shoulder. "You think everyone would leech off their relatives the way you do?"

Celine grins. "It's called being resourceful. And very soon, I'll be the most successful one in my family—I'm very certain of that. They'll all be leeching off me." Then she glances back at me again, her brows rising and disappearing under her helmet. "But why do you even care about your cousin? She's kind of just . . . there."

The funny thing about time is that part of it is always at a standstill, frozen in the back of your mind, waiting to resurface at any given second. Because just those few words and I'm ten years old again, watching the other kids play together at recess, all of them laughing so loud it hurts my eardrums. I'm fumbling for the basketball in gym class because despite my best efforts I can't get it right, and I can see the eye rolls from the sidelines, I can hear the soft snickers when I trip over my feet, my face flushing, eyes burning. I'm walking through the mall with my family and half of the girls in the year are gathered there and I almost go up to them to say hi until I realize that I wasn't invited. I'm trying to smile through my mortification when the teacher lets everyone choose their own study groups and all my classmates are leaning over their desks, reaching for each other, making plans already, and I'm the only one left. I'm shrinking myself down, down, down, as small as physically possible when the teacher forces me to join the group of best friends in the back, like the unwanted product in a clearance sale.

I'm pretending I can't hear when one of them whispers, "God, not her," but maybe the whole point is that I *can* hear them.

It was a little better when Aaron joined. The classes became bearable. I could hope to let myself hope. I tided myself over from day to day with the promise of catching his eye in the hallways.

It wasn't enough, though.

I needed to find a solution. So I started observing my classmates, desperate to find that mysterious, decisive quality that separated them from me. The thing that I was lacking, that made it so I was always picked last, left out, laughed at.

And I came to the eventual conclusion that they were all good at something. Celine was beautiful and witty and intimidating and a humanities genius. Leela was incredibly well-rounded across all her subjects and creative and could carry any conversation with anyone. Even Cathy Liu, who'd always looked up to Jessica, was respected in her own right for her grades.

Clearly, they all thought I was worse than them.

So I had to be better. I had to be so good they couldn't ignore me anymore. If I wanted to be loved, I had to best them all.

"Hey, isn't that Aaron?" Celine says. "I didn't know he could ride."

The sound of his name yanks my thoughts back to reality.

"What?" I say sharply, twisting around—and without meaning to, I tug at the reins too hard. All I get a glimpse of is a blurry silhouette in the distance before my horse takes one haphazard step to the left, then jerks fast to the right again, snorting and dipping his heavy head.

Celine notices. "Whoa," she says, dropping her own reins to hold up two hands in a placating gesture. "Easy. Hold on—"

It feels like the ground has been ripped out from under me. My body pitches forward with sickening speed.

No, no, no.

I know I'm going to fall before it even happens. I can feel myself teetering wildly off-balance, the uneasy pull between the air and the gravity and the creature's movements, the horrible moment when gravity wins. And instead of resisting, instead of grabbing on to the horse's mane or trying to slow him down, I squeeze my eyes shut, my muscles tensing, and think, *Just get it over with. Just don't make it hurt, or make it hurt less.*

But nothing can prepare me for the shock of the actual fall—the terrible swooping sensation in my stomach, and the hard, jarring impact of the ground, the dirt in my mouth. My bones quake with it, and for a second my head goes completely blank.

I can't think, can't breathe, can't feel anything except the bright, obliterating pain. I'm lying flat on my back, the stones scraping against my skin, and I open my eyes in time to see the horse leap over me.

Black specks of dirt fly into my vision. My limbs are suddenly useless, too heavy. I hear the horse galloping away, each distinct, heavy *thud* of its hooves like a heartbeat, sending tremors through the soil under me, before it slows to a stop. And then Celine's yells, Leela's frantic rush of words. Footsteps pounding closer and closer, their faces swimming before me. Celine's eyes are wider than I've ever seen them, and Leela is red-faced, shoving loose strands of hair back from her cheeks, her hand covering her mouth. She looks like she might start crying.

"Oh my god—"

"Jessica, are you okay?"

"Shit!"

"Can you try to move?"

Leela whips around to Celine. "What? No, have you lost your mind? Don't make her *move*—"

"We need to assess if she's broken any bones."

The idea sends a wave of nausea rolling over me, and my fear is more overwhelming than the actual pain itself. My pulse sky-rockets, my breathing coming out high and shallow through my clenched teeth.

"If she's broken anything, she should stay put," Leela's arguing, waving her arms around, her voice rising in pitch. "I read a news story where someone broke her leg and her friend tried to get her to walk to the nurse and the shattered bone ended up piercing her skin—"

A low, embarrassing whimper escapes my lips.

"Look, you're scaring her, Leela," Celine snaps, crouching down on the grass next to me. "Fine, then. Stay here. But we're literally in the middle of nowhere. We can't just leave her lying on the ground—"

"What if we call the ambulance?"

"No ambulance," I croak out. The throbbing in my arm has intensified, and I'm too terrified to look at it, too scared that I really have broken something. Beneath my panic, I feel a spasm of guilt. It's not even *my* body to break.

"Then who?" Leela asks, her round face pinched with concern and urgency. "Do you want us to call your mom, Jessica?"

I'm about to nod, because I do, I want to see my mom, to have her hold me, stroke my hair, scold me for not being careful enough. I want to cling to her the way I used to when I was a child, let her soothe my worries away with the palm of her hand. But then I realize that Leela wouldn't be calling my mom—she'd be calling my aunt.

"No," I force out. "Not . . . her—"

The heavy horse hooves trample the rest of my words down.

"Oh," I hear Leela say, very faintly. "Wow."

With immense difficulty, I lift my head an inch, blinking. Aaron Cai is riding across the wild grass on a beautiful black steed, his dark hair tousled in the wind. He looks like a figure straight out of a poem, a film, a fairy-tale kingdom. He could be a prince. He could be the one good thing left in the world, the only person I can count on.

Then he's swinging his leg easily over the saddle, dismounting in a single swift movement, and running toward me.

"Hey, can you hear me?" he asks.

I swallow, overwhelmed by the sudden, irrational urge to burst into tears. He's so familiar, so reassuring. I feel so safe around him that it terrifies me; I would follow him anywhere without protest. I want to tell him that, want to grab his hand and say, "I'm scared." But the only word I can get out is "Y-yes."

He doesn't look scared at all, though. His expression is

controlled, completely focused. "Can you move your hands and feet?"

"I—I think so." My limbs feel wooden, but I manage to lift my fingers and wriggle them, then my toes.

"Okay. Good." The bright flashlight of a phone flicks on, almost blinding me. "Look over here," he says quietly, raising a finger and moving it from one side to the other. "Follow my finger."

I try to, my eyes watering, the white flare of the light the only thing I can see. After a few seconds, he turns it off again and nods. Then he grabs a bottle of water from the bag fastened around his waist, lifting it to my lips.

"Careful," he tells me. "Slowly."

The water is an immediate relief, cool on my tongue and sweeter than anything I've ever tasted. While I drink, he motions for Leela to hold the bottle for me and turns his attention downward.

"Tell me if it hurts," he says, and brings his black-gloved hand to my ankles, his touch light, barely brushing my skin, then up higher to my wrists. I don't feel anything except the same dull throbbing in my muscles, the stinging in my arm. "Well, it doesn't look like anything's broken."

Leela releases a loud sigh of relief. "Thank god."

"I thought so," Celine says, but there's a slight tremor to her voice.

Then Aaron takes my left arm in two hands, turning it over so he can inspect the damage, and Leela makes a strangled sound. I can't resist the morbid desire to look, either. Bile fills my mouth. Most of the skin stretching from the pit of my elbow up to my forearm has been scraped off. All that's visible is my blood, Jessica's blood, smeared everywhere.

"Fuck," Celine whispers. "That . . . does not look good."

I feel myself shudder. "Am I . . . am I going to lose this arm?" I blabber, my heart hammering inside my chest. "Will you have to saw it off or something? Do we need to go to the ER? Am I dying?"

Aaron shoots me a look that's half curious, half amused. "Nothing so dramatic, I promise."

"Really?"

"Really. Just take deep breaths and let me handle it. You're lucky I have spare bandages in my bag."

I force myself to inhale. Exhale. He unrolls a strip of gauze, and I'm struck by a dizzying sense of déjà vu, but I'm in too much pain to follow the memory, see where it leads. I just stay very still, as still as I can, and concentrate on my breathing. *Inhale. One, two, three. Exhale. One, two, three . . .*

"Did you learn how to do this in Paris?" Leela asks as Aaron works, because she's the kind of person who would strike up small talk at someone's funeral.

"Partially," he replies, wrapping the gauze around my arm. "I already knew some basic techniques, but I had more opportunities to practice."

Inhale. Exhale.

"Did you learn to ride while you were there too? I don't think I ever saw you at the stables before you left."

"They encouraged extracurriculars. The sport's grown on me, though. Helps me clear my head." He stands up, tucking the remaining gauze away. His gloves are stained with blood, and that stirs an old memory as well, like a breeze over a still pool. "All done."

"Thank you," I whisper, and maybe because it's less embarrassing when I'm speaking as Jessica, I add, "You'll make a great doctor, you know."

He falters, just for the briefest moment, and frowns down at me. "Has this happened before? I mean . . ." He seems to be weighing out his words, trying to select the right ones. "I don't know why, I just have this feeling of déjà vu."

I feel a fresh spike of pain under my breastbone, but I shake my head.

"No, I didn't think so," he murmurs, almost too quiet for me to hear. "Strange, then . . . it feels like . . ." But he doesn't finish his sentence. Just busies himself removing his gloves, his back turned to me, the sun tracing out the firm line of his shoulders, and I can only wonder what he was going to say. What else he's remembered.

Eleven

When it has been made very clear that I will not die, the question becomes: How will I get home?

"We're over two miles away from Lakesville Road," Leela offers, tightening the reins as she stares out at our surroundings. It's all tall, swaying grass and aureolin-yellow wildflowers, the early evening sky; the kind of scenery that would be clichéd as a backdrop for a painting. "Maybe we can ride back together."

Aaron speaks up before I do. "I wouldn't advise that she ride with her arm in its current state. Even if nothing's broken, it's still not a good idea for her to use it."

"What if one of us rides with her?" Celine says. "Or Aaron—you can."

He frowns slightly, then turns to me in consideration, and I feel a blaze of heat travel up my neck.

"No," I blurt out, stepping in between them. "No, I'll walk."

Leela snaps on her riding gloves and blinks at me. "For two whole miles? And what about the horses? We can't leave them here."

"I can walk alone," I say.

"It'll be much faster if we ride," Celine points out.

"Yes, but contrary to the popular saying, I don't think I should get back in the saddle," I tell her. "I'd be quite happy to not get back in the saddle for the foreseeable future."

The corners of Aaron's lips twitch, and to my surprise, he steps over to my side. "I'll walk her back," he says. "Don't worry, I'll see that she's safe and cared for."

Leela hesitates, one foot in the stirrups, her head turned back and tilted in question. "You're sure?"

"It's no problem." He makes it sound so easy, so natural. But everything is easy for him.

"We're trusting you with this," Celine says, her eyes narrowed at him. "You better keep your word."

"I promise."

"It's okay, Celine," I say quietly, as if my heart isn't throwing itself against my rib cage at the mere thought of walking two miles alone with Aaron. "I'll be fine."

Only then does Celine swing herself back onto the horse with perfect posture. The animals stamp their hooves, snorting, their coats gleaming beneath the light. With one last glance back at me, Celine clicks her tongue and nudges the horse forward with her heels.

"We'll wait for you," Leela calls over her shoulder, urging her horse forward as well.

I nod and wave and watch as the two of them disappear across the meadow, Aaron's horse and mine trailing after them. My head won't stop spinning. Before today, I would have been willing to bet that Celine wanted something from my cousin—to scare her, or to sabotage her, even. But Celine's concern for me just now had felt too real to be an act.

"Something on your mind?" Aaron asks.

I startle, and shake my head, even though part of me wants to tell him everything. He's the only person I could trust to help me figure out who the anonymous sender is. But then I remember the way he looked at me on the banks of the lake, his disbelief, how his voice had hardened at the mention of my name.

My arm throbs. My fingers itch toward it, to hold it or squeeze out the pain.

"Leave it," Aaron says. "You need to give it time to heal."

I force my hand to flatten by my side again and start walking very slowly, very gingerly through the grass, my body protesting every step. Aaron follows behind me, his presence steady and quiet as a shadow.

"So what happened?" he asks a few moments later.

"What happened?" I repeat. "I fell."

"Yes, evidently." He picks up his pace, so I can make out the outline of his profile in my peripheral vision, the curiosity edging his sharp features. "But you're so careful all the time. I guess I'm just surprised."

"Well, I didn't fall on purpose," I say flatly, to avoid the truth. *I heard your name. All it took was your name, and I forgot myself.*

"I would be very concerned if you did."

I turn to glare at him, then remember that Jessica would never be so thankless, so hostile. So instead I clamp my jaw shut and keep trudging forward, my arm stiff in its bandage, my skin stinging.

As the sun sinks lower, a mist starts to roll in, the white haze washing over the oaks and turning the mountain slopes and wilderness in the background into blurry silver-blue shapes, the shades deepening layer by layer. Everything looks softer this way, like a dreamscape. Even the soil has that musky scent of the woods after a summer rainstorm.

"I'm sorry," I say when enough time has passed for the silence to feel pointed, too uncomfortable to maintain. "I know I'm slowing us down. It'll probably be dark by the time we reach the road."

"It's okay," he says at once. "All the more reason I should go with you, don't you think? And besides," he adds, turning his eyes to the horizon, all the blue rising against blue, "I don't usually ride so far out. It's much prettier here than I imagined."

I gaze over at Aaron and feel my chest ache with everything unspoken between us. "It's beautiful," I agree. "When I was a little kid, I actually used to dream of living in a place like this. Somewhere deep in the countryside, or by the ocean, or the forests, where you could wake up to the most gorgeous views of the grass and the waters and the morning mist. . . ."

He tilts his head. "Really? You did?"

"Yeah. I mean, it was more just a daydream than anything," I say. "But it was nice to think about. I'd have a dog to live there with me and keep me company—a husky, because that's the closest you can get to owning a wolf without owning a wolf. And I'd grow strawberries and apples in my garden and bake pies for lunch and share them with my parents when they came to visit. And then I'd spend entire afternoons just lying on the couch or the front porch, reading in the sun; I wouldn't need to worry about running out of books, because I'd have a whole library to myself. And when night fell, I would stare at the stars and paint and paint. . . ." I trail off when I realize he's come to an abrupt halt amid the wildflowers, his shoulders tense, his black eyes ablaze with some fierce emotion I can't understand, his lower lip quivering. He's staring at me like I might not be real, like I'm someone he might have invented.

"Jenna," he says, and all the blood exits my heart.

I freeze.

"It's really you, isn't it?" he asks. It's a threadbare whisper, a question and a confirmation. "I can't believe it. I didn't want to believe it," he continues, filling up my silence, "but there's no other explanation for this. I know you too well."

The words chafe at something inside me.

I know you.

"Jenna," he repeats. "Say something. Tell me . . . tell me I haven't lost my mind."

"No," I whisper. "You haven't lost your mind." Then, because I can't push down my curiosity, "What convinced you in the end?"

"I couldn't stop thinking about it," he says, walking ahead again, and I make myself catch up. "After that day at the lake . . . I wanted to assume you were joking, but then—it wasn't logical. Why would you joke about that? It would require a truly terrible, warped sense of humor. And then everything started to make sense. I started to comb through all my memories from before I left for Paris and comparing them to the after. I thought at first it was because I'd been gone for so long. People can change, right?

But people can't transform so drastically. I couldn't sleep," he continues, shaking his head. "I just kept replaying our conversations, searching for the differences. Of course, there's also the fact that I haven't seen you . . . Jenna . . . I mean, the person you were—" He breaks off. "God, this is absolutely bizarre."

"I know," I say with a weak little laugh. "Kind of breaks your brain, doesn't it?"

"Is this a nightmare?" he asks. He looks almost desperate. "Is there any way this is all made up inside my head?"

I grimace. Kick at the grass beneath my feet. "If this is a nightmare, we're dreaming the same dream. You know what? Maybe that's what it means," I say, recalling the proverb slowly. "To dream of becoming a butterfly. I didn't understand it when we were studying it in Chinese school, but I think I do now. Maybe it's impossible to tell which is the dream and which is reality."

There is something dreamlike about the view, the yellow flowers lucent against the grass, the mountains dark against the night.

"I tried to look up peer-reviewed journal articles to prove it," he admits after a moment.

This elicits a burst of genuine laughter from me. "Oh yeah, no, I'm afraid this isn't a popular topic for scientific studies."

"But it goes against everything I know about modern medicine," he says. "What separates the body from the soul, the physical from the metaphysical. What can be transferred and what can be kept. It just . . . it opens up thousands of possibilities. Thousands of questions. It could fundamentally reshape our understanding of physics."

I shrug. "I guess."

"Wow," he says, much more like his usual self. "Invigorating response."

"Maybe some things can't be explained by science," I say. "Maybe it's better that way."

"Anything can be explained by science," he insists. "Everything must come with an answer."

"You're so naive sometimes," I murmur under my breath, hating how tender I feel toward him, even at a time like this.

"What?"

"Nothing."

He runs a distracted hand through his hair. "So where's the real Jessica Chen? Have you found anything? Is she okay?" Then, almost in the same breath, as if his brain is leaping ahead of itself, working faster than any ordinary person could keep up with, "Is *that* why you were borrowing those old fairy tales? You think they could lead you to her?" His skepticism is obvious.

"Well, why not?" I challenge. "You haven't had any luck using the *scientific* approach. Can't you consider the possibility that there might be other, more relevant methodologies? Things outside math and physics?"

"So you've had luck with fables and folklore?"

"No," I ground out. "Not *yet*. I don't know." Frustration leaks into my voice. "Sometimes I'll think I'm close, but then I'll hit a dead end. Like, there was this ancient tale about how a man successfully summoned the soul of his long-lost lover, but he had to perform some kind of spell using the soil of her hometown. If I were to try that, I wouldn't even know what soil to use—the soil from her backyard? Or from Tianjin?" I shake my head. "Sometimes it feels impossible. But then, my wish should have been impossible in the first place, and it still came true—"

"Why, though?" he demands, his voice strained, like it hurts him just to say it. "Why would you . . . why would you even make that wish in the first place?"

My breath freezes in my throat. This isn't where I'd anticipated the conversation would go. I don't reply right away, don't know how or where to begin, but the answer flashes like a film reel inside my head.

Every time I walked into an examination hall, handed in a paper, signed up for a club, participated in a contest . . . the mad rush of hope in my blood, only for my optimism to sour into disappointment. Every failure that felt like the apocalypse and has stayed with me since. Every move I made premeditated, but still always miscalculating, offering up the wrong comment or opinion or idea. Days when I was too exhausted to sleep while someone else lived the life I dreamed of. Witnessing everything I'd ever wanted happen for Jessica, knowing it would never happen for me. The report card statements, always the same sentiment rephrased: "Not quite there yet, but has potential," which was what people said as consolation in the absence of true competence. And me learning over time that *potential* was in itself such an abstract term, tossed around recklessly, that more often than not it simply meant you didn't live up to the idea somebody else had of you.

Like the speech night my Chinese teacher had insisted that I would shine in, standing up on that cold, dark stage and trembling, feeling my own lack of presence, my inability to keep anyone's eyes on my face, and not even qualifying for the next round. Sobbing afterward at home until I couldn't breathe, too embarrassed to even tell my parents, my blankets pulled up over my head. Watching from the shadows as Jessica shook hands with beaming teachers, friends running over to gush, the circle that formed around her an impenetrable thing, a private room with windows but no doors, listening to the boasts disguised as self-deprecating jokes and half-hearted complaints.

But somehow trying anyway, believing even when there was nothing left to believe in. Dragging around the terrible knowledge that anything I did could change my life in an instant, but everything I did was futile.

"Because I don't want a quiet life, I want a brilliant one," I say at last. "Because I need to know what it's like to win. To be the best."

"But you don't have to—"

I shoot him a warning glare. "If you give me bullshit along the lines of, 'Oh, everyone is on their own journey, we can all be the best,' I will actually throw a fit. That's nice for a card, but completely untrue in real life."

"I wasn't going to say that," he protests. Then, more carefully, he asks, "Is this because of Harvard? Because you didn't get in?"

I flinch. The rejection still stings. "That's part of it."

"Harvard doesn't matter," he says. "Getting into Harvard doesn't mean you're better than everyone, and *not* getting in doesn't mean you're worse."

And that's what I'd try to tell myself at first. I would come up with a thousand reasons why I could succeed without the Ivy League education. I might even be able to forget about it from time to time, but it would always linger in the back of my mind. One day, ten years from now, I'll be at a party and everyone will be chatting and someone will casually bring up their classes at Harvard and someone else will gush over how smart they are, and in that moment I'll feel so insignificant I'll want to vanish.

"I can tell you don't believe me," Aaron says. "But if you could just—"

"My arm hurts," I declare, and I watch the way he softens instantly, the argument disappearing from his eyes. For now, at least. I have no doubt he'll bring it up again, but my arm really does ache, and the faint scent of blood is making my stomach turn and my head spin and the last thing I want is to dissect my own inferiority like a text analysis, with point, evidence, explain.

"We've already walked a mile," he says. "We're almost there."

He's wrong, though. We still have more than a mile to go.

"Tian ya," my aunt says when I stagger in through the front door, Aaron close behind me. She must have just finished showering; she's wrapped in a fluffy pink bathrobe and she has a facial mask on, leaving very little room to move her mouth. Her next words sound like they've been glued between her teeth. "What happened to you? What's wrong with your arm?"

"Don't worry," Aaron says, helping me sit down on the couch. "She fell off a horse, but she should be fine. She just needs rest."

"You went riding again?" Auntie glares at me. It's hard to take her too seriously with the mask. "How many times have I told you? It's too dangerous. Just because your friends go doesn't mean you should—"

"She won't do it again," Aaron says quickly. "Right, Jessica?"

I can only muster the energy to nod. My arm won't stop throbbing, and through my exhaustion, I can't help imagining what it would be like to come home to my own parents. How much easier it would be, how much safer I would feel.

"Thank you for bringing her back," Auntie says to Aaron. "You're such a good kid. Always looking out for Jessica."

"Of course."

"I'm glad she has you."

My eyes had been close to falling shut on their own, but they snap open at this. My aunt is smiling at Aaron.

"You two get along so well," she continues. "I was just saying the other day, I think of you as my son-in-law. And it's wonderful that you're back home. You should come around more often."

A sour taste rises to my mouth, as if I've bitten into a raw lemon. I'm suddenly, irrationally furious. It's not Aaron's fault, and it's not Jessica's either. But this has always been a deep fear of mine: that they're perfect together, the golden boy and the beloved angel. That Jessica is the main character, and I'm the villain waiting in the shadows, the backup behind the curtains, the monster lurking beyond the village.

"I'm only doing what any friend would," Aaron says, his expression impassive. "It doesn't mean anything special."

"You're a *great* friend to Jessica," Auntie says, eyes crinkling.

I want to throw something. I want to throw up. "Could I have some water, please?" I croak out.

"Mashang, mashang." Auntie adjusts the facial mask that's sliding down her chin and hurries off into the kitchen.

Aaron takes one small step toward me, and I hate how everything in me tightens to the point of pain. How my impulse is to wrap my arms around his waist and press my cheek to his shirt and feel him hold me. I'm weak, I'm injured, I'm so desperate for him it makes me sick.

"Go away," I mumble, hiding my face in the couch cushions. I know it's not his fault, but I still blame him. "But thank you for your help."

"Polite as ever," he says dryly.

I ignore him.

"Are you really going to act like—"

Before he can go on, Auntie comes back with a glass of water.

"Drink up," she says.

I take a sip and choke. It's ice cold. Back at home, the only acceptable water temperatures are warm and scalding hot.

"Zen me le?" Auntie says, frowning at me. "Didn't you ask for water? Or do you want mineral water instead? There should still be some in the cabinet."

"No, no, it's good." I force myself to drink the rest of it, even though it hurts my stomach on its way down. "This is exactly how I like it."

Twelve

It's dangerously easy to make a habit of something.

Every night now, I read Jessica's journal before I sleep, hoping there'll be answers hidden between the lines, waiting for me to find. And that means going all the way back to the beginning.

> *Okay, so this past week has been absolutely wild and amazing. I was invited to this super fancy scholars' conference and apparently I'll be the youngest person there—the others attending are basically all seniors and even college students. And guess what? I get to fly business class and bring my parents with me—and we'll all be staying in a five-star hotel. It's so cool!*

Most of the early entries are written this way: giddy, wide-eyed, her excitement palpable in the wild loops of her letters and the smudged ink, as if she was impatient to jot down her next thought before her previous one had even dried on the page. But as I read on, her enthusiasm levels out into the indifference of someone who was already expecting every good thing that's happened.

I guess that checks out.

Jessica has never been one of those people who need to compare their current selves with their past selves, to show how much they've transformed for the better. She's never really experienced failure—her successes have simply kept growing. She went from being the best in her class, to the best in Chinese school, to the best in our entire high school—and now she'll go on to become the best in all of Harvard, and then the best in the world. Her life is one of exponential growth, the type you can graph out perfectly with a calculator.

My life has never been like that. The only discernible pattern, really, is inconsistency: the second I improve in certain areas, I regress in others. My skin becomes clearer, but my hair becomes thinner. My grades in English rise, but my grades in math fall. I start exercising more in the mornings, but stop doing my laundry over the weekends. One step forward and one step back, and repeat, until in the end, it looks like I've been standing in the same spot for years.

There's another shift in her journal entries starting from around two years ago.

She doesn't sound excited or coolly nonchalant, satisfied or superior to everybody. She just sounds angry.

Like in this one:

> Sometimes I really hate this school. I hate what it stands for, what it chooses not to stand for. I hate that it splashes out ads in Chinese newspapers and recruits students from overseas just so they can pay the more expensive international fees and boost the end-of-year scores, while it only celebrates its legacies and rowing

club heirs. This place has made me miserable, and some of my worst days have been spent trapped inside its halls.

But I also know that when there's a high school reunion three, five, ten years from now, I'll still attend. And not only will I attend, but I'll spend the week beforehand planning out my outfit, mining my life for things I can brag about, just to give the impression that I'm doing well.

I hate this school so much, but I can't stop myself from caring about all the people who go here, from wanting the school to love me, even if I know it's impossible.

And this:

There's a story the teachers like to tell about me. Two years ago I'd come down with a horrible fever the night before our final exams; I was so dizzy I couldn't stand up properly. Eating hurt. Breathing hurt. Everything hurt. And yet I'd insisted on pushing through it; I'd forced my mother to drive me to school and I'd stumbled into the exam halls on my own, gripping the backs of chairs for support, steadying myself against the walls. I don't remember anything I wrote that day, but I ended up with the highest score in the class across all my subjects. And the moral of the story was that sometimes you have to be a little cruel to yourself, that sometimes pain is necessary if you want to succeed.

That's what we do, isn't it? We turn pain into a story, because then it has a purpose. Then, we reason, there was a point to it all along. But sometimes pain is just pain, and there's nothing particularly noble about clinging to it. Perhaps I would have done much better still if I were healthy; perhaps I was lucky I didn't end up damaging my body permanently or fainting halfway through the exam, and the moral is that I should have stayed at home and let myself rest. Only I guess that's not as inspiring.

The ruined skin on my arm has only just started to scab over when another note appears in my bag after school, folded beneath the cover of my textbook.

Everything inside my body goes cold as I pick it up. Read over the handwritten message. It feels like an explosion has sounded right next to my ear, sending my thoughts scattering through my skull. The world slips and sharpens into pieces. The words slice across the torn paper. Whoever is targeting Jessica must be losing their patience, because all the note says is:

If you don't confess, I'm telling everyone in three days.

Three days.

That's hardly anything, and the first day is already taken up by my auntie's planned hiking trip for the weekend.

"Can I not go?" I plead, dragging my heels all the way to the front door. "I still have work—"

"Your aunt and uncle will be there," Auntie says, which I have to mentally translate into my own parents. "And Aaron is coming along too."

Aaron.

He might know what to do. I clamp my jaw down over my remaining protests and quickly slide into Jessica's boots.

Auntie sends me an unsubtle smile. "I thought that might motivate you to join us. Why don't you put some lip tint on? That rose color looks so lovely on you."

Wonderful, I think darkly to myself as I step outside. *I may not succeed at uncovering the anonymous student, or at recovering Jessica's soul, but even if I achieve nothing else, at least I can take comfort in knowing I gave my aunt more reason to believe that Jessica and Aaron belong together.*

There's something both terribly familiar and strangely disjointed about the scene at the bottom of the mountain. My parents are busy applying sunscreen in the shade, and I should be standing with them, letting my mom fuss over the exposed back of my ears and my neck, humoring my dad by half-heartedly following along to his warm-up exercises. Except I arrive in Jessica's fancy car with my aunt and uncle, who are both dressed in designer clothes completely unsuited for physical activity. Aaron is alone, but that's normal; by now, we know to invite his father to these things only out of politeness, rather than any expectation he might actually show up.

"Everyone's here, then?" my dad says, smiling around at us as he fixes the cap on his head. His eyes move right over me, and my chest contracts. *Dad.* I have to shove aside the childlike urge to call for him, like I would when I lost sight of my parents among the crowds at the mall. *It's me.* "Great, great, let's get going. I'll lead the way."

My uncle laughs at him. "You look like a tour guide with that hat. All you need is a little flag to wave around."

Dad makes an unimpressed face. "It's a nice hat. I got it as a birthday present from—" He pauses.

My daughter should be the rest of his sentence. I'd bought it for him three years ago, and he'd sworn to wear no other hat from that point on.

Now he turns to my mom, confused. "Who gave this to me again?"

"Why are you asking *me*?" she demands. "Why do you always expect me to remember these things?"

"Because your memory's better than mine," my dad says, then shakes his head. "Ah, I must be getting old. I could've sworn it was someone important. . . ."

My mouth dries.

"Your memory wouldn't be so bad if you ate more walnuts," Mom insists.

The others are laughing, but I don't feel like laughing at all. I feel like the ground is sinking, like it might crack open at any moment and I'll fall in. How could my dad have just *forgotten*? And what other memories has he lost?

"You bought him that hat, didn't you?"

I startle. I hadn't noticed Aaron walking over to me while the parents started up the mountain steps.

"Yeah," I say, making an effort not to look concerned. "I did."

"You're concerned."

"I'm not," I say, striding forward.

"Don't lie to me," he says. "You might have Jessica's face, but your expressions are still the same—"

"Keep it down," I hiss at him, glancing ahead at the adults. "Do you want them to overhear?"

He shrugs, perfectly nonchalant. "I guarantee that even if they overheard, they wouldn't have any idea what we're talking about, and they wouldn't believe us anyway."

"You could still try to be careful. What if they think we've lost our minds?"

"I've got it under control."

"Oh sure. Because you just have control over everything. You're just perfect and magical like that."

"Well, yes," he agrees.

I would swat his shoulder, except Jessica isn't the kind of person to swat things—not even flies—so I'm forced to take my annoyance out on an overhanging branch. It's darker here on the mountain path, cooler, with the thick spread of trees filtering out the sun.

"How did you even know I bought him the hat?" I ask.

"You mentioned it once," he says simply.

I falter on the next step, something new occurring to me. "But how do you remember? Why?"

"What do you mean?"

"Everyone else has merely accepted that I'm gone," I tell him in a low voice. My parents are already a good few yards away, the distance between us stretching wider and wider; they appear to be racing each other. "The teachers, my friends, my family. They're all under the impression that I went away—except you. You came searching for me," I say. "And you still recall all our past conversations and everything. Right?"

He raises his brows. "Would you like to test me?"

"Eighth grade," I say. "The last day of school. What did I say to you in the parking lot, before we left—"

"That Old Keller was being too harsh with his marking," he says easily, not even pausing to think. "That you felt like he singled you out in class all the time, and you actually *were* listening, you just don't enjoy staring at the teachers when they're lecturing because you find the eye contact awkward."

I stare. "I—yeah. I mean, exactly. How did you . . . I can't believe you actually remember that."

He clears his throat. For the first time, he looks flustered. "You ought to give me more credit."

"Xianzai de nianqingren tili buxing ya," my dad calls, spinning around. *The youths are so weak these days.* "You two need to get your heart rate up. Move your limbs. Where's your energy?"

In another life, I'm sure he would've been a sports coach.

"So how are you feeling about college, Jessica?" my dad asks when we draw closer. "Harvard. *Harvard.* Your parents raised you so well."

Cue the instant protests and humble-but-not-humble smiles from my aunt and uncle.

"Don't be modest," he says. "This is a very big deal, yes? Tai you chuxi le. You will be set for the rest of your life, you understand that? With a great education, you won't have to worry about money or job security or buying a house ever again. You can be anything. Whatever you want to be. We never had that kind of freedom when we were younger, did we?"

My uncle nods, his forehead shining with sweat. He's evidently having difficulty keeping up with my dad. "No," he says. "When we were . . . their age . . . we had two choices: pass the college entrance exams, or—"

"Stay in our town forever," my dad finishes. "To be honest with you all, I've always been proud of us: we were one of the only families where *both* sons made it out. I like to think we're successful, in that regard. But Jessica's success—that's beyond anything I could have ever imagined. Did you imagine this?" he asks my uncle, waving a hand at me.

"No, no, not at all," my uncle says.

My dad beams at me. "See? She's the pride of our whole family."

This, I think to myself, breathing in the crisp air like someone smelling a fresh bouquet of azaleas, letting the sweetness fill my lungs. For a few moments, I feel whole, the sense of solidity spreading down to my tingling fingers, my toes, as if I'm a sketch colored in at last. This is why I crave success, why Jessica's life will always be better than mine. Success is such a beautiful thing. It's so intimate, so heartachingly personal, I can feel it in my very blood. It's the closest you'll ever fly to the sun. The closest you'll ever get to immortality. Who cares about a bit of pain and sacrifice when you could—if only for a few fleeting days in your already short life—know what it's like to be a god?

"But Aaron has enjoyed plenty of success too, hasn't he?" My dad claps Aaron on the back. "He's going to be one of the best doctors in the world. If anything happens to me in the future, I'll go straight to you."

Aaron absorbs this with the perfect amount of confidence and humility. "Well, you're very young and healthy, shushu. You'd be welcome to ask me for anything, but I doubt you'll need me."

"Oh, please. You flatter me."

"Just telling the truth, shushu."

My dad sighs. "Ah, you're such a good kid. If your mother were still here, she would be so happy. . . ."

I immediately tense and glance over at Aaron. His expression hasn't changed—he's too good at hiding his emotions for that, too used to carrying these kinds of conversations with well-meaning adults who don't understand him. But I notice how his fingers shift, curling around air.

"That reminds me," I say loudly, stepping in between them. "There's a question I wanted to ask our brilliant future doctor."

Aaron blinks, and his hands relax. "Yes?"

I deliberately slow down on the path, waiting until my dad and the other parents have tuned out of our conversation and started complaining among themselves about inflation before continuing. "It's about Jessica. There's someone who's been sending her these strange messages. . . ."

"What kind of messages?" he asks, frowning.

I recount everything I know, all my flimsy guesses and incomplete clues.

Surprise washes over his face, but it quickly settles into contemplation. "You can't find the sender's address?"

"I thought to check," I say, "but the first email seems to have been sent from an untraceable email provider or something. It's too hard to track them down."

"What about the handwritten notes?" he prompts. "You said you found them folded between your test and your notes, right? And that was in—"

"Our world politics class," I finish for him, following along. "That's why I thought it was Celine before, since she seemed kind of . . . I don't know . . ."

"Jealous?" Aaron raises his eyebrows. "You're probably just sensitive to the fact because you're experiencing it firsthand, but I definitely wouldn't count it as suspicious. Almost everyone's a little jealous of Jessica, including her best friends."

I'm just as bad as everyone else, I admit to myself, shifting my gaze away, guilt squirming in my stomach. *I'm worse, because I'm closer to her, whether by blood or by the years I've known her, and I still can't control my jealousy.* Whenever I think of her, I see three different images: there's my cousin, who'd catch my eye across the dining table while our relatives gossiped loudly and make the long dinners more bearable; there's my friend, who'd line up with me at the mall just to try out the newest ice-cream flavor and buy us both hot drinks afterward, when our teeth were chattering from the cold; and then there's bierenjia de haizi, someone else's perfect child. The only person who'd understand the pressure to succeed, and the last person I'd want to tell all of this to.

"We can narrow it down to the people sitting around you in world politics," Aaron is saying. "That's around fifteen people."

"But I only have two days to figure out who it is," I tell him, my throat tight.

"What about if you tried to match the handwriting?"

"I've considered that. The problem is that half the class takes notes by hand; everyone else just uses their laptops. And I'd need to have a sample of their handwriting for long enough to actually compare it."

"A sample . . . ," he repeats slowly. Then his eyes widen. "Wait. I think I've got it."

The roar of blood in my ears.

"You do?" I say, not daring to hope but hoping anyway. "What?"

He hesitates. Unexpectedly, inexplicably, color rises to his cheeks. "Remember that birthday card you gave me when I turned fifteen? The one you asked everyone in our grade to write a message on?"

Of course I remember. I can't believe that he does. I had started preparing it a month in advance, hand-painting the dozens of flowers on the front and chasing down every single classmate with a pen, even the people I wouldn't normally dare approach. *Nothing is too long or too earnest,* I'd reminded them. Most of the girls had been all too glad for a chance to say something sweet about Aaron, and for once, I hadn't minded it. I knew that the card wasn't enough. That it couldn't compare to having both parents around to blow the candles out. That on those particular days—his birthday, Mother's Day, the Spring Festival—the grief would wrap around him like a damp scarf and the shadows would fall sharply on the empty spaces his mother had left. But I just wanted him to feel less alone.

"I've kept it by my bed—I mean, in my room," Aaron says, rubbing his neck. "I can send a photo of it to you when I go home, and then you can compare the handwriting, side by side."

"Oh my god." I skid to a stop. "*Oh my god*, Aaron. That might actually work. You're a genius."

"I know," he says. He stops too, standing directly beneath a faint trickle of sunlight through the trees, and turns back to glance at me, his grin quick and beautiful as a lightning strike.

And time fractures. Reverses in on itself. We're both on the cusp of fifteen again, and it's autumn, everything soft and ephemeral and molten gold, the leaves crinkling underfoot. We're in the same mountains but deeper. The air is cold. We've been walking for hours already and Jessica's run ahead as always, leaving just us here. Alone. Privately, I'm grateful, then feel so guilty, so foolish for my gratitude—what do I expect to happen?—that my tenderness splits into irritation.

"Are you tired?" he asks, noticing me falter.

"No," I grumble, though my limbs are aching, and my breathing is shallow, labored. The sky is starting to darken, the pinkish light dying beyond the horizon. I watch it change through the gaps in the foliage. I've never known how to witness dusk without feeling a dull sense of grief: another day gone, another day lost where I'm still the same.

"We can rest for a while, if you want," he offers.

I shake my head. "It's too late. You know my mom will kill me if we don't get home in time."

"I'll tell her you were with me. She trusts me."

"A little too much, I think," I mutter, forcing myself to walk on.

He waits until I've caught up before moving too, his paces even with mine. "What do you mean?'

"You know what my family thinks of you."

"I don't," he says, sounding genuinely curious.

"Aaron, the golden child," I mimic, unable to hide the envy in my tone. "Aaron, the good influence. Aaron, the future doctor. They adore you. They think you're going to save the world and eradicate all misery and disease."

He cocks his head to the side, considering. "If it bothers you so much, I could always be a bad influence."

"Oh sure." I snort.

"Really."

"I doubt you'd even know how, to be honest."

"I can. I could be terrible," he says, voice suddenly low, suddenly too quiet, and leans in. My heart runs away from me, thudding so hard that it feels like punishment. "Jenna."

"Y-yes?"

"Should we sneak into a bar tonight?"

I stare at him for a beat and burst out laughing. "God, I can't stand you," I complain, but I'm smiling wider than I've smiled in a long time, and he's gazing down at me, his raven-black hair windswept, his eyes dark with amusement, and I think I might go mad from all the emotions boiling inside me. I've never wanted anyone so badly. I can't imagine ever wanting anybody else like this again. My throat aches from it.

"I'm afraid you'll have to," he says. "Unless that's why we're in these mountains? Is this all an elaborate plot to murder me?"

"Don't expose my plans, please. It took a lot of effort getting you here."

"Is Jessica in on it too?"

The mention of her name hits me like ice water. I deflate, and the wilderness in the background sharpens into focus again, the sound of sparrows chirping and small creatures scurrying through the thornbushes. Jessica Chen. There's an unspoken equation here: the three of us versus the two of us. Friends versus something else. Maybe that's why he brought her up—to remind me that we can't be anything else. I tug the sleeves of my sweater down over my fingers and walk faster, my eyes trained on the dark blue slope of the mountains ahead, still and silent as a slate sea.

Then a sharp pain tears through my left calf.

I freeze, and the first thing I register isn't the branch twisting into my skin but Aaron's expression, his eyes widened slightly, his jaw tight. He's beside me in an instant, one arm sliding around me to support my weight as I lower myself down onto a boulder.

"Let me see," he says, and I don't even think twice about it, just nod. My mind feels fuzzy at the edges; everything stings. He could ask anything of me in that moment, and I'd probably agree.

Very slowly, he wraps his long fingers around my bare ankle, stretching my leg out a little before him, and inspects the wound.

I hiss. Blood is flowing from a fresh gash the length of my thumb, the red so vivid I can't imagine it's something that could come from my own body. It looks almost artificial, like food dye or acrylic paint.

"You'll be okay," he murmurs.

And for some reason, even though I'm bleeding up in the mountains miles away from home and I can barely see the sun anymore, I believe him.

"I should clean this out first, though," he says.

I flinch. "Wait. What?" My voice rises an octave. "That, um—that sounds really painful. Will it be painful?"

"Only for a bit. It's better than an infection."

I manage a weak scoff. "You sound like a doctor already."

He smiles then, or tries to, but only his lips move. The rest of his features are hard, focused, his eyes burning with a rare intensity. "Maybe hold on to something—that should help. I'll try to be quick."

Without thinking, I grab his shoulder, and I feel the surprise flicker between us, the air rippling like water, though we both do our best to hide it. Act like nothing's happening, when everything is. At least for me. I watch him as he takes out the bottle of water he's been carrying, unscrews the lid with steady fingers, his movements fast and certain. Then he splashes it over my leg.

The pain is instant. I clench my teeth around a yell, my nails digging into the fabric of his shirt, so tight I know it must be hurting him, but he doesn't utter a single word of complaint. Instead he's apologizing, his voice low and hoarse. "Sorry," he keeps saying, one hand still wrapped firmly around my lower calf. "Sorry, almost done now. It's going to be fine."

Through the hazy film of tears, I stare at him, the white of his neck, the intense concentration in his eyes, and it takes me a delayed beat to realize that he's scared. Maybe even more scared than I am, when I didn't think he could be scared of anything. My blood quickens in my veins. I imagine reaching out across that cold space and touching his cheek. Just once, gently. I imagine wrapping my arms around him when he's done, leaning all the way against him, thanking him the way I want to. Nobody else would know, except us and the sky and the trees. At the mere thought of it, I feel a rush of longing so violent it almost strangles me. *Will it always be like this?* I wonder, squeezing my eyes shut, feeling the places his fingers touch my skin. *Is this as close as we'll ever be?*

"Jenna," he calls, a second or a lifetime later. "Jenna."

"Jessica."

Time resets itself, like a dislocated bone. I'm someone else, and someone else's mom is waving me over.

"Look at this," my aunt is saying, pointing ahead of us at something in the shrubbery. "Did you see the butterfly? I've never seen one with so many colors in its wings before. It was right here."

That old saying floats across my mind again. *To dream of becoming a butterfly.* I've been busy deliberating why the dream started, but I'm not so sure if I'm ready for the dream to end. Would the butterfly be relieved to turn back into a human? Or would the butterfly miss being able to fly too much?

Thirteen

On our climb back down the mountain, my aunt insists on inviting Aaron over to stay for the rest of the afternoon.

"You must have some tea and fruit after that long hike," my aunt says. "And I'm sure Jessica would be very happy to spend more time with you."

I'm slightly horrified by this overt attempt at matchmaking, and it couldn't have come at a worse time. With the note's threat looming over my head, the idea of having afternoon tea feels as frivolous and ill-advised as throwing a party while a tsunami is visibly approaching from the shores.

"That's really okay," Aaron tries to say, exchanging a pointed look with me, but it's futile. Once my aunt decides something, even the gods can't change her mind.

She isn't known to be very subtle, either. As soon as we're back home, she makes a vague excuse about needing to buy something from the supermarket and all but ushers my uncle out the door with her.

"Jessica, make sure Aaron feels right at home," she instructs. "And call if you need anything."

Then she winks—actually, blatantly winks—before leaving us alone together.

I feel somewhat violent.

"You can sneak out now," I tell Aaron. "I'll make up a convincing excuse about why you had to go back early. Don't worry," I can't help adding, my tone sharpening on its own. "I'll let her know how much we bonded."

But he doesn't leave. "What will you do?" he asks, suddenly serious. "After I send you the card, and you've confirmed who the sender is? You're not planning on confronting them alone, are you?"

I stare at him. "What else am I supposed to do? If I get anyone else involved, then they'll find out whatever it is Jessica's hiding—not to mention that I'd have to explain the *slight* complication with the me-being-in-her-body thing."

"But it could be dangerous," he protests. "You don't know what they'll do."

Don't say anything you'll regret, I warn myself. *This is not the time for that. Just don't say anything—*

"Is it really me you're concerned about?" I blurt out. My muscles are sore from the hike, and my clothes feel sticky on my skin. Maybe that's why it's more difficult than usual to control my tongue. "Or is it only because I'm in Jessica's body?"

He goes completely still.

"It's because of her, isn't it?" I guess, heat flooding my cheeks. "Well, don't worry. I'll do everything I can to protect her, so that when Jessica returns to her own body, you two can have your happy reunion and life will go on as it should. My aunt will be absolutely ecstatic, and I'll be sure to get out of your way—"

"I don't like Jessica," he cuts in.

The words don't register at first. I'm still talking. "I'll be nothing but supportive. Everyone at school thinks you're perfect for each other. Leela and Celine do as well. It makes so much sense; Jessica's the best. She's gorgeous and talented and smart, and so are you, and there's no reason why . . . what did you say?"

"I don't like Jessica," he says, enunciating each syllable. "I already like someone else."

My heart stops beating. "Who? Is it . . . is it someone you met in Paris? Or someone from our school? Or—"

"Are you pretending you don't know?" he asks, the sharpness to his tone matching mine now. "Because I fear I've already made it painfully obvious. I mean, I left the *country* because of you."

Wait.

Pause.

Hold on.

"That makes no sense," I tell him. I think I'm laughing, or shaking my head, or stepping backward. I don't really know anymore. I don't know anything. "You . . . you left because you hated me. Because you rejected me. Because you didn't care—"

His eyes flash. "I left because I couldn't bear it."

"What?"

"You," he says, and the air escapes my lungs. He runs an agitated hand through his hair. "What I . . . felt for you. How much I needed you. I thought I would lose my mind if I stayed any longer, if I . . . if we—" He cuts himself off, breathing hard.

"What?" I repeat, but this time there's no anger in my voice, only shock. I blink at him, uncomprehending. I'm scared to speak again, to make even the slightest sound, scared he'll take the words back and tell me I imagined it.

"Surely you must have sensed it," he says, coming to an abrupt stop, his expression distressed, almost desperate. "Even just a little. I know . . . I know it took me too long to start looking at you the way you wanted. But near the end—once I did . . ."

"All I know," I say very slowly, to make sure we're speaking the same language, "is that you pulled away from me. Don't you remember?" *Because I do,* I want to add, though it's hard to summon that old, humiliating rage when he's looking at me this way. *I remember every detail, even now. It's all I've been able to think about since you left.*

"Because I was scared," Aaron says, gazing across the space at me like he can feel all those years burning between us. All those nights after he left, when I would wait until the house was quiet before crying into my pillow, my knees hugged to my chest, trying to dull the ache there. "I thought . . . if we ever became something more, I was sure I was going to disappoint you."

"That's—how would that even be possible?" I demand. "You're perfect, and I'm me, and I—I fell for you first. I've liked you for almost half my life, and you basically just admitted that you only saw me as a friend for most of that time—"

"No, you *think* I'm perfect. You think everyone's so much better than they really are, and you think you're so much worse than you really are. I was only a goal to you," he tells me, swallowing. "I was a dream, someone unattainable, something you built up inside your head. You forget how well I know you, Jenna. There's nothing you want more than to want—you'll obsess over something, and convince yourself that so long as you get it, you'll be happy, but then once you do, you're immediately dissatisfied and want something else."

"That's not true," I start to protest, though I feel my tongue falter.

"I've seen it happen," he says. "When you were thirteen, you begged for this dress for months and months, as if it was the only thing you could ever look beautiful in, but after you got it for Christmas, you only wore it once because it wrinkled too easily. I remember when you made it your goal to get over eighty percent on your end-of-year exams, and you were happy for maybe a couple hours after you achieved it. Or when you claimed that all you wanted was to place in the top three for the school's essay contest, but before your certificate had even been printed, you were wishing out loud that you could come in first for next year's contest. And if I'd let myself kiss you that day—" His breath hitches. I watch him try to steady himself against some invisible emotion.

"Maybe you would've been glad at first. Maybe you would've agreed if I'd asked you out. But what would have happened after two days? Two weeks? After you discovered that I'm not perfect— that I'm a coward, that I'm awful at making decisions and regret half the things I've done, that it's nearly impossible for me to warm up to new people, that sometimes I'm hit with grief so heavy I can't do anything except lie down in silence? After you realized there was no point wanting me anymore, because you already had me?"

I feel stripped to the bone, so exposed I wouldn't be surprised if my skin was rubbed raw.

"If I'd kissed you," he goes on, "you would have wanted me for an afternoon, and I would have wanted you for the rest of my life. But even though I knew it wouldn't work, I also knew that if I stayed, I wouldn't be able to stop myself from kissing you anyway." The bitter crack of a smile. "I only have so much self-control."

"So . . . you left for Paris," I whisper.

"I fled to Paris," he corrects. "They'd sent me an invite to their gifted kids' program months before, and I'd planned to decline, but then it seemed like the perfect opportunity to clear my head and stop myself from doing something I regretted. But you see . . . it was absurd," he says quietly, resting his head back against the wall. "There I was in this new city, free to go anywhere I wanted, without anybody to tell me what to do, and I felt so—trapped. Almost claustrophobic. Every time I thought of you, of how far away you were, the last time we were together, the room seemed to shrink around me."

My voice catches over my next words. "What are you saying?"

"The world just felt smaller without you," he tells me. It's the kind of sentiment most people would be afraid to say out loud, but he looks me straight in the eye when he speaks, his chin lifted a few degrees, as if in challenge. "Or maybe you have a way of making the world feel bigger. I missed you. I'd miss you everywhere I went: in the car and at the mall and in the winter. I know I stayed there for a full year, but you must realize—by the end of the first week, I was ready to fly back. It was only out of pride that I didn't. I still kept everything . . . I would check the time and weather back here—back home, where you are. I thought . . . I tried to convince myself again and again that there would be an expiration date on what I felt. That I only had to push past a certain point and I would be better. I wouldn't want you so much. I wouldn't need you so badly."

"And?" I whisper. "Did it work?"

The corner of his mouth rises higher, a smile laced with self-mockery. "What do you think?"

I'm speechless.

I'm hallucinating. I must be hallucinating. There's no way at all—

"I was completely wrong," he says, and he moves forward. I freeze and stare at him as he bows his head before me, vulnerable, sincere, pleading. I'm definitely hallucinating. "The second I saw you again, I realized there was no avoiding it. I was going to want you either way. Even if you only cared for a day and then moved on . . . I could make myself live with that. I'm sorry I understood too late, I really am. I promise, as soon as we find a way to undo this . . . curse of yours, I'll make it up to you." He lets out a shaky breath. "But I can't let you find this person alone. I'm concerned about *you*. Your soul. You have to be safe. I can't—I can't lose you again."

"I will be safe," I say weakly. "You can come with me, if you insist. I just . . ."

When he looks up at me, I can see the dark shadows of his lashes. The hope in his eyes. "Yes?"

"I think . . . I need to process everything," I stammer, desperately trying to reorient myself. But there are too many limits to what I can say or do. If I tell him everything I want to, everything he's right and wrong about, it'll be Jessica's lips forming the words, Jessica's eyes he'll be gazing into. So far, her life has felt like an escape from my own, but in this moment, it feels more like a cage, one I can't claw my way out of. "There's so much going on right now. Can we . . . can we please talk about this later?"

I track the movement in his throat, the way he attempts to hide his hurt. "Sure," he says at last, reaching for the door behind him. His fingers fumble around the knob twice before he grips it, his knuckles white. "Anything you want. I'll be here, always."

It usually takes twenty minutes to walk from my cousin's house to Aaron's.

But only ten minutes later, my phone chimes with the photo.

I zoom in on the birthday card, the two anonymous notes spread out on the bed next to me, my eyes flicking back and forth between them, trying to match them up. I go over every single birthday message, but none of them looks exactly like the handwriting I'm searching for.

Had we guessed wrong? Had I somehow missed a person in our year when I was organizing the card?

I slump back on the mattress and hold the notes up against the light, until the ripped paper turns almost translucent, the dark orange shadows of my fingertips visible through it, and the letters seem to float over the surface. *Think. What am I missing here?* The notes look like they were scribbled out in a rush, but maybe that was the point. Maybe they'd thought to change their handwriting so I wouldn't recognize it.

Which means that it's—

Impossible. The word forms in the sound of Aaron's voice, in the shape of an old memory. Fourteen years old, the soft days of summer just behind us, the oak trees outside the library burning gold. We were studying, or he was—I had flipped my sketchbook open to a random page and was testing out my new fine-liners.

"Do you want to see something cool?" I asked, tugging lightly at his sleeve. Only the very edge of it, where he'd rolled up the fabric; I was scared to brush his skin, as if it were possible to transmit feeling through touch alone. A simple graze of the hand, and he'd know of the nights I'd stayed awake, delusional, dying beneath the weight of what I wanted. "See, there's this cursive font. . . ." My brows scrunched up in concentration as I looped my letters together. "And then there's this block font . . . and this formal font that should look good on school forms. . . . Which one do you think I should use this year?"

I'd hoped he would be impressed, but he'd just turned his head and laughed at me, the sun settling behind him, lighting the silk strands of his hair the same brilliant orange as the autumn trees. "I like them all."

"You *have* to choose one, Aaron," I'd insisted. "This is important. They're completely different styles."

"But they're all still your handwriting. I'd be able to tell it's yours even if you mixed it with a hundred other people's."

I frowned down at the paper. "That can't be true."

"It's like how every artist has their own recognizable style, even when they're painting a new piece," he said, shrugging. "It's impossible to really hide the person behind it, so long as you know where to look."

My body bolts upright. I hadn't wanted to agree with Aaron then, but now I can only pray he's right. I squint at the handwriting again, except this time, like it's another painting. Every artist has their own style, their way of holding the pen, of interpreting the world, capturing it in pieces. Even if they tried to mask their identity, they should still have left behind telltale signs. So whose style is it?

When I finally find the answer, shock ripples through me.

I double-check it again, just to be safe. But the signs are there. Subtle, but distinct. The same swoop of the Ys, the same dash instead of a dot above the Is, the same cut of the Ts, like they're running out of time.

It's her.

It has to be.

Fourteen

The waiting is always the worst part.

I do not absorb a single thing in our world politics class the following morning. It's excruciating enough not to glance every second in the direction of the suspect, not to push my chair back and march up to her and demand answers. Looking at it now, it all seems so obvious. I can't believe I didn't notice it sooner.

The clock moves so slowly above the whiteboard I have to wonder if it's broken, the minute hand stuck. My stomach heaves and twists around nothing; I had skipped breakfast, unable to shove down even a morsel of bread through my chattering teeth. My legs cross and uncross themselves so many times that eventually Celine elbows me in the ribs.

"What's up with you today?" she whispers while Ms. Lewis drones on and on at the front of the classroom. "You've been fidgeting all class."

"Sorry," I croak out. "Had too much coffee."

The fifty-five minutes before my next move are almost as painful as the wait before the Harvard email.

My anxiety accumulates steadily over the course of the lesson.

When the bell rings, I nearly jump out of my seat, my heartbeat ticking like a bomb. Still, I don't look at her. Not yet. I glance back over my shoulder and lock eyes with Aaron instead, who gives me the faintest nod.

"I'll see you two after the break," I tell Celine and Leela as I fumble for my books. "I'm, um, meeting the physics teacher to go over a few questions."

"Do you want us to buy you a snack?" Leela asks.

"No, no. All good." My smile takes so much effort it hurts my cheeks. "I'm not really hungry."

I hurry to the library alone, my footsteps echoing up the spiral staircase to where the bookshelves fan out into polished panels and private rooms. The walls here are thicker, soundproof, built for the language orals students take at the end of each year and all the practice sessions leading up to it. Whenever a door opens a sliver, you can hear fragments of French, German, Mandarin floating out from within.

Sunlight falls drowsily through the stained-glass windows when I enter one of the last empty rooms, casting a latticework of shadows over the plywood desk. It reminds me of the art project Leela did last spring, when we were asked to experiment with mediums. She had chosen watercolor on shattered mirrors, a painting that changed the composition of whatever was reflected within it.

I breathe in sawdust and spearmint, and brace myself. The closer you get to the end, the harder the waiting becomes, every possible distraction chiseling away until you're left only with the apprehension pumping thick through your blood. I run my finger over the broken nail of my thumb, catching on the jagged edge. Aaron should be leading her up here any minute now.

My mind falls away to imagined scenes: him, approaching her after class, asking so politely and sweetly for her opinion on his oral presentation. She would be proud enough to agree, since the school's star student rarely asks for help for anything. He accompanies her up those creaking steps, past the seated, sleepy students, chatting aimlessly the whole way about the weather, which is pleasant, or the topic for our next essay, which isn't, then down the aisle, until he slows just outside the room and—

The doorknob turns.

Cathy Liu's face is blank at first, confused. Then her eyes focus on me, and comprehension flares to life behind them.

The waiting is always the worst part. Now that it's over, I feel a strange clarity settle within me. I motion for Aaron to wait outside, returning his concerned look with a light shake of my head. Then I step around Cathy and close the door.

"I know it was you," I tell her. "I understand that your preferred way of communication seems to be through vaguely threatening cryptic messages, but I thought maybe we could talk. What are you after?"

"What am I after?" she echoes, her expression twisting with incredulity. "I mean, isn't that obvious? I want you to confess."

"Confess to *what*?"

"Oh my god, seriously, Jessica?" She leans back against the wall. "Did you think I wouldn't recognize my own thesis? You're the only one I told it to—I showed you my entire essay outline. I guess that was my bad; I was naive enough to think I could impress you with how smart I was, as if you're ever impressed by anyone else. But then, how was I supposed to predict you would copy my thesis? You stole it, Jessica. You stole it from me, and you don't even have the guts to admit it. Or maybe you just don't care. Maybe you think it's *hilarious*. What was it that you said in the interview again?" Her lips curl, revealing the white knife of her teeth. "Copy and paste is your friend?"

I blink, stunned.

It can't be true. Of course I'd assumed it was something terrible, something shameful, or else Jessica would never have written that journal entry. I had even contemplated the possibility of manslaughter. Yet it hadn't crossed my mind to think of this:

Jessica, *cheating*. Plagiarizing someone else's ideas. If I'd found this out before I made the wish, I wouldn't have believed it, even if someone was holding the evidence right in front of me. Why would Jessica Chen feel the need to cheat when she's never even failed before?

But then my memory hooks around the disappointment creasing my aunt's face, the way Ms. Lewis had held me back after my test results came out, the shocked glances from my classmates when I gave the wrong answer in physics class, the unspoken question *What happened to you?* screaming through the silence, and I think I know why.

"Why didn't you just tell the teacher then?" I ask Cathy.

She lets out a short, shrill laugh. "You think I had a chance to? Mr. Keller kept me back after class to lecture me about the *striking resemblance* between my essay and yours. But of course he assumed that *I* had copied you, because how could someone like you cheat? Smart, perfect Jessica, the model student who can do no wrong. What is that like, by the way?" she adds, the bitterness in her voice changing to something almost akin to wonder, to awe, and I'm gripped by the absurd terror that she's going to lunge across the space, shake me by the shoulders, sink her nails into my face. "What is it like to just go around knowing that everyone loves you, and believes in you, and wants to be you?"

I smother my surprise before it can show. Her words are too familiar, shooting and landing with lethal, uncomfortable precision; I've wondered the exact same thing to myself countless times.

"It doesn't always feel like that," I say, as honestly as I can.

She falters, but only for a moment. "You know, it's kind of insulting it took you so long to figure out it was me," she says, stuffing her hands in her blazer pockets. "When someone's out to get you, you should suspect your competition before anyone else. I guess that's the problem, isn't it? That's the worst part." Her dark eyes flash. "You never considered me a threat. I always had a clear view of *you*; you were always first, and I was always second. But you didn't even see me coming, because you never thought to turn around. I'll never know what it's like to be you, and you'll never know what it's like to be me. To want something so deeply, so desperately that it hurts you."

I do, I reply silently. *I know all too well.*

Because to me, wanting has always been indistinguishable from pain.

A clenched fist around my heart. A blunt dagger through my stomach. Cold hands around my throat. Whenever I saw the news about the sixteen-year-old who already had everything I'd ever wanted, the fifteen-year-old who had her whole life paved in gold. It was like that with Aaron as well. Whenever he was next to me, so beautiful it ached, his hair falling perfectly into place, his face like that of a young god, smooth and tragic and made for eternity. Whenever he smiled at me and I had to keep my hands fastened to my sides, had to stop myself from saying what I truly felt. Whenever I imagined the impossible, of us together.

Living Jessica's life has dulled that pain slightly, blurred out that particular part of my memory—similar, maybe, to how quickly you forget the stuffy discomfort of a fever once you recover. Because it is no longer relevant. Because your body believes the terrible thing is behind you.

But now it all comes rushing in again, like floodwater, rising instantly to my lips. The pain of insignificance.

"It's just not fair," she whispers, dragging her sleeve roughly across her eyes. "It's not fair. You cheated and you're still heading off to Harvard, and I've done everything right, and I was *wait-listed*."

I stare at her. In a flash of clarity, it all makes sense. "But in class, you acted like you'd gotten in . . . I saw you nod—"

"Yeah, well, obviously." Her voice cracks. "What else was I meant to do? Announce to the whole class that I had *failed*? I mean, do you know how embarrassing it is? I was supposed to be the gifted one. I was *so talented*, so special—that's what they all told me, when

I was still playing with dolls and didn't know what an Ivy League was. I didn't even want to skip two grades, but the teachers said it'd help me realize my full potential faster, and my moms believed them. So then I was thrown into your classes, and I wasn't special anymore, even though I studied harder than I ever had before, and after all that, you're the one who made it. You're headed off to my dream school, and the really funny thing is, Jessica, that you don't even . . . you don't even *need* it."

If she had been clinging to any last ounce of composure before, it crumbles away now. Tears slip between her fingers and drip from the tip of her nose. I'm struck suddenly by how very young she looks. How much younger she is than we are. "You got into every Ivy you applied to. Your family has money. You could simply choose to go to another school and then there'd be room for me—they'd let me off the waitlist. This would be an absolutely incredible, life-changing thing if it happened to me. But for you? It's just another accomplishment, isn't it?"

I swallow. I don't know what to say—not because I can't fathom her logic, but because I can. It's the mantra we've all been fed since we were kids: *study hard, get into a good school, be better than everyone else, and you'll have a better life.* Because a school like Havenwood might be a cage, but at the end of the day, a cage is still a shelter, and we all want to be valued, to be protected, to be safe, to prove that we deserve to be here. Because the chances of success are so suffocatingly small, and the pressure to succeed is so overwhelmingly great, and there are only a handful of people, distant as deities from the rest of us, who hold all the power.

"It doesn't have to be like this," I tell her eventually.

She sniffs. "Yes. It does. You shouldn't be going to Harvard—it should be *me*."

"If you're waitlisted, you might still get in, whether or not I'm going to Harvard too," I say, my voice even. I should be angrier; her messages have kept me up countless nights, filled my lungs with dread and terror, made me flinch at the shadows. But as I watch her wipe her nose, her body shaking, I realize that she hadn't acted out of malice so much as desperation, a need to convince herself that there was still an opportunity to alter her future. Softer, I say, "And even if—"

"Don't." Her fists clench, and I take an automatic step back. "Don't *pity me*."

"I don't pity you. I only . . ." I hesitate. "I've been in a similar position before, that's all. So I . . . I get it, I really do. It's so easy to fall into the assumption that anything someone else gains is something you lose. To think of success as some lavish party with only a limited number of invites. To convince yourself that if you could only make it to a certain point in the distance, you'll finally find a place to rest. To feel like there's always more that you can do. But I mean, look what's being done to *us*—to our self-esteem, to our pride, to our bodies. We're all exhausted and on the verge of breaking down at any second and somehow . . . somehow we're expected to just keep going.

"Even if you don't get into Harvard," I tell her, as gently as I would speak to a younger version of myself, the words seeming to float up from somewhere deep inside me, "you can still be happy. You can still live your life. But I also know . . . I know I shouldn't have copied your idea. It's just—there have been a lot of bizarre, unexpected things happening recently, so I'm not in the best position to give you an answer. If I could have more time . . . I promise," I say, praying she can hear the sincerity in my voice, "I'll figure out how to make this right."

And maybe she does. She slowly unfolds her arms and frowns. "Why?"

"Why what?"

"Why are you comforting me?"

I offer her a small smile. "Because if we don't try to understand each other, then who will?"

There's no reply at first. I'm not sure if she's even heard me. But when I gather up my books and turn toward the door, she says, so low I almost miss it, "A week. I'll give you one more week." She doesn't look at me; she simply remains standing in the shifting, blue-tinted light of the library, her eyes on the sky.

"How did it go?" Aaron asks as soon as he sees me, pushing off from the railings, his brows drawn with worry.

"As well as it could've," I tell him. I feel shaken, like I've just stumbled down a flight of steps. "She was . . . upset. Kind of rightly so. My cousin . . . she . . ." I hesitate. I want to tell Aaron everything, but it's still Jessica's secret.

"It's okay, you don't have to give me the full story," Aaron says. "I just need to know if you're safe."

"I mean, she didn't try to hurt me or anything. And she agreed to drop it—at least for one more week."

He doesn't relax. "Are you certain—"

But before he can continue, the familiar sound of Ms. Lewis's heels clack up the staircase. "I was just looking for you, Jessica," she says, waving me over.

I quickly rearrange my expression as I walk toward her, Aaron following behind me. "Hi, Ms. Lewis. What did you need me for?"

"You know the art exhibition happening tomorrow evening?"

"Yes," I say slowly. My self-portraits were meant to be displayed at the exhibit, but I'm not sure what that has to do with Jessica.

"Havenwood's school director, Mr. Howard, will be attending." Ms. Lewis's smile is huge, her eyes shining with excitement. "You know how rare his visits are, and well, he's asked to meet you."

"Meet me?" I repeat.

"Yes, he's heard all about your achievements, and he wanted to congratulate you *in person*. It's a real honor, one that few students will ever get to experience," Ms. Lewis gushes. "You should be so proud."

I do my best to inject the same enthusiasm into my voice. "Oh, yes, I'm definitely honored. I'd love to go." I really am honored, or I know I should be. It's an opportunity I would have killed for, if only to hear others talk about it afterward. *Did you know the school director personally requested to see her? No, really. That's how successful she is!*

"Perfect," Ms. Lewis says, and nods at Aaron. "Guests are encouraged to come as well, by the way."

"I'll be there," he replies right away, his gaze locking on mine.

And I'm certain in this very moment that if I had to walk deep into the woods, into a burning house, down into the depths of hell itself, he would still accompany me, just to make sure I don't leave his sight.

But I'm less worried about what Cathy will do now than what will happen if I still haven't found my cousin's soul by the end of the week.

Fifteen

On the night of the art exhibition, I stand before Jessica's wardrobe, considering my options.

There are plenty, when it comes to clothes and accessories. The prettiest dresses in silk, satin, cashmere, with delicate floral lace patterns and puff sleeves and ribbons wrapping around the waist. Ironed tweed jackets and sleek leather coats that look like something models might wear on the runway. Twenty different kinds of bags in twenty different sizes, the smallest one so tiny it can hold only mascara and lipstick, the largest one big enough to contain an entire folder and textbook. Three dozen pairs of earrings glittering from inside a glass display, laid out on crimson velvet, designed in the image of the sun and the moon, two broken hearts, studded with real pearls and emeralds and what might be real, actual diamonds. Stilettos and platform shoes and thigh-high boots.

I feel spoiled, greedy, almost guilty to be able to afford such luxury. The act of choosing what to wear always used to be an exercise in self-criticism, a reminder of my own inadequacies. Sorting through the old, lumpy sweaters and ill-fitting skirts to find something that didn't look too terrible. I was almost always in a worse mood afterward, and too busy scrutinizing the way the clothes looked on me to enjoy whatever event I went to.

That's no longer a problem.

Now, anything I try on looks incredible, and it's not only genetics; I have this other theory that accomplished people instantly become more attractive.

No moisturizer in the world can compare to the sheen of success, the glow of glory. No contacts or eyelash extensions can make the eyes glow brighter than immediate validation. No rouge can ever replicate the flush of victory.

Don't get too attached, I remind myself. Now that I've spoken to Cathy, the most urgent matter is finding Jessica's soul.

"Jenna," Aaron calls from below. "Are you ready yet?"

I fluff out my hair and hurry downstairs as fast as I can in two-inch heels, nearly tripping over myself. "You can't call me that," I warn him.

He's waiting by the front door, sleeves rolled up, arms crossed over his chest. "The house is empty. Nobody is around to overhear. And," he adds, his eyes bright, "it shouldn't be a problem soon."

I pause. "What do you mean?"

"I think I've figured it out," he says. I've never seen him so hopeful before. "How to undo everything before the one week is over. It's actually so simple that we'd overlooked it."

"I . . . what?"

"You said you made a wish that night," he tells me, so patient, so gentle, so sure of himself. "Maybe that's all there is to it. Maybe you just have to close your eyes and wish for yourself to change back. Ask for your old life. For Jessica to return."

"Right now?" I ask. Those are the only words I can produce. My mind feels empty, slowed down, like the world has split off into two timelines and I'm stuck in the one that's running behind. *Right now? Before the art exhibition?*

He loosens a huff of laughter. "When else? Don't you want to change back right away?"

"Yeah," I say, but my voice comes out less certain than I intended, wavering up at the end. "Yes," I repeat, and this time, it manages to sound somewhat convincing. "I do. Of course I do."

"So go ahead." He gestures to the open space. "I'll be here in case anything goes wrong."

"Okay. I mean, I feel kind of ridiculous doing this, but . . . sure." I clasp my hands together. *Make the wish.* I scramble to find the right words, to repeat them inside my head. *I wish to be myself again. I wish for my cousin to come back.* But it's like I'm reading lines off a teleprompter. The wish doesn't feel like mine, and the air doesn't change, the universe doesn't respond.

I squeeze my eyes shut so tight that when I finally blink and lift my head, the white lights of the living room streak across my vision.

"Did it work?" I ask Aaron, already knowing the answer. My feet are starting to ache. The heels, while gorgeous, are too narrow at the front, and too stiff at the back.

"No," he says. He conceals his disappointment well; if I were anyone else, I wouldn't even notice it. "But maybe it's because there are other factors to consider. Maybe you need to make the wish at the exact same time as you did the first, or you need to replicate the exact conditions, or there's an object involved—like when you make a wish as you blow out a birthday candle . . . or when there's a shooting star. Remember?" he asks, with dawning recognition. "There was a shooting star, the night you disappeared. I was there. We all saw it in Jessica's backyard. Maybe it also has something to do with that."

"Oh yeah." I swallow. "Good point."

He pauses. The way he's staring at me, as if he can see right through me, makes my stomach pinch. He doesn't speak for a long time, too long, and then he says, quietly, "You don't actually want to change back, do you?"

Blood roars through my skull. My lips form the shape of a protest, but my throat closes. I can't deny it, because it's true. It's the secret I've buried in the deepest soil of my thoughts, the secret that I prayed he would never find out, that I couldn't even admit to myself. Now he knows what I am: weak, twisted, selfish. "I can't help it," I whisper, afraid to meet his gaze. "I'm sorry. I'm really sorry. I *do* want my cousin back, I swear, but I don't . . . I just don't want to return to my life. If there were any other way to reverse the wish, even if it meant walking across the country on bare feet, I'd make myself go through with it. I really, really would, but I can't wish for something I don't want. I simply can't force myself to believe with my whole heart that I'd like for everything to go back to how it used to be."

Another horrible beat of silence.

He must hate me, I think. Maybe he already regrets confessing his feelings to me, or coming back from Paris early. Maybe he won't even want to talk to me again.

The soft jingle of car keys jolts me back to life. "Let's continue this conversation in the car," he says. There's no disgust or resentment in his voice. Only resolve. "If you're not going to change back now, then we still have to get to the art exhibition."

I swallow and nod quickly, following him all the way to the car. Dusk is falling, the sky a watercolor spread of deep blue, the horizon fringed with the faintest shade of yellow. Without another word, he pulls open the door to help me inside, before walking around and settling naturally into the driver's seat. As he places his hand on the wheel and starts the ignition, I curl up around the seat belt, hugging my knees.

"I just don't understand," he says at last, steering the car onto the main road. "I know you've always compared yourself to Jessica, and I would get it if you just wanted to try out her life briefly, like when people talk about what celebrity they'd like to be for a day. But *this* . . ."

"Of course you don't understand," I tell him. "But you know, someone like Cathy Liu would. Can you believe that?" My laughter tastes bitter on my tongue. "I have so much in common with the girl who's been blackmailing my own cousin."

"You're not like Cathy," he says firmly. "You're nothing like her."

"I am. I'm just as jealous and insecure, though I wouldn't even have the guts to threaten someone else. But you—you're exactly like Jessica. You're a genius. You're so talented you don't even have to try, while all I *do* is try." I grit my teeth until they hurt, until I feel something inside me splinter. The greenery rushes past us, the light bleeding out of the sky. "I try again and again and nothing happens. Nothing comes of it. I'm never going to be first. I can't even be *second*, like Cathy. Nobody would care if I came back—"

"Why does it matter—"

"*Because.*" I almost scoff out loud. *There are no stupid questions,* the teachers always like to remind us, but what a ridiculous, non-sensical question this is. That's like asking why we need to breathe. Why we need water. Why the ocean exists. "That's the one thing I've worked for my entire life—to be someone who matters. That's why my parents moved to this country. That's my purpose. If I can't do it, then *what's the point of anything*? What's the point of me? What possible value could I provide?"

He's silent.

He's silent for so long I can hear the air tremble against my lips. I can hear my heart thrumming, the blur of brown noise from out-side the car, the wind moving over the windows, the world tipping on its axis. I can hear my own resentment, expanding, the corro-sive truth eating away the space between us.

Finally he says, "There are far worse things to be than un-talented."

"I'm aware, but—"

"Are you really?" The heat in his voice shocks me. The burr of anger. "Because you act like the worst fate for a person is to be mediocre, to go about their lives without accomplishing anything

234

significant enough to leave behind a lasting legacy. Do you even know—" He inhales.

"You say I'm a genius? Okay, fine. I am. You're correct. School comes easily to me; it always has. I can memorize anything I see. I can ace an exam without studying. I'll head off to an Ivy League, and I'll be admired by my classmates and my professors, and I'll be able to get into medical school, and I like to think I'll still be at the top of my class. But I would trade all of that—*any of that*—to have what you have."

"What do I have?" I whisper, because I'm genuinely confused, genuinely curious. What could I have that he wants?

"Oh, I'm not entirely sure," he says, his sarcasm sharp enough to cut, his grip tightening over the wheel. "Maybe a family? Maybe a mother who's alive, a father who actually cares?"

I flinch.

"I wouldn't even want to be a doctor if not for my mother," he continues. "I just . . . that's the best I can do. That's the most and the least I can do. To find a cure that could have saved her, to be the person who stops someone else from losing their mother. But for her—for me—it's too late. And I will have to spend the rest of my life grieving, in pain. Do you know what that's like?"

"Aaron, I'm sorry. I'm really sorry," I say, and I could die from my shame. It's burning the skin off my fingers, my face. Because of what I've said. And because of what I'm going to say next. "But I . . . I can't make myself do it. I can't . . . I can't change the wish—"

"*Why not?*"

"I just can't."

"That's not an excuse!"

My heart is in freefall. "I don't need to explain myself."

"I deserve an explanation," he says fiercely. "Just tell me *why*. Please. It's driving me mad—"

"Aaron, drop it."

"You can't just avoid the subject forever. Why—"

"Because I hate myself too much."

There.

The real, full, humiliating truth. It feels like someone's extracted a tooth, removed a vital organ. It's the same raw feeling I get after I've been crying for too long.

"Are you happy now?" I demand, my skin stinging. "Is that answer good enough for you?"

I glance over at Aaron's face, terrified of the pity I might see on the features I know so well, but he doesn't look remotely sympathetic. He looks livid.

He's always been exceptional at concealing his emotions, at smiling even when he's suffering; he's the kind of person who could take a beating with a complete poker face. But he doesn't seem capable of hiding anything now. Everything is laid open in his gaze. His frustration, his grief, his confusion.

His hurt.

Like someone holding out their bloodied hand after they've been cut. The space of the vehicle is suddenly too small, too intimate, the doors locking me into this conversation. I can't escape it. I have to face him.

When he speaks, his voice trembles. "You really don't know yourself at all, do you?"

"What do you mean?"

"You have no idea," he goes on in a furious whisper. "You truly have no idea what you mean to me. You can't see yourself from anyone else's perspective; you don't even really know yourself. You're so stuck in your own skewed version of your life, and it's not . . . it's not *real*. You're incredible."

I actually laugh. Slap the dashboard in my hysteria. "Oh my god, okay, seriously. We're not doing this—"

"No. Let me continue," he says, his eyes flashing. "You are incredible. You see the world like an artist. You notice every color in the sky, you stop and marvel at the sight of a sparrow flying by or a ripple in the lake or an autumn leaf in the sun. You're always the first person to sense if someone else is having a bad day, and you can't watch a sad movie without crying, and you always skip the ending if you know it's going to be tragic, so you can make up something better in your head. Once, you teared up after your elderly neighbor asked you to read the expiration date on a loaf of bread for him because his eyesight was fading. You also tear up every time you watch that cereal commercial about the border collie who runs away from home. When we found a dead bird in the forest, you insisted on building a grave for it out of twigs and wildflowers. You hate small spaces, but you still came to sit with me in the attic for hours when my father was mad at me. You're sarcastic, but never in a mean way. You're dramatic, and you can make anything sound like poetry. You're sensitive, and maybe that means you feel pain and fear and humiliation more sharply, but you also feel joy more beautifully and completely than anyone I know. You make me feel the same joy just by looking at you."

My heart is pounding fast, so fast.

"And you're always showing up at the right time and place. Like speech night in tenth grade," he continues. He's twisted around slightly in the driver's seat, even though he keeps his eyes on the road ahead of us. "Do you remember? We all had to get there early for rehearsal, and when everyone else was waiting for their parents to arrive, and my father couldn't make it that night . . . you came over and stood next to me. And suddenly—suddenly I didn't feel alone. I realized I would never have to be alone again, if you were there."

Speech night. Tenth grade.

I remember Jessica Chen getting all the awards she was eligible for. Top achiever and the academic award for every subject she took and the Diana Bagshaw Award for contributions to the school.

I remember the teachers organizing the seating according to the awards we'd received. Those who had one or more were seated at the front. Jessica sat first. Those who had none—those like me—were ushered to the very back.

I remember Aaron sitting with her. I remember watching them from behind, the bright, glaring lights of the stage limning their silhouettes. *They look so perfect together,* I'd thought to myself. And I'd made sure I congratulated them both. I'd been the first to tell them how happy I was for them, and I'd helped them hold their bags while my uncle and auntie took pictures, proud and beaming ever so wide.

But I don't remember this part at all. That scares me. It makes me wonder what else I've forgotten, what else has slipped through the cracks. If I'm forgetting myself too, like everyone else has. Except him.

"That was ages ago," I finally manage. "It doesn't even matter—"

"It does matter. You matter," he interrupts, jaw tight. "And maybe . . . maybe there's a selfish part of me that just wants to see you again. I want to do all the things I used to mock from the movies. I want to have picnics by the lakes with you and walk down the corridors with your hand in mine and call you up late at night." His eyes darken, deepen. "I want to kiss you—"

The car lurches sharply over a bump in the road, but even after it's behind us, my stomach still feels like it's forgotten gravity. "No," I say. "No. Don't do that. You're not playing fair."

"I'm not playing fair? You're literally defying the known laws of physics."

"You know it's my weakness," I breathe out. "You know you're my weakness."

"Then come back to me," he says, softer, his voice pained now, pleading. I'm unprepared for how quickly it unravels me. I had been braced for a war; I had entered the car with my armor on, my weapons sharpened. I can do that. I can fight him if I have to. But not this. Not him with his guard lowered, his sword dropped to his feet, his palms open, empty, searching.

And he senses it.

Always so observant. He's always known me so well.

"I can help you, really," he says. "I can figure it out. You said it yourself—I'm a genius. Just say the word, Jenna, and I'll do anything. Please, I'm begging. If you don't really believe in the wish, I'll come up with an entire list of reasons your old life could be good. I'll remind you of it every single day until you can make the wish and mean it. Everything will be fine."

Just say the word.

My lips part, but the word won't form. Not the right one, the one he's hoping for.

"Jenna?"

"No," I whisper, even though it physically hurts me to say it.

"Do you realize what you're saying?" he demands. "You can't stay like this forever. And what about Jessica? It's *her* life—if you don't make the wish, she won't be able to return."

"*I know that,*" I cut in, tears of frustration prickling my eyes. "I know the consequences. But I don't know what I'm supposed to *do*, Aaron. It's how I feel; it's beyond my control. I wish I could brainwash myself. I wish I didn't have these thoughts at all. I wish I was kinder, and selfless, and convinced that I could be happy back in my life, with you. But there's no point pretending it's all I want when it's not. It's just not enough for me." I swallow. "It's not enough."

The silence in the car is terrible.

"Nothing is ever enough for you," Aaron says, gazing over at me.

I'm not sure what I would have replied then. Maybe I would

have admitted that he was right. That I don't know how to do any-thing except crave what I don't have. I don't know how to be content, to sit with myself and my life and let it wash over me like daylight. But before I can say anything at all, a dark blur appears in my periph-eral vision, approaching fast, heading straight toward us—

I gasp. *"Watch out!"*

Aaron's eyes snap back to the road.

He yanks the wheel hard to the left.

For a moment the ground seems to drop out from under me, the car swerving so fast the world spins, tires shrieking against asphalt, and I would scream except my head hasn't even caught up to what's happening.

We jolt to a stop against the curb just as the other vehicle whiz-zes past us, honking twice.

I don't think I'm breathing.

My heart is hammering so hard I'm terrified it might break my ribs or tire and stop altogether. I'm gripping the door handle so tight the joints in my fingers ache but I can't let go. Finally I man-age to unfreeze just enough to glimpse Aaron's face. He's shaken as well, and doing his best to hide it. He wipes a hand over his fore-head. Licks his lips.

"We could have died," he says, more in disbelief than anything.

"But—but we didn't," I say shakily.

"I . . . probably shouldn't be driving like this." He rubs his eyes and reaches for the door. "We're better off walking the rest of the way."

"Aaron . . ."

He pauses and glances back at me, his gaze gentle, despite everything. "Yes?"

"You're not leaving me here?" I whisper. "I mean . . . aren't you angry?"

The look in his eyes changes, hardening to resolve. "You think you can get rid of me so easily?" He steps out and walks around to open the door for me. The cold air rushes in, surrounding me like a frozen embrace. "Come on. Let's go."

Sixteen

Silver balloons and banners guide the way to the art center, in typical Havenwood fashion. It's hard to decide whether the decorations are impressive or just overly pretentious. Teachers wait by the entrance in stiff suits, fake-friendly smiles glued to their faces, no doubt waiting just to greet Mr. Howard when he arrives and then retire for the evening. Professional photographers weave their way through the students with their heavy equipment, taking pictures of everything except the actual art on display, most likely so the school can use the photos for future advertisements and promotional newsletters.

And then there is the exhibit itself.

Art on every white wall, every surface, every stand. Oil paintings and sculptures and charcoal sketches.

"Surely you miss it?" Aaron murmurs under his breath as we make our way around the room.

"Miss what?"

"Doing this," he says, gesturing to a framed painting I recognize instantly as Leela's. It's of her mother, brushing her little sister's hair. The colors are subdued, the background drawn in simple strokes. But golden sunlight streams in from a window just beyond the frame, and I have to marvel at how she's done it. How she's found the exact shade and color of the sun itself and captured the precise way it changes fabric and marble and illuminates every strand of glossy black hair. Her mother is focused, not necessarily smiling, but one look and you can tell how gently she's holding the brush. There is something so peaceful about the piece, a quiet, tender quality I've come to observe in Leela herself. Like dawn air, or lake water.

I wish I could do that, but I've never known how to paint from a place of happiness. I only paint what I want to change or what I don't already have.

"I can still paint," I say quietly, and hope he can't hear my voice falter.

"The way you used to?"

"Sure."

"Have you tried?" he challenges.

"Well, who cares if I can't? Painting isn't a useful skill," I continue forcefully, repeating the same words people have flung at me a thousand times before. "The only way to be valued as a painter is by being the very best there is, and I simply can't be, even if I were to spend the rest of my life trying."

The girl admiring the painting next to us shoots me an offended look.

"Sorry," I stutter. "Not talking about you—I'm sure your skills are very useful. . . ."

Aaron scoffs.

I spin back to face him, my face heating. "What?"

"I just find it incredibly fascinating," he says. "How you can say something you don't believe in with such conviction. Were you always such a good liar?"

"I'm not lying," I insist, stepping past Leela's painting to a still life of a broken porcelain vase. Instinctively, I find myself assessing the brushstrokes, noting how the artist has layered the shadows. What appears to be plain black at first glance is in fact a collection of colors: midnight blue and navy and lavender. "Art can't give me the kind of validation I want. It's too subjective, too unstable, too temporary. Even if someone likes your art, they'll inevitably move on."

"I would never move on," Aaron says softly. "I would never take your paintings down."

I pause, and almost lose my next thought in the depths of his eyes. Aaron, as my first and final audience. Aaron, as my muse. It sounds so tempting, but—

"There's no point," I say, "if my paintings are not known and loved by everyone."

"I see," he says, without judgment, but without agreement. Then he catches sight of someone in the entrance, and his brows rise, just as a burst of high-pitched laughter travels toward us, cutting through the lukewarm chatter. "Looks like Mr. Howard is here."

I've only seen Mr. Howard in formal photos and that painting of him they've hung outside the assembly hall, which always gives the misleading impression that he's dead. He's much shorter in real life than I would have thought, with a jovial face and uneven brows, and unlike the teachers, he hasn't bothered to dress up for the event at all. He could have dropped by the school on his way back from the local pub.

That doesn't stop my muscles from tensing when Ms. Lewis leads him inside and waves me and Aaron over.

Because even if Mr. Howard came here dressed in a garbage bag, it wouldn't change the fact that he's important. His approval matters.

". . . our best student," Ms. Lewis is saying excitedly. "Just got accepted into Harvard not too long ago, had to turn down a bunch of Ivy Leagues—they all wanted her, you see. She's won a bunch of awards too; I lose count of them all, honestly." She points to Aaron next. "And this is another one of our best students. He was chosen for a *very* selective medical program in Paris—you know the one— and came back recently. The very pride of our school, these two. Both will go on to do incredible things, we're all sure of it."

Mr. Howard barely seems to be listening. "Is that so?"

"It's lovely to meet you, Mr. Howard," I say, smiling Jessica's best smile, the one that could make world peace possible if she directed it at the right person.

"Nice to meet you too," he says, then pauses. Looks at Ms. Lewis in question. It's a quick look, but I catch it, because I've seen it hundreds of times before. "Jessica . . . Choi, was it?"

A sinking feeling hits my gut.

I don't know why I'm still smiling, why it's so important to maintain my facade of politeness. "Jessica Chen," I say.

"Jessica Chang," he says confidently. "Right, right. Actually, I believe we've met before—aren't you also the one leading the orchestra? The violinist?"

My smile threatens to collapse. Jessica plays the cello and the piano and the guzheng, but not the violin. He's thinking of Cathy Liu. "No," I tell him. "Sorry, that wasn't me." I don't know why I'm apologizing, either.

"Ah, really?" He frowns, like he's wondering if perhaps I've suffered a brief lapse of memory and forgotten that I am, in fact, the same violinist he's talking about. "I could have sworn . . . We even shook hands."

"Must've been another person," I manage.

He shrugs. Looks toward something over my shoulder. "Well, keep up the good work, yes? Study hard."

And that's it.

He brushes past me to speak to Sarah Williams, and I catch pieces of their conversation. "At your aunt's old beach house" and "How is dear Susannah?" and something about a Christmas party and the club on the other side of the city. He looks infinitely more engaged, laughing outright at whatever Sarah is saying. He remembers her name, and her mother's name, and even her family friend's name.

I feel like I've missed the instructions on a test. Like I've done something wrong, made a fatal miscalculation. Wasn't this supposed to be the moment I was proven right? That I became worthy at last, having received approval from the person in power, the man at the top of the school? But there's no vindication here, no sense of satisfaction. Only confusion.

Aaron tugs lightly at the corner of my sleeve. "Let's keep moving," he says. "There's not much left to see here."

I follow, unsteady, my mind clambering around for clarity that isn't there.

"What, are you really that surprised?" he asks me, but his tone is gentler than it was before. "You could win the Nobel Prize, and I'd bet he would still have trouble remembering who you are. All that matters to him is that they can market your results and encourage more students like you to enroll in the school."

"I understand that," I say, frustrated. "I mean, on some level, I obviously understand that it's a business. But I still . . . I don't know." Humiliation singes my throat. "I just thought it'd be different."

He doesn't say anything.

At first I think he's given up on trying to reason with me, or perhaps he's preparing to laugh at me for my naivety, but then I realize he's staring at the series of paintings on the wall before us.

"They're yours," he says. "Aren't they?"

They are.

Or they were, once. I had painted a collection of self-portraits, close-ups of my face at different angles. I can remember every stroke, every shade. There should be a portrait where I'm staring directly at the sun, another where I'm holding up a hand as if reaching through mist, another where I'm resting my head against my forearm, my eyes dark and weary.

In order to capture my features, I'd spent way too long scrutinizing my appearance in the mirror, until I grew unbearably bored of my own face and hated what I saw—and that had come through in the paintings. I didn't look remotely happy in any of them, and the colors I'd chosen were just as depressing: the deep blue of an ocean in the storm, the silver of a jagged mirror edge, the maroon of a rusted door.

But now, in all of them, half my face is gone.

Erased.

As if painted over with dark acrylic, hiding my eyes and nose.

It's a self-portrait of a stranger, someone unrecognizable, someone who might not even exist anymore.

There's no artist statement underneath it either. No name.

"Excuse me," I say, turning to the closest art teacher I can find—Ms. Wilde, a woman with glittery butterfly clips in her graying hair and huge emerald rings on both bony hands. She was always hanging around when I'd go in to work on my pieces during lunch breaks and after school. "Excuse me, sorry, but I was just wondering about these paintings. Do you know who they're by?"

Ms. Wilde shakes her head. "They've just been lying around in the art room. We figured we would put them on display. They're not bad, huh? There's something just slightly ominous and unsettling about them. . . . I can't quite put my finger on it. A shame that we don't know who the artist is."

I swallow. My voice comes out shrill, shaky. "I hear . . . I hear it's by Jenna Chen."

She stares at me, mystified. Blinks twice. "And . . . who is that?"

My stomach drops.

"An art student here," I try.

"Never heard of her," she says mildly.

"Jenna Chen," I repeat. "You must have seen her around the art classroom. She knows who you are."

"You're mistaken, my dear," she tells me. "Now, I have to go check on the others. . . ."

"What will you do with them?" I blurt out. "If—if nobody comes to claim the paintings?"

"Throw them away, I suppose," she says. "It would be a waste, but we certainly can't keep them stored around forever."

Ice creeps through my veins. It's happening even faster than I thought—I'm disappearing. Every trace of me, every memory, everything I've made and left behind. And then something else dawns on me. Another way to check what's going on, to confirm my worst fears. I'm trembling when I take out my phone and scroll through my photos and find the one I took of the painting in my bedroom, and my breathing stops. It's changed, the same way the other portraits have. Most of my face has been covered, the smudge far bigger than it was before.

My eyes go back to the paintings on display before me, and I understand what Ms. Wilde meant about them being *unsettling*. They're wrong, eerie in their anonymity, almost sinister looking.

This is all wrong.

"I need to go," I tell Aaron, who's been following close behind me this whole time, his eyes sharp, his mouth closed. "I—I need to see something at my aunt's house. Can you drive again?"

He tilts his head a little, then holds out his hand. "Let's go."

★★★

"I'm not entirely sure what you're planning," Aaron says as he walks me up the stairs back at Jessica's house, "but I just think we should talk it over."

I kick the bedroom door open. "Sit down," I tell him, pointing to the spare chair next to the desk.

"What?"

I take out my earrings and unclasp my necklace and run a rough hand through my hair to loosen it. My high heels are discarded by the closet. My heart is discarded in the corridor. "I said, *sit down*. I'm going to paint you."

He looks bemused. "You're going to—"

"Yes. Paint you," I say impatiently, trying to calm my thudding pulse as I fumble around for brush and paint. Jessica barely has any art supplies, just a half-dried tube of dark blue paint, but it'll have to do. "I haven't drawn anyone in ages, and I need to prove that I still can."

Somehow I am convinced that this is the answer to everything. That if I can still paint, if I can still hold a brush the same way, then I will still exist. I won't have to give anything up.

Greedy, a voice whispers in the back of my head. *I thought we'd established that a long time ago*, I retort silently. *That's the problem. I'm not sad because I don't love life enough, but because I love life too much. I always want more of it.*

"How should I pose?" Aaron asks, lowering himself into the chair. He has one long leg stretched out in front of him, his arms crossed casually over his chest, his chin tipped up to look at me.

"Whatever makes you comfortable," I say. I sit down as well, one of Jessica's notebooks flipped open to a blank page and balanced against my knee, the brush in my hand. I've done this god knows how many times before. There's no reason for me to feel so unsteady, so unsure of myself. "Just hold still."

He obeys.

He goes so still he could be a sculpture, and I let myself study him like a painting. I take note of the orange glow of Jessica's bedside lamp, how it softens the line of his lips and turns the ring of his irises warm brown, how it stretches across his collarbones and deepens the creases of his shirt. I collect with my eyes the bluish hues of the night sky beyond the curtains, the way a few strands of hair fall free over his forehead, the shadows draped over the rug beneath him.

But when I lower the brush to the paper, all of that is lost.

The difference is almost laughable. The beauty is gone. It's nothing but a collection of messy, haphazard strokes. I hold the brush tighter, as tight as I can, the muscles in my fingers aching from it, but it doesn't work.

"It's not working," I whisper out loud, gazing at the sketch in despair. It's so ugly I have the violent urge to rip it apart. "I can't get it right."

Even though I *know* exactly what the painting should look like. I can picture it so clearly in my head it's maddening. Why can't I just transfer the image onto paper? It was never this hard.

"Have you tried painting something else?" Aaron asks. "Or someone else? Maybe—"

"No," I tell him, certain of this, at least. "If I can't paint you, I can't paint at all."

I don't realize what I've said until his expression flickers. What I've just confessed to. Because I have all of Aaron's features memorized; I could conjure up his face with my eyes closed and the curtains drawn and the sun down in the distance. I paint him privately, with just my mind, every time we're together. I know him better than I know anyone.

He clears his throat but says nothing.

"You're not rubbing it in?" I ask.

"Now's not the time for that," he says.

"Saving it for later then."

A faint smile. "For later, yes."

I throw the brush aside and bury my face in my hands, rubbing my palms into my eyes until my vision goes fuzzy. "Aaron?"

"Yeah?"

"I don't know what to do," I admit.

"I know," he says quietly.

Silence settles between us like sediment. There's only the faraway sound of cars rolling through the suburbs and this room I didn't grow up in, this house that isn't my own, this boy who can't be mine.

Suddenly Aaron stands up—to leave, or to comfort me, I can't tell. But before he can do anything, he knocks the leather journal off the corner of the desk, the pages falling open with a loud flapping sound. The sound startles us both.

I pick it up first, the blue paint on my fingers smearing the page.

"This is Jessica's," I tell him, meaning to close it, but my eyes land on a few lines written in the margins, now half smudged with oil color. I must have missed it before; it's so short it hardly qualifies as its own entry. But it's dated to the night Jessica received her Harvard acceptance. The night of the gathering. The night where everything changed.

And this too will change everything. I realize it as I read over the words, my whole body frozen, my blood churning faster and faster, a building roar in my ears.

"Sometimes I get so tired," she'd written, her usually neat handwriting almost illegible in her haste.

> Everything gets so heavy. I wish somebody else
> would just come and take over my life. Live it for me.
> Please. If the universe is listening; if the stars could
> grant me any impossible wish, then all I ask for is this:
> I don't want to be Jessica Chen anymore.

Seventeen

When I enter the library the next day, everyone is glued to their laptops, faces pinched tight with apprehension. The air is unusually hushed. Only Leela glances up when I drag myself over to the seat she's saved between her and Celine.

"Wow, someone didn't rest well," she remarks.

I grimace. I hadn't slept at all last night, even after Aaron left the house. I couldn't stop thinking about Jessica's journal entry.

"Who can blame her?" Celine says without lifting her eyes from the screen. She stabs the refresh button in her inbox with one manicured nail. Hits it again and again and again. "Though there's not much suspense for Jessica."

Leela snorts. "There's not much suspense for you, either."

"Of course there isn't," Celine says, even as she continues refreshing her inbox with the fervor of someone possessed. "If the teachers don't choose me, I'll riot."

"You can't *threaten* teachers into choosing you."

"We can't all flatter them the way you do," Celine says, reaching behind my chair to give her a shove. In a voice that sounds remarkably like Leela's, she mimics, "Oh hello Ms. Lewis, oh you look absolutely stunning today, is that a new shade of lipstick? I found yesterday's lesson so very fascinating. If you had any extra questions for us to do—"

"Shut up," Leela says, laughing—maybe louder than she normally would. "As if you don't charm people."

"I reserve my charms for people I want to make out with," she says.

"Is that how you ended up with the model last summer? What was her name again?"

"Juniper," Celine says distractedly. "Yeah, she was nice. It might have worked out if she wasn't always trying to push me into doing a liberal arts degree."

"You mean a degree in your *area of passion and expertise*?"

Celine shoots Leela a look. "I mean a degree that can't bring me any stability. She didn't understand that—she thinks people only head to university for the *experience* and the *memories you'll make* and learning doesn't require any practical application. Easy to think that when your parents are billionaires." Each word is punctuated by the sound of Celine's nails tapping the keys. "Like I said—she didn't understand, but you must."

Leela heaves a sigh. "Unfortunately. Yes."

"Damn it," Celine mutters, pulling her laptop screen closer. "Where is that *email*? Or—" The faintest quiver creeps into her voice. "Or has it come in? Have you gotten anything?"

"Don't worry, I haven't gotten it either," Leela says.

It takes me a beat to identify the source of tension. *Awards.* They should be announced this morning. If I weren't so preoccupied with my more pressing supernatural-existential situation, I would be just as nervous.

Academic awards are a big deal at Havenwood. Fewer than ten awards are given out to the best students in each year for their performance across every subject. Winning one doesn't really promise you anything except praise and a free outdated encyclopedia, but *losing* an academic award is a humiliating ordeal that can wear away at your confidence for a whole year. The only remedy is to win the academic award the following school year.

I've received it just twice before, in seventh and ninth grades, when most people weren't quite as intense about their studies. Both times, I had the overwhelming suspicion I'd barely made the cut.

Jessica's won it every year, though. Of course.

"Oh!" Celine makes a squeaking sound so high in pitch I'm scared I've stepped on a mouse. "Oh my god, I think it's—No." Her tone sours. "No, it's just that cursed student feedback survey. What do they even want us to answer? 'How's your mental health?' Terrible, thanks. 'Would you feel comfortable speaking to staff members if any issues were to come up in your personal life?' I barely feel comfortable asking Old Keller if I can go to the bathroom in the middle of class. 'Do you know what is expected of you in your subjects?' Yeah, I'd say the issue is that I'm *too* aware of the expectations . . . Hang on, I got it," she says suddenly, her mouth splitting into a grin as her eyes move over the screen. "I got it. I mean, I *obviously* knew I would. But it's nice to have the confirmation—and to finish the year on a good note."

"Same here," Leela says, smiling at her screen too, her shoulders sagging with relief.

Celine turns to me. "What about you, Jessica?"

"Oh, um . . . let me check." I pull out my phone and refresh Jessica's inbox. Sure enough, it's there: an email from the principal congratulating me on winning not just the academic award, but also the STEM award, the humanities award, and the Betty Robertson Award.

"Wow." Celine peers over at my screen. She falters for a moment, but the smile that rises to her lips is genuine. "Figures that you'd win all of them."

"All of them?" Leela says, craning her neck as well. "Oh my god. Jessica. That's incredible. You don't understand—that's like, ridiculous. No one scoops up an award in every single category." She stops reading and scans my face. "Why aren't you happy?"

Why aren't I happy?

Is this how Jessica felt when she got accepted into Harvard? Empty, instead of ecstatic?

"Probably because she's already used to it," Celine says.

"No, no, it's definitely not that," I say in a hurry. "I am happy. I think I just need to process it."

"Well, *we* need to head to class," Leela tells me, slinging her bag over her shoulder. "But enjoy your success. I hope you know this means you're treating us to a very nice dinner."

"Sure," I say weakly. "You got it."

The two of them head out the doors together, already deep in conversation—most likely speculating who else received the academic awards and who didn't and why and whether they'll be upset about it. It's a sadistic little game all Havenwood students hate but participate in anyway. We're so invested in each other's successes and failures, so insecure that we need to repeatedly compile and update all the evidence we can find that we're doing well in comparison to everyone else.

But I'm suddenly not so sure I want to keep playing.

I manage to study for about twenty minutes after Leela and Celine leave. And by study, I mean I attempt to do a practice test with the answers lying wide open next to me.

"Hey! Jessica Chen!"

I startle and look up to see Lachlan Robertson marching across the library toward me.

This in itself is shocking enough that the students sitting near me have also swiveled around to stare. Aside from the debate, I've probably spoken to Lachlan a total of three times before—we operate in such different social circles. He's a legacy kid, the youngest son in a family of entertainment attorneys and chief financial officers; his world is one of trust funds and lavish pool parties and holiday houses off the coast of Italy. Whenever I catch sight of him around campus, he's always laughing with the other guys in the halls, tossing a basketball around on the court, or making loud, obnoxious phone calls in the parking lot.

"Yes?" I say, tentative, half convinced he's looking for the wrong person. I can't imagine a single reason why he'd want to talk to me.

He doesn't slow his steps until he's towering right over my desk. It's not a particularly flattering angle.

"That award was meant for me," he says, not bothering to keep his voice down. The words echo in the vast space, and suddenly all the muted activity in the background dies down. More heads turn toward us. It's so quiet I can hear my own sharp breath of surprise.

"What award?" I stare at him. "What are you talking about?"

He makes an impatient gesture with his hands. "The Betty Robertson Award. It was created by *my* grandmother. It wouldn't even exist if it wasn't because of her."

Slowly, understanding trickles in. "Um, thank you? To her?"

"The award is meant to go to someone who embodies the school spirit. She wouldn't want it to go to someone like you," he says, his pale eyes narrowing.

"Well, if that's the case," I say irritably, "then maybe you should go talk to your grandmother instead of me. You can complain about it together."

Somebody snorts from the desk behind me, and his face flushes.

"But you have to agree that it's wrong," he says, like this is a fact. "I mean, listen, you can take all the academic awards you want, all right?"

"What do you mean? They're already mine."

He continues on as if he hasn't heard me. "I just think you should stay in your lane, is what I'm saying. Stick to the math tournaments or whatever. That's what you're most suited for, you know?" He pauses and offers a smile closer to a sneer, his mouth twisting at the sides.

I feel something inside me go cold. With forced nonchalance, I start to close my laptop, tidy my notes, my fingers quivering slightly over the papers, all the equations I'd been working on bleeding together. Nobody moves. The quiet is punctuated only by the screech of the chair as I stand up. It doesn't make much of a difference—even with my back straight and my head lifted, Lachlan is still tall enough to block out the chandeliers hanging from the ceiling. Tall enough to cast a shadow over me.

"I should get to class," I tell him, and I have to marvel at how steady my voice sounds, how perfectly controlled, even when I think I might be sick.

He doesn't stand in my way. But as I stride away from him, my books hugged tight to my chest, my leather shoes squeaking over the floor, he calls after me, "There's nothing remotely special about you."

Ignore him, I urge myself. It's what my mother would advise. *Don't talk back. Don't get into any drama. Don't make a mess. Nobody will stand on your side.* I can hear her voice now, in the back of my mind, firm and coaxing. *There are plenty of things in life that are bitter, Jenna; you must learn to swallow the bitterness and continue on.*

Yet I skid to a halt, my heart pounding, the cold feeling in my stomach spreading out to my fingers. Transforming into heat. I clench them as hard as I can, my nails digging into skin.

"Nothing that stands out," Lachlan goes on. "I've met plenty of people like you before, you know, and most of them end up crashing and burning out the instant they step into the real world. You don't even have a personality. The school just gives you these awards because you're the more diverse choice. You don't actually deserve it—"

I twist around on my heel, the library a dark brown blur in my peripheral vision, and fling my notebook at the wall behind him. The sound it makes is louder than I'd imagined, a solid *thud* that seems to ring and expand through the space even after the notebook has fallen to the floor, its cover bent like the broken wings of a bird.

Gasps rise from the other students. A girl cries out.

Lachlan flinches, his eyes wide, the look on his face not one of fear or outrage, but pure disbelief, like he's not sure what's happening. He wasn't expecting it. Certainly not from me.

I let my hand drop back down to my side, adrenaline buzzing through my blood. I can still hear my mother's voice in my ear, warning me against making a scene. If I were really the one Lachlan was insulting, I might be able to listen. But this is my cousin he's talking about. My cousin he's attacking. The girl who I understand better than I ever have before.

My mouth opens. This is the time to say something profound, something that could express all my rage and resentment and grief, but I'm jarred by the limitations of the English language, the very history and design of it weighed against me.

And in the end I don't get the chance to speak.

Ms. Lewis steps forward from the teachers' desks, and I'm gripped by the absurd, terribly inappropriate urge to laugh. Her lips are pursed in one tight line, her face pale. From her expression, you'd think someone had just been brutally murdered right inside the library. "Jessica Chen," she says, in a tone I've never heard her use on Jessica before. "Come to my classroom now." She pauses, and glances over at Lachlan, who's staring at the spot where the notebook hit the wall as if it's the scene of a grisly crime. "And you too, please."

As Ms. Lewis shuts the door behind her, trapping us inside the dim classroom, I realize that I've never gotten into trouble at school before.

Even when I wasn't always the best student in the class, or even the second best, I was still considered well-behaved. Most parent-teacher conferences were so anticlimactic as to be a waste of time, the comments always the same: Jenna Chen is attentive, you can tell she tries really hard, she seems to be following the curriculum without much trouble. . . .

It used to be a major point of frustration, listening to their canned, polite responses, then comparing the lackluster experience to Jessica's. Once, a teacher had grown so emotional in describing how simply *remarkable* Jessica was and how *very privileged* she was to teach her that she'd burst into tears.

There was nothing very remarkable about me. But now that I really think about it, there was nothing wrong, either.

Not until now.

"I have to say, I'm quite stunned we're even here," Ms. Lewis begins, sitting down behind her desk, her bony hands folded in front of her. There's a significant stack of test papers waiting on the side, most of them already marked with red. *Our papers,* I realize, noting the familiar-looking questions on the first page. And despite the dire circumstances, despite the fact that I've just threatened one of the most powerful people in our school, I can't resist the impulse to peek at the scores. Kevin Cheng received seventy-five percent. Leela received ninety-eight percent—

"In all my years of teaching at this school," Ms. Lewis says, her lips a bloodless white, "I have never witnessed such terrible behavior."

I yank my gaze back and remain standing.

I know this is probably the part where I'm meant to bow my head in shame and dissolve into inconsolable sobs, but all I can think is: *Really? This* is the worst behavior she's ever seen? Not when one of our old PE teachers was "transferred" to another private school after he harassed a student in his class? Not when someone in the year above ours scribbled a slur in permanent marker on the bathroom walls? Not when Tracey Davis posted her ex-best friend's home address online after an argument, and trashed her locker with raw eggs and chicken blood? Not when two boys in our class fought each other in the parking lot over some girl they both liked, until one ended up with a broken nose and the other with a fractured arm?

This manages to top all of that?

But already I can imagine the answer. To them, violence doesn't look like blood and broken bones. Violence looks like the disruption of power.

"What were you thinking, Jessica?" Ms. Lewis asks sharply. "You could have hit Lachlan."

A few feet away from me, Lachlan slides into one of the seats by the open window, his long legs sprawled out. He hasn't uttered a word since we left the library.

"Well?" Ms. Lewis presses.

I swallow and try to think of how Jessica would respond, except of course *Jessica* would never be in this situation in the first place. So when I speak, I speak as myself. "Did you hear what he said to me?"

She blinks. "What *he* said? Are you honestly making excuses for your actions?"

"Fine," I say, folding my arms across my chest. Suddenly all my anger has wilted, and all that's left is heavy, bone-crushing exhaustion. I don't want to be here. I don't want to explain my hurt, dissect it in a way that'll make them understand. "So maybe I scared him a little."

"Maybe—"

"But what else was I meant to do? Just stand there and take it? Ignore him? Walk away and be the better person?"

Her eyes flash. "Yes, Jessica. I'm frankly appalled that I even have to answer that question. Yes, that's exactly what you should have done. That's what we would expect of a model student like yourself."

I clench my teeth and face her fully. She stares back, her disappointment palpable. A sharp, twisting pain tears through my chest. I remember all the times I watched Ms. Lewis stop Jessica after class to compliment her, just to tell her she was doing a great job. I think of all her kind smiles, her words of encouragement, her subtle nods of approval from the front of the room. Jessica Chen has always been one of her favorites—everyone knows it.

But now, within a matter of moments, because of one mistake, it's like everything has been erased.

And I realize, with a deeper pain, that this is the difference between being accepted and being tolerated. Even Jessica isn't an exception. None of us are.

"What exactly is your definition of a model student?" I ask her.

She falters, but I already know what she's thinking.

A model student causes no trouble. A model student makes no noise. A model student gives everything they have and asks for nothing. They simply keep their head down and study and get the best scores on behalf of the school, and then they graduate as valedictorian, with their perfect winning streak, and they head to the best universities in the world to train even harder to become a model citizen, so they can continue to be *good*. They're so good that nobody bothers to notice when something's wrong. They're so good they're an afterthought. They're so good they might as well not exist, except to be used as evidence that success is possible, that the system is perfectly sound, that anyone who struggles can only blame themselves.

"Well," Ms. Lewis says at last, with a sniff. "For one, they would never resort to *violence*." She turns her attention to Lachlan, and her voice instantly grows softer, the way you'd speak to a young, defenseless child. "How are you feeling, Lachlan?"

Lachlan makes a low grumbling sound. "I think . . . I think I might need some time to recover—"

"From the notebook sailing over your shoulder?" I demand incredulously.

He glowers at me. "It could have hit me. It could have *killed* me."

"Yes, sure. It's entirely likely that the notebook would have ricocheted off the library wall twenty-five feet behind you at a perfect hundred-degree angle, shot back through the air with the speed and force of an arrow, and hit you perfectly in the back of the neck with the corner of the soft cover, hence shattering a bone near an artery—"

"Exactly. It could have," he says, sniffling. Either he is incapable of comprehending the sheer absurdity of his accusation, or he's so shameless as to not care if his claims are ridiculous, because he believes everyone will side with him anyway.

"If that's your understanding of physics," I say sweetly, "I'd suggest paying more attention to the teacher instead of ranking the hottest girls in the class with your friends."

"*Jessica,*" Ms. Lewis snaps. "Seriously, what's gotten into you?"

"I didn't hurt him," I say, because if she believes I'm guilty either way, I might as well speak up for myself. "I didn't even touch him. I threw a *notebook*—"

"I want to call my father," Lachlan says, straining his voice to be heard over mine. "I'm going to tell him that I don't feel safe at this school anymore."

An audible snort escapes my lips, but beneath my incredulity, I feel the first prickling of fear. If Lachlan refuses to let this go, the school will have to step in. Maybe they'll message my aunt and uncle. Maybe they'll tell Harvard, and they'll rescind my acceptance. *Jessica's* acceptance. The thought makes my stomach contract. I've always envied Jessica for being better, but I've never wanted to make her life worse.

Ms. Lewis visibly freezes. I can almost see the mental calculations she's doing, her need to protect Lachlan's feelings warring against her need to protect the school brand—and, ultimately, losing.

"Now, Lachlan," she says, her tone softening, changing tactics in an instant. "Jessica has a point. I can see no signs of physical harm, and in accordance with our school guidelines, this would only count toward a warning strike."

Lachlan slouches back in his seat, his brows furrowed. Behind him, the window opens out to a sweeping view of the manicured school oval, half of it bathed in golden light, the other half cast in shadow. Clusters of friends are spread out over it, blazers sliding off their shoulders or cushioned beneath them like rugs, whispering and falling back on the grass, laughing hard. I wonder if news of the incident has already spread. It must have.

"There's really no need to turn this into a big . . . event," Ms. Lewis continues carefully. "I understand you're upset, of course, and Jessica will apologize."

"I will?" I ask.

Ms. Lewis pinches the bridge of her nose. "Will you . . . not?"

My heartbeat picks up. How far can I push this before it completely blows up in my face? "I'll apologize only if he apologizes first for insulting me."

Her hands flatten over the desk, her lips moving soundlessly—no doubt cursing me for making her life difficult. "Lachlan?"

Lachlan shrugs. "Sure, sure, sorry."

Ms. Lewis breathes out and twists her head back to me. "And Jessica?" There's a note of warning in her tone, a weight to the hardness of her gaze. "Can you apologize now? I really shouldn't be asking twice."

The words crawl up my throat like bile.

"I'm sorry," I grit out, and Lachlan's sulk immediately vanishes. This is all he's after, really. To feel like he's won, to feel like he has power. To him, this is the balance of the universe restored.

"For?" Ms. Lewis prompts.

"For throwing an extremely thin notebook at the wall," I say.

"And what else?" she asks.

Lachlan waits, visibly gloating.

My next word turns to dust between my teeth. It feels like someone's struck a match, set my blood on fire. I clench my jaw so hard I imagine my bones fissuring, the pressure spreading down through my neck, my stomach, my arms.

And I think: *screw it. Screw all of it.*

"I'm also sorry," I say, before I can stop myself, "that your very fragile feelings were hurt."

Lachlan frowns. "Wait—"

"And I'm sorry for not protecting your precious ego, the way everyone else has your whole life. I'm sorry you're secretly ashamed," I say, "because you *know,* deep, deep down, that you aren't as great as you've been led to believe."

His face has turned a shade of crimson so unnaturally bright it could make the news. "My father will—"

269

"Actually, yeah, go right ahead and tell your father," I say. It's not something I imagine would ever come out of Jessica's mouth, but maybe that's just it. I am not Jessica Chen. And maybe Jessica Chen herself isn't either. Maybe nobody is. The very idea of her is a construct, a myth, a distraction, the dream we're forever reaching toward but can never quite grasp. "The bigger deal you make of this, the more people will find out that it all started because you didn't get an award, so do with that what you like. Can I go now?" I ask Ms. Lewis, though I'm not really asking. "I still have class to get to."

Before she can reply, I smooth out my skirt. Tighten my ponytail. Turn around and walk away, without so much as glancing back to see their reactions.

Eighteen

The second I step outside, I start running.

I don't know where I'm running to, or what I'm running from. I don't care. All I know is that I want to get out of here. I have to escape; I have to put as much distance between myself and the campus and the memory as possible. My feet pound over polished wood, then steep cement steps, then faded cobblestones. The cold air hits my face, stings my throat when I swallow. My breaths come out in sharp, frantic bursts. My blazer flies behind me, my skirt rippling in the wind. I tear the buttons loose, freeing up space for my arms to move.

I'm already at the gates when somebody calls me by the wrong name.

"Jessica."

It's the voice, rather than the name, that makes me freeze. It's the only voice I care about now, the only thing that could stop me mid-step, that could stop the whole world in its tracks.

Aaron strides up to me calmly, as if this is our usual way of greeting each other. Only his brows are faintly furrowed. "Where are you going?" he asks in a light voice. "I heard that you—" He pauses to make exaggerated air quotes. *"Got into a violent fight with Lachlan?"*

"I didn't even touch him," I snap. My anger is misguided, but I can't control myself. "And he was the one who came up to me."

Aaron doesn't react with shock or disapproval. He just nods, like he'd been expecting as much. "A sore loser, isn't he?"

"Y-yes," I say, overcome by a sudden, bursting feeling in my chest, like my own emotions might overflow and drown me. "Yes. You could say that."

"So why are you trying to run away from class?" he asks, tilting his head now.

"I'm not," I tell him. "Not from *class*."

"Then? If I'm going to cover for you, I need to at least have a few details."

"I . . . I want to undo it." It's not until the words surface in the air between us that I realize what my intention has been all along. More firmly, I continue, "I have to go back to myself—my own body, my life, whatever it is. You were right. I really, truly believe it this time. They were never going to accept me. I can't live for the recognition or the applause or the illusion of a dream life. I—I have to live for myself. I *want* to live for myself."

His frown deepens. "What are you talking about?"

"I know you're still mad at me," I say. Try to smile. Try to ignore the gnawing, sick sensation in my gut. "And I'm really sorry. I'm sorry about everything—"

"Why would I be mad at you?" He doesn't sound like he's taunting me. The truly horrifying thing is that he sounds serious.

"Because of . . . because of what I said," I stammer. "Yesterday, in the car. You wanted me to undo it and I couldn't and—"

"Undo what?"

I feel as if I've been shoved. My ears ring. "The wish," I repeat slowly, because maybe he hadn't heard me. Maybe I'd spoken too fast. That's all. "*The wish*. About being Jessica Chen."

I wait for understanding to wash over his face. But he merely stares at me as if I might be joking. Suspicion sneaks under my skin, grabs hold of me. I don't want to even consider it. *Please.* Anything but this. Anyone but him.

"Aaron," I say. It sounds like I'm begging. "Aaron. Who am I?"

"What kind of question is that?" He lets out a breath of laughter.

"Tell me," I insist. "You have to tell me. Who do you . . . think I am?"

"You're Jessica Chen, of course."

No.

No.

The moment seems to crawl to a standstill. There's Aaron, gazing at me without really seeing me, confusion growing over his features. The sun, close to disappearing behind the clouds. The eastern wing of the school building looms behind him, turrets touching the sky, ivy spreading over smooth white walls, the bronze hand of the clock tower suspended in place. Everything like a dream from another life, a memory from a nightmare.

"Aaron, please," I choke out. I really am begging him now, desperate. Dread threatens to strangle me. "You can't do this. You can't forget."

"Can't forget what?"

"I'm Jenna," I say. "I'm Jenna Chen."

For the barest second, the mist in his eyes seems to clear. He stiffens. Opens his mouth. "Je—" But then the clarity is gone, as if his mind has been wiped clean of it by a violent hand. "Jessica," he says instead.

"*No.*" I stamp my foot hard in frustration. "You have to . . . you have to remember. We went to school together every single day for years. You would walk home with me. You'd open any bottle for me without asking and then hide it behind your back to annoy me." I'm shaking; I can barely keep track of what I'm saying. I just need to keep talking. I need him to come back to me, I need him to help me.

"Please. It's me. I'm *Jenna*. I—I'm not the best student, but I'm a good painter and I'm a good friend and I'm my parents' only daughter and there's nothing I wouldn't do for the ones I love. I'm messy and disorganized and I can't memorize all the dates in history class but I've never forgotten a birthday before. I keep a jewelry box of every card anyone has given me, and I hand-paint every single card I send out. When I set my mind to something, I always go through with it. I would get into heated debates with you over the most ridiculous topics, like . . . like whether a vampire apocalypse was more deadly than a zombie one, or whether death from heartbreak was a real phenomenon. I've always wanted to visit Tianjin because I love the sea and you said there was a steamed bun restaurant you went to as a kid. . . ." I trail off at the look on his face.

His expression is carefully controlled, a deliberate mask of neutrality. He only looks like that when he's assessing something, deciding his next move. He doesn't remember me.

Pain of a sort I'd never imagined before, never experienced—not even when he left without warning—wrenches its way through my heart. It feels like someone's prying my ribs apart.

"I'm sorry," he says at last. "I really don't know what you're talking about, Jessica."

"Stop calling me that." Tears scald my eyes. I wipe them angrily with my blazer sleeve. "You can't do this to me. You can't, you can't. . . ." I'm a child throwing a tantrum, crying incoherently just to be heard. I'm a person drowning, waving my hand in the air, right before the currents drag me under again.

He looks mildly alarmed. "Don't cry. Whatever it is, I'm sure somebody can help you. . . ."

But that's how I know. It's too late; the damage is irreversible. He never would have spoken to me like that if he knew I was Jenna. I draw in a harsh, rattling breath that sounds like my body is cracking from the inside out, and think back to the afternoon after our final exam scores had come out. I'd been crying then as well, almost as hard as I am now. I had stuffed the test in my bag and run out of class to hide in the back of the parking lot, but Aaron had sensed something was wrong. He'd followed me, and when he found me, he didn't ask what had happened, didn't tell me to stop. He'd merely covered my eyes with his hands—gentle, always so gentle—and said, *You can cry as much as you want. Nobody else will see you.*

"I'll bring her back," I say, stepping away from him. "I—I'll make you remember again."

"Remember *what*?"

I don't answer him. I just spin on my heel and keep running.

I go home.

My real home, not Jessica's house.

The front door is unlocked. It swings open when I push it, and the smell of chrysanthemum tea and fresh mangoes envelops me at once. The news is playing in the background, a soft hum of sound, the volume dialed low enough to allow for conversation. The afternoon light leaks through the windows and turns the rugs canary yellow. It's all so achingly familiar that I start to cry again, muffling the tears with the heel of my hand.

But as I walk deeper inside, I realize that something's different. The furniture has been rearranged. My study desk is no longer sitting in the corner of the living room—the desk my mom and dad had carried down the stairs for me, because I once made an offhand remark about how my bedroom was too cold to study in during the winter. The cards I'd hand-painted for my mom's past five birthdays have been taken down from the refrigerator door. My section of the bookshelf has been emptied out and filled with encyclopedias and travel guides instead.

A new fear races through my veins. I trace my fingers over the wall behind the kitchen door, searching for the crack in the plaster from when I'd slammed the door too hard in a fit of anger. We'd been talking about how Jessica was chosen for the school's academic extension program, and I wasn't.

You have to pay for it, my mom had yelled when she saw the damage later. *Do you have any idea how expensive it'll be to repair this? The entire house value will drop.* I didn't know anything about real estate values, but I'd made the unfounded calculation that it would probably cost a million dollars. I'd run up to my room sobbing and searched frantically online for the fastest way to make that kind of money without having to donate any vital organs. The next morning, I'd devised a grand plan that involved teaching abstract art to young heirs, but my parents never mentioned the incident again. They didn't end up fixing the crack, either.

Except now the surface is completely smooth, unnervingly cold against my skin. It's as if I was never here.

As if I'd never even existed.

My eyes close. *I wish I was myself again.* I scream the words into my mind. *I wish I could reverse my wish from before.* It should work—I've never meant anything more. But nothing changes.

"Jessica?" My mom comes downstairs to find me weeping over a random spot on the wall. I can understand why she looks so concerned. "Tian ya, what are you doing here? Why are you crying? What's wrong?"

I shake my head, the tears falling faster.

She pauses, then cleans her hands on the towel draped over the oven and rests them on my shoulders. "Where's your mom? Does she know you're here?"

I mean to keep quiet. I'd come here for answers, not comfort, but—

"Mom," I sob. "*Mama*. It's me."

She blinks. "I . . ."

"I'm your daughter." I look up at her, willing with every single cell and nerve in my body that I can somehow make her remember. "I'm your only daughter."

No recognition surfaces. Just bewilderment. "You . . . have always been like a daughter to me, yes," she says politely.

"That's not what I'm saying. Listen. You have to listen to me—"

Her hands fall from my shoulders. "I'm going to call your parents," she says, and starts to turn away, her alarm growing visibly by the second.

"No, Mom." My throat is hoarse. "Bie bu li wo ya." *Don't ignore me. Don't neglect me. Don't forget about me.*

The door swings open behind us, the sound making me jump. Then I see who it is. My dad is home.

"What's happening?" he asks, staring at me.

My mom makes a helpless gesture with her hands. "Buzhidao zhe haizi shou shenme ciji le." *I don't know what's gotten into this child.*

"Shouldn't she still be in school right now?" Dad asks over my head. I'm a guest to him. An outsider.

"Well, she won't say anything. She just keeps crying. . . . I've never seen her so distraught before."

"Should we call someone?"

"I was just about to . . ." Mom grabs her phone from the kitchen counter. The news is still playing from the speakers.

". . . rare meteor sighting expected tonight. Viewing conditions are favorable. Stargazers should travel to a dark location to get away from light pollution . . ."

My blood freezes. Everything seems to slow, to sharpen. Nothing feels real except this.

Rare meteor sighting . . .

A shooting star.

That was what Aaron had been talking about. Could it be that? The moment that cleaved my life in half, the moment after which everything went wrong?

No, not just that, I remind myself. I had headed home that night as well, and I'd smeared paint all over my self-portrait. That could be another factor. Maybe I just need to retrace every step I took.

"I have to get something," I decide out loud, straightening. For the first time today, I feel hopeful. My head is clearer, my thoughts reshaping themselves around my new plan. I have a course of action. A path forward.

My parents both stare at me, startled, but they don't stop me as I sprint up the stairs and burst into my old bedroom—

I freeze, my gut sinking.

No.

The bedroom is empty. There's just the single bed, stripped down to the mattress. My clothes have been thrown out, my photos taken down from the walls, my books and bags and brushes missing. The night-light isn't plugged in anymore. The faint pencil marks on my closet—the ones that my mom used to keep track of my growth spurt, the wobbly lines she'd draw out as she chided me to stay still and stop cheating by standing on my tiptoes—have been erased as well. My paints are gone. My self-portrait is gone.

It's all gone.

"What did you do?" I demand, running downstairs. I don't keep my voice down. I can't control my panic, which feels like it's something alive and clawed, thrashing around inside me. "Where did you throw everything?"

My mom gives me a blank look. "Throw what?"

"The things in the . . . in the room upstairs," I choke out. "Where is it?"

"The guest room, you mean?" Dad asks with a frown. "There was a bunch of stuff cluttering it up. We think it might have been left behind by the old tenant or something. It's all lying around in the garage; the town should be sending someone to collect—"

I'm already out the door. We never use the garage; at best, we treat it like a storage space. Dust tickles my nose when I step inside, coughing and blinking hard to adjust to the dim light. The air has that old, stagnant smell of an abandoned house. There are cobwebs sticking to the ceiling corners, and dark spots stain the carpet beneath my feet. All my stuff is here, stacked unceremoniously in a pile. I do not know what to feel first: grief, or relief. I do not have time for either. I drop down to my knees and rummage through the shirts and half-used oils and sketchbooks until I find the rough texture of canvas.

The self-portrait is hardly a self-portrait at all now.

It's the vaguest impression of a person, a mess of smeared paints, unrecognizable to anybody except for me. The face is almost completely covered, save the corner of my mouth. It's enough. It has to be enough.

I fold it under my arm and pocket a spare brush and oil tube, then kick the garage door open. But I don't leave right away. I linger outside my house, unable to resist glancing at my parents one last time through the windows. They seem to have forgotten about my sudden appearance already. In the kitchen, my mom is marinating the ground meat, my dad washing the plates and pots from lunch.

As I watch them move around the room, I'm seized by a memory so sudden and vivid it freezes me in place. The strangest thing is that there's nothing special about it at all. No tests, no awards, no results. It was years ago; we were all in the living room, me and my parents and Aaron, who'd come over for dinner. We were making dumplings together, the ground meat prepared in a metal bowl, the dough soft and smooth and rolled out into flat, round pieces and dusted with white flour.

My mom had been attempting to teach me how to wrap the meat properly. "You have to pinch the corners together, like this," she'd said, demonstrating, then glanced over at me and frowned. "No, no, Jenna—that dumpling looks so sad."

"It looks like it's dying," Aaron remarked helpfully from the other side of the table. Smiling, he'd then held up the dumpling he made. Of course it was perfect, like something you would see featured in a food magazine.

I'd glared at him while my mom gushed.

"Oh, it's beautiful," she said. "You're really good at everything, aren't you?"

And even my dad, with his usual stern expression, had nodded in approval. "Do you practice often?"

"Not really," Aaron said with a shrug, the very image of humility. But the second my parents looked away, he'd flashed a grin at me. I chewed my tongue, a flush of heat racing up my neck.

"Jenna has always been a little clumsy," Mom said. "Not like Aaron—you have such steady hands. You'll make an excellent doctor."

"I don't think my dumplings are *that* bad," I grumbled, picking up another piece of dough.

My parents had exchanged a look, while Aaron's grin widened.

"You're right," Mom said in the voice you would use to coax a child, her lips twitching. "Your dumplings are so . . ."

"Unique," Dad offered.

"Artistic," Aaron said.

"Exactly," Mom finished, and by that point the three of them were visibly trying not to laugh, and the kettle was boiling in the kitchen, the air warm with steam, and the dusky, roseate light was shifting through the translucent curtains, and everything was ordinary, familiar, serene, and everyone I loved was in the room with me.

Nineteen

The sun is falling behind me.

The dying light drapes shadows over the mountain path, the air burning the back of my neck. I push my feet faster, tearing through the wild twigs, letting them scrape and snag at my clothes, my cheeks, my hair, not slowing even when I bleed. I have to outrun the darkness. I have to reach the peak of the mountain before night arrives, catch the meteor before it leaves.

My breath rattles in my throat. The painting knocks clumsily against my stomach, slipping against my clammy fingers, but I don't dare loosen my grip.

I'm gasping when I reach the lookout, my body trembling from exhaustion, my ponytail tumbling over my shoulders. Sweat stings my eyes. Dampens my palms. There's a stitch in my side, so sharp it feels like I've been stabbed, and for a second I want nothing more than to collapse on the ground and sink into the dirt, but I force myself to stay standing.

I can see everything from here. The shine of the lake and the long winding roads and the Victorian houses and the stables with the grazing horses and the meadows Aaron and I walked through. The air feels colder this high up, tastes colder, sweet like the sugar cubes I'd melt into my jasmine tea. Night is arriving, fast. Above the familiar jagged landscape, I watch the sky turn from hazy violet to indigo to the darkness you find behind shut eyelids, like the world is closing its eyes.

I've taken this path up the mountain a hundred times before, but I've never been alone, never stayed behind so late. The black branches look twisted and ominous, the misshapen boulders waiting around in packs.

Too late, I remember someone talking about wolf sightings up in the mountains.

Fear worms its way through my stomach, but I force myself to focus. I set the canvas down, using my phone as a flashlight, and uncap the tube. Dip the brush into the blue paint. Then, trembling all over, I lower it to my self-portrait and begin to draw over all the places that have been covered.

The rough shape of a nose. The slight bump on the bridge.

The arch of my mouth.

Every individual eyelash, curving up.

The freckles dusted over my cheeks.

The shadows under my temples.

My fingers—Jessica's fingers—still won't obey me. No matter how much control I try to exert over the brush, it seems determined to run away from me. It's little more than an approximation of what I could do before. Nothing is exact. The strokes are messy, uneven. The excess paint runs down the canvas like fresh tears. I frantically wipe it with the edge of my sleeve, but I only end up smudging it further.

A scream of frustration escapes my throat.

"Damn it," I hiss. In the dark, the paint smeared over my hands looks curiously like blood. "Work. Please, please. This has to work."

And then it's no longer a matter of painting, but waiting. Waiting for the shooting star to appear. I search the sky and sit in the cold with the canvas and wait for what must be hours, until my bones start to ache.

"Please," I whisper to nothing. "Please."

A glimmer of light in my vision.

I stop breathing. Even the mountains seem to fall into quiet.

It appears like a miracle. Like magic. The meteor streaks through the night in a beautiful, radiant blaze of silver, quick as a blink, distant as a dream. I clasp my hands together so tight it hurts and present the painting like an offering and pray and pray and pray with all my strength: *Let it go back to the way it was. I don't want to be Jessica Chen anymore; I wish I could be Jenna Chen again. I'm Jenna Chen. I'm Jenna.*

Please, I miss it.

I miss everything.

I miss my room, our garden that never grew anything but was still lovely to gaze at, the view of the stars from the balcony. I miss the sound of my mom calling me down for breakfast, scolding me for going to sleep too late, all her concerns disguised as threats. The jar of sea glass sitting on my nightstand, a collection of every trip down to the beach. Walking past the kitchen and smelling chili and cumin powder in the air and knowing Mom was making lamb skewers for dinner. My dad driving us home at night, the windows rolled down a sliver and the radio on, the streets painted purple and stretched out ahead of me like infinity. The mid-autumn festival at my house, the mooncakes split into thirds, the sweet lotus-paste filling and the golden salted egg yolk always given to me. Picnics in the park, basking in the ocher light, listening to the sparrows sing.

How we sat together on the damp grass one Saturday afternoon and unpacked our basket: steamed, half-warm pork buns and packets of chips; tuna and avocado sandwiches, dressed in tight layers of cling wrap; fat slices of apple that were already starting to yellow. How we passed the food back and forth between us on cheap plastic plates and watched the sun rise over the trees, the leaves burning white-gold as though held to flames. How I strolled by the lake with Aaron, back when we were too young to know what it was to really want something. And him skipping pebbles over the water, the stones casting ripples everywhere they touched, his wrists flicking, the pale bones of his hands exposed. A doctor's hands.

I miss him, even if every moment we shared together was a reminder that he wasn't mine. Chasing after him across the oval, his shadow stretching out behind him, never quite close enough to touch. Standing next to him under a flickering streetlight, the moon lopsided and silver through the foliage, spilling over his midnight hair. When he was around, the world seemed safe, the kind of place that was worth everything, all the little disappointments and injustices and chips at my pride. The kind of place that could be beautiful if we really tried.

But more than anything else, I miss myself. The thrill of creating something, of stepping into the art classroom, past all those half-finished paintings, the sketches in charcoal, sharp shapes and bursts of color and memories in motion, photo references taped to desks. Opening a fresh tube of oil paint, blending two shades just right to create the sea or a wild plain or a sweep of snow, time bleeding away in the background, then finally stepping back and seeing something there, a physical impression of the scenes inside my head. Walking alone through the golden fields, watching the contrails over the horizon, stopping to tuck a wildflower behind my ear. Waking up at noon during the holidays to make pancakes, dicing fresh strawberries and dusting powdered sugar over the top. The scent of my cardigan fresh from the laundry, the cool softness of my blankets against my bare ankles, the dandelion stickers I had glued to my walls when I was eleven and couldn't quite scrape off no matter what I did. The long, languid summer days, the liquid blue of the sky, clear enough to swim through.

I miss it all. I miss my life, because even when I felt like I had nothing, I had everything. I just didn't know it at the time. You never do, until it's in hindsight.

The light disappears.

A cold wind whips through the trees, and nothing happens. It suddenly feels foolish—all of it. The self-portrait and the meteor and my own wretched hope. The stars are gone, and I'm just another girl, praying alone in the darkness for the impossible.

I don't remember falling asleep. I only remember crying, tugging at my hair until my scalp burns, eaten alive by my regret.

"I get it now," I scream at the sky. "I *get it*. You've made your point."

The sky doesn't reply.

And when my throat is hoarse and I can't form another word, I sob into my hands, the horror of my situation truly registering. I will be trapped like this *forever*. I'll have to act like Jessica Chen for the rest of my years. I'll have to treat my own parents like strangers. My memories of my old life will haunt me like ghosts, visible to my eyes only.

I don't remember falling asleep, the same way I wouldn't remember my birth. I can't tell when the nothingness begins or ends. But very briefly, in the moments between, there's color: burning roses and sage, ceruleans and lavender, the soft canary yellow of my childhood, the viridian of the sea, the first flush of dawn.

Twenty

Sunlight.

The world sharpens in fragments. The musky scent of soil, the crisp green fragrance of pines. The hardness of pebbles against my skin. The sun dragging itself up over the horizon, painting the silhouette of the mountains gold. Birds singing from the trees.

I cough. Rub my eyes.

My whole body is stiff, and my mouth feels like it's been stuffed with sand. I sit up very slowly, as though waking from a long, disorienting dream. Something feels different. Despite the pain in my joints and the dirt in my hair, I feel . . . lighter. Like I've finally taken off a soaked, oversized coat and slipped into my own shirt.

Then I see Jessica standing above me.

Jessica.

Shock spears through my chest. I'm blinking, blinking, my head spinning so fast it makes me dizzy. She's wearing the same clothes I was in yesterday, her school blazer wrinkled at the sleeves, her fingers covered in blue paint. Her face is pale, her eyes wide.

"Jenna?" she says.

I lurch to my feet, more awake than I've ever been. My heart kicks against my ribs as I lift my hands to the air and inspect them. There are calluses on my palms and my index finger, marks from all the nights I spent painting alone in my room. *My hands.*

I exist again.

"Oh my god," I say, and it's the sound of my own voice. I could sob. "Oh my god."

"What happened?" Jessica asks, looking as dazed as I feel. "I just woke up and we're on a *mountain* and . . . what is this?"

I open my mouth, but I have no idea where to even begin. "I was you," I manage at last. "I—I made a wish and I was you. I became you. I had your appearance, your life, your family. Can you remember anything? Do you know? I . . . I tried to look for you but . . ." I trail off, a sudden, overwhelming wave of guilt crushing the words in my throat. *But I've failed, so many times.*

"I kind of remember," she says, massaging her temples, her brows drawing together. "It's hard to describe. The last night I recall clearly is . . ." She closes her eyes. "The night of the Harvard acceptance. Aaron had come to visit—yes, and you were there too. Then you left and I went to bed and everything was normal and the next morning I woke up. . . ." Her eyes snap open again. "It was like I was watching a movie play out from far, far away. I had some vague impression of everything that was going on, but I wasn't myself. I was . . . suspended in a place in the back of my own mind. Just hovering there, weightless, in a closed room. I couldn't control my body. It was . . . freeing."

"Wait. So you were there? This entire time?" Despite the warmth from the sun, my skin goes cold. "You were just . . . trapped?"

"Not trapped, exactly," she says. "There were these few moments early on when it felt like the door in my mind wasn't fully locked, when it seemed possible for me to break through, if I really wanted to. Like when you called my name. But I was—scared. I wanted to stay in that room and just . . . rest. And the longer I stayed there, the harder it became to remember why I needed to leave at all."

There's a certain kind of fear that comes not before or during, but *after* an event has passed. The same fear that comes after you've swerved the car out of the way a second before it crashed; of missing a step and catching yourself right as you're falling; of noticing a mistake on your test and correcting it before the teacher collects it. The sharp, heart-pounding realization of what *could* have happened, of how fragile and arbitrary life itself is, of how one moment, one mistake, could have the power to change everything.

"I'm sorry," I babble. "I'm really sorry. It was my wish that started it all . . . it should have never happened—"

She waves the apology away briskly, without resentment. I'd almost forgotten that about her. Jessica Chen doesn't like to dwell on platitudes and well-wishes and empty sentiments. "It was my wish too," she says. "And besides, I'm more curious *how* it happened. Have there been any . . . I don't know, any conspiracy theories about this? Has this sort of phenomenon ever been reported before?"

"I don't think so," I say slowly. "You know, I used to have this theory that if I wanted something badly enough, the universe would make sure to keep it just out of my reach. Like a cruel joke, or a trick. But . . . maybe the cruelest trick the universe can play on us is to give us exactly what we wish for."

She shivers, rubbing her arms. "Really? You believe that? That the universe is listening?"

"It's possible." I shrug. "I mean, how much do we actually know about the universe and what's out there? Maybe anything could happen. Maybe all those things people speculate about—time loops and parallel universes and whatnot—could all be real. Maybe somewhere on the other end of the world, someone else also has the ability to wake up in another person's body, or to foresee the future, or turn invisible."

"I wouldn't usually agree with that," she says, "except it did happen."

"It did happen," I echo. I run a hand through my hair, shaking out the loose leaves and twigs, marveling at the impossibility of it all. That we're standing here on the peak of the mountain and watching the clouds shift colors in the light and having a normal conversation about this.

Jessica shoots me a curious look, like something's just occurred to her. "And you really wanted to be . . . *me* that badly?"

"Oh, not at all, not anymore," I say, then pause. "Um, no offense."

This time, she bursts out laughing, and the tension cracks. The sheer absurdity sets in. We're both in hysterics, clutching our sides and gasping for air.

"So what's next?" she asks at last. "Do we . . . I mean, what, we just go back to our old lives?"

Before, the idea would have completely depressed and terrified me. *What is there to go back to?* I would've asked. *There's nothing waiting for me.* Now I can't imagine anything better. "We go back," I confirm, my face splitting into a broad grin. "We go home."

I've barely set foot in my house when my mom marches up to me.

"Where were you?" she asks shrilly. She's still wearing her pajamas, an old bathrobe pulled around her narrow frame, her hair unbrushed. She's not smiling at me politely like a host or a distant relative. She's scowling fiercely, her lips set into a furious line, her eyes glowing with rage. When she starts talking, she doesn't stop. "Where did you go, you xiong haizi? Do you know how scared we were? Your dad and I were searching the whole house—your bedroom was completely empty. No note. No message. No letter. We thought you'd been *kidnapped* or eaten by a *bear* or run over by a gigantic *truck*. We were just about to head down to the school to interrogate them. Your dad has high blood pressure, you know that? Did you want to give us a heart attack? What will you do if we both die, huh? You can't even do your own laundry; your shirts come out all wrinkly. You think our life insurance is going to cover you? Why do you look so *happy*?"

"Because I am really, really happy," I say, beaming so wide the muscles in my cheeks hurt. "Mama."

"What?" she asks.

"You're my mom, right?" I ask, only to hear her say it. "I'm your daughter?"

She stares at me for a long beat, silent, and just when I feel a familiar trickle of fear, she reaches out and swats the back of my head. "What kind of nonsense is that? Are you looking for another mom? Because if you have any complaints—"

"I don't have any problem with that," I say quickly. "None at all."

She frowns again, and presses her forehead to mine for a second. "Are you running a fever?" she mutters. "Why are you acting so weird?"

"I'm not," I say, then crane my head to scan the house. Everything's gone back to the way it was. The family portraits, the desk in the corner, the books on the shelves. "Where's my dad?"

"He was about to start the car. Aiya, I better get him—" My mom whirls around and yells, "*Laogong!* Haizi ta ba, she's back. She's back. She's okay." In the same breath, she turns to me and seizes my shoulders. "You are okay, right? You're not injured anywhere? Youmeiyou zhaoliang? You're wearing so little— zhen shi de, bu zhidao leng re. I'll boil you some ginger water after this—"

The door creaks open.

"Where did you go?" My dad walks straight over to us. I had expected him to be angry, even angrier than Mom, but all he looks is relieved.

"I was, um, exercising," I say. "Up in the mountains with Jessica." This was the story Jessica and I had agreed upon before we parted ways outside my house. It's the truth, in a way, and it's the best explanation for why there's dirt smeared on my clothes and my shoes.

"Exercising?" Dad repeats in disbelief.

"You're always telling me to exercise more, aren't you?"

"Yes, but—"

"I woke up super early in the morning and just felt really, really inspired to start right then and there," I tell him. "And Jessica— well, you know, she's always been very fit and likes to do her workouts at dawn. So I called her up and we went hiking. I thought you'd be pleased."

Dad exchanges a glance with Mom and then heaves a sigh. "Next time," he says, "you *have* to tell us beforehand, okay?"

"Okay," I say.

His bushy brows lift. "That's it? Where's your usual attitude? Aren't you going to protest?"

I shrug, hardly suppressing my joy. "I'm in a very agreeable mood today." I feel like it's the last day of school, the promise of summer flung out ahead of me. There is no greater or simpler joy than this: I can go anywhere I want—the glittering lakes, the singing cliffs by the sea, the wide, wind-rustled meadows—and I can always come back home. "Wait. Can you make wontons for dinner tonight?" I ask my mom, clinging to her arm. "Please?"

She laughs at me. "You're craving them?"

"I've been craving them for ages," I say honestly.

"All right." She exchanges an amused glance with my dad. "I'll defrost the ground meat."

"I'll help you mix it," I promise, giddy at the very prospect of dinner, of being able to eat with my own parents, inside my own house. It's bizarre, how everything that had once seemed so ordinary to me now feels uniquely, unbearably precious, and everything that had once seemed so vital now feels so trivial. "Can we also have egg-and-tomato soup another day?"

"Yes, yes," she says, laughing harder. "Is that all, ni zhege xiao chihuo? Anything else that you'd like to have?"

I think about it for only a moment, then shake my head.

"Well, let's feed you some breakfast first. Oh!" Mom snaps her fingers. "Before I forget, we should also tell Aaron. He'll want to know Jenna's home."

The very sound of his name jolts my heart inside my chest. "Aaron?"

"Yes," Mom says, frowning. "It was quite strange. He called the house first thing in the morning—that's what woke us up. He sounded incredibly frantic. I don't think I've ever heard him so worried before. I'm not sure what's going on with that boy. He kept asking for you and saying he needed to see you right away. I'll give him a call back—"

"There's no need," Dad interrupts, pointing to the driveway beyond the window. "It appears he's already come here."

I close the front door behind me and wait for my pulse to calm down. It doesn't; it only hammers faster and faster as Aaron strides up to me. Grabs my wrist. Pauses mere inches away from me. His scent is so familiar—like gardenias and spring storms and the air rising through the mountains on a clear, moonlit night—that I find myself inhaling deeply. It feels like breathing for the first time.

"Jenna," he says. I thought my mom might have been exaggerating, but his voice is every bit as distressed as she'd described. "Jenna. Thank god. You're here."

"Do you remember now?" I ask him, searching his face.

His eyes widen a fraction. "So it wasn't a dream. You really were . . . you were gone. You were Jessica. All of that was real?"

I nod.

He releases a sharp, shuddering breath. He still hasn't let go of my wrists yet. His skin is blissfully warm around mine, his fingers firm but tender. "I woke up and I wasn't sure—I just heard your name. That was the only thing that mattered. I knew I had to find you."

"And you found me," I say simply.

"Yes," he says, gazing down at me. He gives his head a little shake. "You're really her?"

"Do you want to test me?"

"Are you being funny?"

"For once, no," I say. "I'm serious. Test me. Any memory we have. Something only I would know."

He deliberates on this for a moment. "The week before I left for Paris," he says, and I can see the memory come alive in his expression. I can almost feel the rain on my skin again. "When it was raining, and we were standing beneath the trees . . ."

We're standing beneath the trees now, the wisteria spreading its branches around us, the soft purple petals brushing the top of my head.

"What did you ask me, then?" He's studying me as intently as I'm studying him.

"I asked you—" It's hard to speak past the lump in my throat. "I asked you if you would ever hate me. And you said no. You said never."

"You're right," he says, voice low, and it occurs to me that this is the first time the two of us have really been alone since before he left for Paris. Maybe the same realization has struck him as well, because he swallows, hard. Drops his hands. "Well," he says. "Good. As long as you're back now."

There's too much unsaid between us. Too much that's passed already. Too much I want. His gaze flickers once to my lips, and all the blood in my body rushes through my veins with the speed of wind. I'm lightheaded, dizzy with anticipation, with longing, with relief. But he doesn't move closer.

Instead, he rights himself. Casts one last, long look at me.

And turns to go.

No, I want to say, and in that split second, something else occurs to me: that life doesn't have to go back exactly to what it was before.

"Wait," I blurt out.

His footsteps stall, and that's all I need. I rush toward him and wrap my arms around his torso from behind, just like I've always fantasized about, my body pressed so tightly to his I can hear his uneven breathing. I'm stunned by my own bravery, but I bury my face in his shirt, in the space between his shoulder blades.

"I know exactly what I want now," I tell him, my voice holding even, despite how hard my heart is pounding. "And that includes you. I promise you're not just some dream for me to chase. I promise I'll never stop wanting you—"

I don't have the chance to finish. He spins around, and his hands are in my hair, his lips are on mine, and my heart is on fire. I can't believe it's happening, even as I kiss him back, urgently, recklessly. Even as my fingers find the collar of his shirt to pull him closer, closer, closer, bridging the months of absence, the years I loved him in private. And I'm stunned by how *right* it is, how natural it feels. I've dreamed of this for so long that it seems impossible the reality of it could ever match up to the vision I'd been building inside my head, but it's somehow even better.

He pulls back just to look at me. His eyes are the deepest black, a shade I can never seem to replicate with oils or watercolors. He lifts his hand and tugs my hair once, lightly, teasing, testing, as if he needs to confirm that I'm really here. Then he runs one gentle thumb over my cheek, and I think I lean in. I think I stop breathing.

"Jenna, you're all I've ever wanted," he says, quiet. Perfect. "It's always been you. It can only be you."

The sun is bursting through my chest, breaking past my lips. *It's my life,* I think with amazement, *and it's beautiful, and I can paint it any color I want to.* Right now it's drenched in the brightest shade of gold. I have the brush in my hands, and the canvas is mine. It's all mine.

Twenty-One

Unbelievably, I still have to go to school the next day.

I brush my hair and shrug on my blazer and pack my lunch as if everything is normal. But I pay more attention now. I finish the entire bowl of congee my mom makes for me and ask for seconds, with more pork floss and century-egg slices on top. ("Has my cooking improved?" she marvels, to which I answer, "Of course!") I wave at my dad on the way out.

The sky is a pure, perfect blue, and I pay attention to that too, the feeling of the sun on my face, even though my bag is weighed down by homework and mock papers.

My first class is art. I don't realize how much I've missed it until I'm sitting at my usual table, my paints and paintings spread out in front of me. All of my self-portraits have been restored to what they were before, my face showing, every brushstroke in place.

"Morning."

I spin around at the familiar voice. It's Leela, her ponytail swinging over her shoulder as she drops into the other seat, and I can't stop myself. I reach out and pull her into a crushing hug.

"Oh my god," she says, laughing, but she hugs me back. "What's with the sudden display of affection?"

"I just had a bad dream," I say, squeezing her arm. "I'm still a little spooked."

She snorts. "Is it as bad as that dream you had where Old Keller transformed into a spider and started scuttling around on your desk so you couldn't finish your English essay?"

"You still remember that?"

"Um, *yeah*, you traumatized the hell out of me with that story." She shudders, then pulls back to study me. "Why are you smiling so wide?"

"Am I?"

"Very wide," she says. Then she glances over at the self-portraits and claps her hands together. "*That's* what I was looking for. Of course."

"What?"

"It's so weird," she murmurs, "but the other day, I suddenly thought of this series of paintings I loved. I had like, the vaguest impression of them; I couldn't even tell you what they were about, only the feeling I would get when I looked at them, like this—this tightness in my chest, right where my heart is. It drove me mad that I couldn't remember who the artist was and what they were called. I even tried to Google it. But this is it. It's *your paintings* I was searching for. Have they been here the whole time?"

"Yeah," I say. "The whole time."

"I really love them," she says. "Like, genuinely."

"That's good, because I was thinking of adding another self-portrait to the series."

But this self-portrait is different.

I start on the sketch, shaping my nose, my eyes, the contours of

301

my cheekbones. I'm not looking directly ahead or up at something I can't have, but at someone over my shoulder, and I'm smiling. The colors are softer, plum-purple and pale lavender and carnation pink for the collar of my dress, buttermilk yellow for the sunlight streaming in behind me, old rose for the shadows under my collarbones. I mix and blend the paints and run my brush across the canvas and it's like the world disappears. I don't even realize the period is over until Leela nudges me, giggling.

"Looks like someone's come to see you."

"Who?" I ask.

The answer is waiting by the door, hair falling perfectly over his eyes, his eyes falling straight on me. He's holding his books in one arm, the other propped against the frame. He looks so beautiful that I can't believe he's waiting for me.

I make my way toward him, and I'm surprised to find him grinning. "Hi," I say, uncertain.

"Hello," he says, then leans in. My heartbeat skyrockets, but he stops inches away from my ear and whispers, "You have paint on your face."

I shove him back, and he's laughing. "I thought you were going to start being nicer to me," I grumble, mortified.

"What do you mean? That *was* nice of me," he says. "Or else you would've headed off to English with red smudged on your cheek."

I wipe my face roughly. "Still there?"

"Yes. I think you made it worse."

People are moving around us, streaming in and out of the classroom. A few girls pause to sneak not-so-discreet glances at him.

Aaron doesn't seem to notice them. "Let me," he whispers. "Don't move."

I couldn't move if I wanted to. I'm too nervous, frozen to the ground as he brings his thumb to my cheek and swipes it very gently over my skin. I hope he can't feel me trembling.

"There," he tells me. "All better now."

We're gathering at Jessica's house again on Saturday.

We bring braised beef this time, and a bag of fresh mangoes. When the door opens, I smile up at my aunt and greet her without thinking, "Hi, Mom." Then immediately wince at my mistake. Some habits really are too easy to form.

My mom pokes my forehead. "Xia jiao shenme ne? Your mom's behind you."

"Sorry," I apologize to them both. "I, uh, was just kidding—"

"Jenna is so funny," my aunt says cooperatively. "Young people and their sense of humor these days."

"Yes, yes, just hilarious," my mom mutters, poking me again.

"We have mangoes for you," my dad offers.

"Aiya, you're too polite," Auntie says, as she always does. "I tell you every time, you really don't have to bring anything. . . ."

"How could we come empty-handed?" my mom protests.

This process repeats itself a few times before we finally make it into the house.

"Jessica's out in the yard, by the way," Auntie tells me. "She should be happy to see you."

I'm not sure the latter is true, but I do find her sitting on the back porch, ankles crossed, hair blowing back in the breeze, the kind of graceful I could never fully emulate, even with her body. At the sound of my footsteps, she turns her head a fraction toward me, her eyes wary. It still feels strange, to have her here, this blood-and-flesh person, this separate entity from me. It feels like I'm looking at myself, or looking at another version of myself.

"You're here," she says.

I hesitate, then move to join her, encouraged when she does not protest. "How has . . . everything been?"

"Good." She tucks her hair behind her ears. "Strange. I don't know. I'm not sure if it's just my imagination, but people are treating me . . . differently. Lachlan and his friends don't seem to like me much."

I grimace. "That's, uh, my bad."

"No, it's fine. I never liked them much either," she says with a little smile, and I feel myself relax. "And I don't really mind how other people are acting now. Like I'm—a real person, you know what I mean? I didn't feel fully real before. I didn't think I would ever have a chance to."

Another breeze floats past us. I lift my head up, letting it fan my face.

"You know what used to bother me most about you?" I ask.

"What?" she says.

"You were proof," I tell her, and only when the words are out do I realize how true they are, how long I've been carrying them. "You were proof that it was my fault."

She frowns. "I don't get it."

"If people didn't like me," I explain, "or if I didn't get a particular offer or acceptance letter or award, if I was excluded or ignored or underestimated, if I didn't get the life I wanted . . . I could only blame myself for not being good enough, because *you* were there. You came from the same city, the same family, and you managed to achieve everything I couldn't. It was simple, really: you were successful, and I wasn't, so either I was doing something wrong, or there was something wrong with me." It's still a little embarrassing to admit, to draw out the clear differences in our lives and point at everything she did better, but the pain I'm braced for doesn't come. Steadily, I continue, "You were, like, the better version of me that I could never be. You were what everyone else thought I *should* be. You were the standard."

Jessica blows out a long breath and stretches her legs over the grass, processing this. "God. Jenna, that's . . ."

"But I didn't realize how lonely being used as the standard was," I say. "How hard it was for you. How utterly *exhausting* that gets. I was so caught up in feeling jealous and insecure that I didn't even think about it. I just assumed . . . I assumed all the wrong things. I'm sorry."

She's silent for a moment. Then she makes a soft, half-choked sound. "I'm sorry too. I knew people compared us sometimes, and I knew it must have bothered you, but I—I didn't know how to talk to you. I was scared that I'd only make things worse." Her voice grows smaller. "That you wouldn't want to be around me anymore."

I blink. "You were worried about that?"

"Of course," she says. "You're my cousin."

"We have other cousins," I point out. "We have at least a dozen, I'm pretty sure. Another one was born just last year. And they're all very nice—except maybe Liuwen. He still won't admit to stealing my money from the spring festival."

Her eyes widen. "Hey, he stole my red pocket money too."

"Oh my god. So he has this whole criminal business going on."

"Evidently," she says, with such indignation that we both pause, and dissolve into laughter. "You see," she adds. "I might have other cousins, but you're my favorite cousin. Just don't tell the others at the next big reunion."

"Don't tell them that you're my favorite cousin too," I say, and I find that I really do mean it. "And not just because you're super smart or most likely to buy a mansion and invite me to visit your home theater or whatever. But because you make the most incredible lemon cookies, and you always give the best fashion advice, and I can trust you to come with me to take back our red pocket money."

"I'm very honored."

"You should be."

When our laughter subsides again, she offers me a tentative sort of smile. "So . . . no hard feelings?"

"That depends on you. Have you forgiven me for taking control over your body and ruining your perfect streak across every subject?"

"I can't believe it. I can't believe this is real life, that we're even having this conversation. But yeah. Yes." She hesitates, tracing a line in the gap between the planks. "You know, I spoke with Cathy yesterday about her essay thesis, and . . . I'm going to confess."

"What?" My head jerks up. "Are you sure?"

"I've already made up my mind," Jessica says. Sighs. "Even if nobody had found out, it's been gnawing at me ever since I did it. I—I don't know what I was thinking, honestly."

"You were under a lot of pressure."

"Yeah, but it was still wrong," she says quietly. "I just don't want to start at Harvard in the fall carrying this awful secret with me. I don't want to pretend. I'm too exhausted to go on the way I have these past years. I've burned through all I have to offer, and I've run out of fuel. And if they revoke my acceptance because of it . . ." She swallows. "Then I'll learn to live with that, somehow. I thought I needed to be the kind of person who'd sacrifice anything for success. I thought sacrifice was a *good* thing, that it proved you were determined, dedicated. But there are some things I have to keep for myself. Like, my integrity. Like my dignity. My sanity."

"That's . . . really brave," I tell her.

Surprise dances across her face. "I don't think anyone's called me that before."

"You are," I say firmly. "And no matter how it goes, I'll be here."

She smiles. "I know."

I smile too, and set my eyes on her garden. The lavender has started to bloom, the magnificent purple petals rising above a sea of silvery-green leaves, all of it as beautiful as a painting. "I'm going to miss this yard. And this porch," I muse aloud. "I miss my own bedroom a lot more, though."

"If you ever miss it, you're always welcome here," Jessica says. "We're family."

And I've never felt so grateful for it, so happy that we're related, that when we all moved here from Tianjin we took a piece of home with us. That thousands of miles away, we can still have gatherings, and homemade food, and fussing parents and petty arguments and inside jokes.

"Jenna!" My mother calls from inside the house, and my grin widens. "Jessica! Wash your hands—it's time to eat."

"Okay, coming," I yell back.

"Hurry up, the noodles are sticking."

I push onto my feet and hold out a hand to Jessica. She takes it, straightening her plaid skirt in one quick, elegant motion, and as we walk back into the house together, the living room warm and hazy with steam, our mothers adding last-minute pinches of cut coriander and chives to the dishes, our fathers setting the floral-patterned bowls down around the table one by one, it's like we're kids again, back when we'd play outside before dinner and fold tiny stars out of paper. *Make a wish,* Jessica would always tell me, and I always did.

But right now, there's nothing else I'd wish for except this.

Acknowledgments

By the time you're reading this, *I Am Not Jessica Chen* will be the fifth book I've released into the world. Each time, I'm deeply humbled by how much goes into transforming a story from a rough idea in my Notes app to a book you can hold in your hands, and it wouldn't be possible without the following people:

A huge, heartfelt thank-you to my extraordinary agent, Kathleen Rushall. Thank you for always believing in me and advocating for me—there aren't enough words to express how lucky I am to have you in my corner. Thank you to the wonderful team at Andrea Brown Literary Agency for all your support.

Thank you to Claire Stetzer for your passion and your sharp editorial eye and your faith in my writing. I'm eternally grateful for you. Thank you to Sara Schonfeld for your guidance and for helping turn this book into what it is today. Thank you also to everyone at HarperCollins for your tireless efforts and expertise: Catherine Lee, Jessie Gang, Erin DeSalvatore, Gweneth Morton, Danielle McClellan, Melissa Cicchitelli, Kelly Haberstrom, Audrey Diestelkamp, and Lisa Calcasola.

Thank you to Kim Myatt for your breathtaking art and for

giving me the most beautiful cover I could've possibly asked for.

Thank you to Taryn Fagerness at Taryn Fagerness Agency for your enthusiasm and brilliance.

Thank you to all my friends who've celebrated the highs with me and comforted me during the lows. You know who you are.

Thank you to my parents for your endless encouragement and patience, even—and especially—when I make some questionable decisions in life. I love you.

Thank you to my sister, Alyssa, for being my first reader and biggest fan throughout all these years. There are often times when it feels like you're the older sister, and I'll only say this once, but you're so much wittier and wiser than I'll ever be.

Thank you to my incredible readers for picking up my books and sharing them and supporting me in more ways than I could possibly count. You've really, truly changed my life, and I can't thank you enough.